MW01032564

LADIES NIGHT

LADIES' NIGHT

Elisabeth Bowers

THE SEAL PRESS

Copyright © 1988 by Elisabeth Bowers.

All rights reserved. No part of this book may be reproduced in any form without prior permission from the publisher, except for the quotation of brief passages in reviews.

This is a work of fiction. Any resemblance to real characters or events is entirely coincidental and unintentional.

Library of Congress Cataloging-in-Publication Data
Bowers, Elisabeth.
    Ladies' night / Elisabeth Bowers.
        p.   cm.
    ISBN 0-931188-65-2 : $8.95
    I. Title.
    PS3552.087197L3 1988
    813'.54--dc 19   88-19897
                                                                 CIP

Cover illustration: Clare Conrad
Cover design: Deborah Brown

Printed in the United States of America
10 9 8 7 6 5 4 3 2 1
First edition, October 1988

Seal Press
P.O. Box 13
Seattle, Washington 98111

Acknowledgements:

No book begins and ends with the author. But I would like to thank, in particular: my father, who bought me a typewriter; my co-workers at C.R.S., who gave me time off to complete this project; and Arnie, for his editorial assistance and unfailing support.

LADIES' NIGHT

CHAPTER ONE

Where did it start? Sometimes it's hard to draw the line between the end of one case and the beginning of the next; they seem interlocked like links on a chain. One thing keeps leading to another.

But that was the year I was so goddamn broke all the time; when everyone was predicting a new depression and I spent my spare time juggling my bank accounts, shoving my petty cash from one to the other, trying to cover my bills. That was the year my son Ben got his first job, and that was the year my daughter Katie left home, after dithering for months, worrying that I'd be hurt because she wanted to live without me. It never occurred to her that the feeling might be mutual, that I'd been longing for the day when I could escape her supervision and have a life of my own. Yet another of our failures in communication. My name is Meg Lacey. Yes, I am a mother. Also a private eye. A combination you may find indigestible.

This case began with Stan Kubicek. He showed up one fine spring morning—a grizzled misery of a man, one of those people who is determined to accept the worst that life has to offer, and gets it, as a result. His wife had died not two years previously, and now his daughter had run off—vanished into the city's maw, leaving no breadcrumbs behind her. Fifteen years old. The police had already done their best and were still keeping her name on file, but as the officer at the police station told me when I spoke to him about it, fifteen-year-old

3

runaways are a dime a dozen and they don't usually turn up until they're good and ready to. Lillian Kubicek had packed both money and clothes and was, from all accounts, both brash and worldly, unlikely to get lost. But her father wanted her back. He missed his morning cup of tea (no one made it like Lily), her garish clothes and loud laughter. He wanted her to return to school, although, as her teacher told me, of late she'd been more absent than not.

I heard a lot about Lily. Her father virtually took up residence in my office, and I visited less partial acquaintances: friends, teachers, relatives—who gave me a rather different account. According to them, Lily was reckless, outspoken, intractable. "Impossible," according to her guidance counsellor; "really wild," in the words of a friend. And her father had no influence over her whatsoever. "There was nothing really wrong with the girl," her home room teacher told me, "except that she had no interest in what we were offering her." "Do you know what did interest her?" I asked. The teacher sighed. "Boys, sex, movies, clothes. I don't think she thought much further than that. If she hadn't run away we would have had to dismiss her. She was too disruptive."

One of Lily's friends told me that she'd been talking about running away for a long time; another said that some woman had offered her a screen test. This sounded pretty farfetched and when I said as much, the friend agreed. "Lily always exaggerated," she admitted, dismissively. "Everybody knows you gotta be skinny to get into movies. Lily was too fat." I gave the girl a look; she was a little overweight herself and she had the grace to look uncomfortable. She was probably jealous. Lily, after all, was now the talk of the town. Her friend had probably harbored similar ambitions, but had more sense of self-preservation.

However Lily was not my idea of movie star material. Her father had obliged me with enough photographs of her to fill an album, and for a long time I kept one of the more recent ones with me in my wallet to pass out to people that might have run into her. She was a freckled, big-breasted girl, good-looking by virtue of health and high spirits rather than any composite of features. I spent a lot of time looking for

4

Lily; I earned every penny I got—but I never really expected to find her. She sounded like the kind of girl that would find a niche somewhere (though not necessarily somewhere nice), and the better I got to know her father, the better I understood her reasons for staying away. Poor old Stan. He was such an irritating man, so lugubrious and self-pitying, always looking at you out of the corner of his eye to see if he'd hooked your sympathy; he drove me right up the wall. Or, more accurately, back out into the streets to see if I could find hide or hair of his daughter and get rid of them both for once and for all. But I never did.

He kept me on the job for over six months, although after the first month I told him it was futile. "You can't find someone that doesn't want to be found. Give her time to grow up and she'll probably come back on her own. I know it's hard, but I think you're going to have to wait it out."

But Stan shook his head. "It's not like Lily. I feel sure in my bones something's happened to her. You try all the hospitals?"

"I've tried them before; I can try them again."

"And the bus depots. I can just picture her sitting in a bus depot."

"Six months after she left home?"

"You keep looking," Stan insisted. "I don't mind the money. Money's no object in this case."

Which was why I kept working for him.

After a while though, he too began to flag, and we agreed that, for a retainer fee, I would keep my eyes and ears open and her photograph on file—but abandon the official search. The cops, of course, were providing the same service for free, but Mr. Kubicek mistrusted bureaucracies and preferred to pay me for my more personal service, which mostly consisted of listening to a long list of his forebodings over the phone once a week. And to be fair to him, he had reason to be worried. In my estimation, Lily was fair game for the prostitute rings on Davie Street, where minors are the best-selling commodity on the market. I'd looked there, of course; but in that area of town people take care of their own (for better or worse) and don't answer questions unless they can see what's in it for them. When I make inquiries on Davie Street I get very helpful answers, every one of them a runaround.

So I put Lily Kubicek on the back burner and scraped by on a couple of divorce cases, but by the following spring, I'd reached an all-time low. The only case on my books was Talney vs. Talney, which wasn't going to pay me anything until the court awarded costs. Bad business, you might say, but Carol Talney was an acquaintance of mine, my hairdresser, to be exact, and I figured she deserved a break. She comes from Jamaica, arrived in Vancouver ten years ago, married a white guy, Mike Talney, has two kids and a case of clap for every year she's been married. How's that for marital bliss? Her husband was a real sweetie, as I had reason to know, having been tailing him for some time. I'd collected a dossier on him that I hoped would outweigh his well-oiled connections, his handsome face and pretty manners. He was not only contesting the divorce, he wanted custody of the kids. But fortunately for us, it hadn't occurred to him to change his ways; despite the impending court battle he was still out hustling twenty-year-olds, while Carol stayed at home doing the laundry, cooking supper and reading stories to his progeny. Some people learn the hard way.

Anyway, that's about all I was doing at the time, watching Mike Talney usher his secretaries in and out of motel room doors, and in a lousy mood as a result, wondering, as I often do, how I ever got myself into such a sleazy occupation. Divorces are my bread and butter. Nothing too glamourous about sitting in hotel lobbies, keeping vigil in parked cars, peering through bedroom windows. Telling tales. Even when I'm working for as deserving a client as Carol, I don't like what I do. I'm paid, for the most part, to betray other people's secrets. Sometimes I refuse. Sometimes I can't afford to. Sometimes I refuse whether I can afford to or not. But not too often.

Which is why I willingly put up with people like Stan Kubicek. Or with anyone, for that matter, who isn't asking me to find out whether his wife votes Liberal, whether his son's a homosexual, whether her daughter is dating "that Jew down the street." I get requests you wouldn't believe. And I've often been tempted to remove that word "confidential" from my business card. It brings out the worst in people.

More than a year after his daughter had gone missing, Stan phoned me to ask if I would accompany him to the morgue. I told him the cops must have made a mistake. I was wrong. Poor brazen Lily, out to conquer the world and found dead behind one of the logs on Sunset Beach with needle tracks up both arms. When they pulled back the sheet, I was shocked to see how young she looked: freckles on her cheekbones, a smooth forehead, chapped lips. Stan Kubicek identified her and was led away weeping; I stayed to ask a few questions, then accompanied him home.

I attended the inquiry, heard the testimony given by the school counselor, an aunt, a teacher, one friend I'd spoken to and another I'd never seen before, the cops that found her, the medical examiner. They'd found no one, I noticed, who admitted to having seen her since the day she disappeared from home. Stan was called into the box, but was excused, being incoherent. The coroner arrived at a verdict within an hour. Death by misadventure, a heroin overdose; the lab tests had produced incontrovertible results. The needle tracks testified to a history of heroin injections; her character and morals (combined with the character and morals of our Society, which were nowhere mentioned) had probably landed her a career on Davie Street. To listen to the coroner, you would have thought the process inevitable: sex, junk, death, in that order. One wiggle of the hips and you're a goner, you deserved it. Though he was too tactful to say it outright in front of her father.

But poor old Kubicek barely understood a word of it. I spent the rest of that day trying to make him understand how it was his daughter had died. "Suicide!" he kept protesting. "My Lily would never have committed suicide! A ray of sunshine, that girl; never down for more than a minute and she'd pop up like a piece of toast."

"No one's saying it's suicide," I repeated for the tenth time. "When you buy street heroin, you never know what you're getting; you don't know what it's cut with; you don't know how strong it is. You get a good bag; you fall asleep, go into a coma—and that's the end of it. At least it's painless."

But he couldn't—or wouldn't—hear me. "But she was such a happy girl; everybody liked her. She had so many friends. All on her lonesome, that's not like my Lily. Where did her friends go?"

When he said that, I glanced up—because that had struck me too. "Life of the party," a friend had described her and everyone else had agreed; not the kind of girl to go for a solitary walk to Sunset Beach. Lily, as I understood her, should have died at a party, in a friend's house, in a car packed with teenagers—but Christ, everyone gets impulses to be alone sometimes. And maybe she'd changed. Life as a junkie must have come as a shock to her; most fifteen-year-olds—most adults—don't take kindly to the knowledge that few people in the world could care less if one lives or dies, and how much one suffers in the process. Lily had been forced to grow up fast, and may well have regretted it. For many junkies, an overdose can become a very tempting solution.

The case was now closed. There was a horrible, tasteless funeral, well-attended by school friends, teachers and neighbors, most of whom seemed to have come to say "I told you so"—in which the minister encouraged them. He waxed eloquent on the evils of sex and drugs (and made no distinction between them); "poor Lily" was his theme, an example to her entire community. I was glad to hear she'd served some good purpose. Most of us don't.

I drove home depressed, partly thinking of Lily, but also of my bank account, which had seen the last of Stan Kubicek's checks. I've often thought of that drive since—had I no premonitions? I was surprised she'd died alone—no syringe, no teaspoon; she must have shot up elsewhere and then set out for the beach. But after all, I'd almost predicted it—predicted, at least, that a runaway teenager that never thought much further than immediate gratification was in danger of ending up on the streets. No, despite my reservations, I accepted the coroner's verdict: another inexperienced junkie, going for the ultimate high, had overshot the mark.

It happens all the time.

CHAPTER TWO

THE FOLLOWING month I did almost no work at all. About once a week Carol Talney would phone to tell me that her husband was working late, so I'd hustle on down to the plate-glass phallus where he worked and wait in the lobby to see who he was escorting through the elevator doors tonight. He stayed home with his kids an average of two nights a week; if he won custody he'd have to re-marry at once, find some other sucker to sit home and babysit, mend his socks and watch the late shows. He'd find one without difficulty; I should know, having tailed half a dozen of them.

I met some real winners that month, like the guy that wanted me to tail his wife while he was out of town on business conferences. There was something fishy about him, so I made him a cup of coffee and encouraged him to get chummy. I discovered that his wife wasn't a wife at all—she was his mistress. He also had a wife, but he wasn't worried about her; she was, in his words, "as straight as a die." (He was proud of her.) But his mistress was another matter; he was convinced that she was two-timing him.

"But you're two-timing her," I pointed out. "*And* your wife."

He didn't agree. When I declined to do business with him, he threatened me with the Better Business Bureau and called me all manner of names, none of them new. It's for occasions like these that I've found it worthwhile to decorate my office with photographs of myself in full black-belt regalia, disposing of blurred bodies. My clients glance round my walls, gain faith in my capabilities. In fact I've never actually used my skills more than twice in my entire career, although I continue to practice regularly. I teach Aikido when I get the chance; I give martial arts demonstrations in high schools, to Y.W.C.A. groups and Girl Guides. I think they should know that there's more to survival than tying knots.

I had another client that month (yep, I was busy). He was a Chinese kid, about eight years old, all ribs and skinned knees; so cool he smoked cigarettes, so tough he carried a flick-knife. He'd lost a dog he called Radar, and proposed to pay me in beer bottles. Having not too much else to do that day, I phoned the pound and the S.P.C.A., then provided him with felt pens and helped him compose ten signs: "Lost in this neighborhood: short-haired dog with brown and white patches, one bit ear; one brown eye, one blue eye. Sometimes answers to the name of Radar. If you see him phone Sammy"—and then he wanted me to put down my telephone number. "Put down your own phone number," I objected.

He shook his head, looked stubborn.

"You don't have a phone?"

"My grandmother doesn't speak English."

"But they'll be talking to you—not her."

He continued shaking his head.

"All right," I said. "We'll write: 'If you see Radar, leave message at this office number.' Then I'll call you."

"But you *can't* call me!"

"Why not?"

He said nothing.

"You sure you own this dog?" I asked. "Or did you borrow him?"

"He's mine!" Sammy insisted. "He didn't belong to nobody. He was starving!" He sniffed and scrubbed at his nose, glared at me accusingly. I gave in.

"O.K. You check in here once a day—only *once*—you hear? And I'll tell you if there's any messages. But if I catch you hanging around here any more than that, the deal's off. Got it?"

He got it. And in the end, he proved useful. Had it not been for Sammy I might have given up coming in to the office at all. As it was I was right there, feet propped on my desk, reading my horoscope when Gloria Chase called.

She'd obtained my name from a mutual acquaintance: our dentist (of all people), for whom I'd once done a particularly unpleasant piece of business. He'd had the kindness to recommend me. But Gloria Chase wasn't trusting anyone sight unseen; nor did she care to darken the doors of my office. She wanted me to come to her house. That kind of service costs, and I told her so. She said she didn't care. At this my spirits lifted; I drove out to North Vancouver that evening with my fingers crossed.

She lived in one of those new suburbs that sprawl high up the North Shore mountains, in a house that was typical of the neighborhood: large, ostentatious—with two patios, three balconies, a swimming pool and a tennis court. When I rang the doorbell, chihuahuas barked; I could hear them leaping and scrabbling at the other side of the door. It was finally opened by Gloria Chase, who examined me doubtfully before letting me in.

Her husband more than made up for her lack of enthusiasm. Fred Chase had a salesman's smile and a politician's handshake; he poured me a drink, invited me downstairs to inspect the sauna and the swimming pool, then out onto the patio to admire the built-in, gas hibachi—big enough to braise a side of beef. I praised the view. In their living room they had a television screen that must have been six-foot square, and in the den they had enough video cameras, monitors and cables to furnish a television studio. For the next half hour Fred ran around flicking switches and spinning dials (it turned out he was in the video business), gave me a "hands-on" demonstration while his wife sat on the sofa, picking at her cuticles. They both acted pretty nervous. And since they didn't seem about to tell me what their trouble was, I decided to ask.

Again it was a daughter, gone missing without notice. I suppressed a sigh. But Alison Chase had a lot more going for her than Lily Kubicek; she was nineteen, not fifteen, and she had financial resources of her own. She had merely moved out, and left no forwarding address. She'd taken clothes, books, even her blankets. She was a student at the local art college, her mother showed me samples of fabrics she'd designed. They were weird, but quite beautiful. Her parents described her as a quiet, cautious young woman; a little lacking in self-confidence; *too* quiet, her father said, but his wife didn't agree. "She's like me," Gloria explained, turning her back on her husband. "Alison's more thoughtful, the creative type."

"Damn inconsiderate, I call it," Fred pronounced. "Why not tell us if she wanted to move out? That's what other kids do. You'd think we were jailers! Why sneak out and leave us worrying? She could be dead for all we know!"

But they didn't think she was dead. They hadn't phoned the cops, and they'd waited two weeks before they'd phoned me. All they wanted, they said, was to know where she was.

As stories go, it was pretty threadbare. I had the feeling I was missing a few pages. "If Alison, as you say, could have moved out—why did she run away? What was she running away *from*?"

"Well that's just it—!" Fred began, but Gloria interrupted him, waving him away like a wasp.

"We didn't *want* Alison to move out of home," she explained. "We're a close-knit family. Our eldest daughter lived at home until she married, and even now she lives less than a mile away and visits us several times a week."

"With her kids," Fred put in. "Oh those kids—what a handful!" He shook his head indulgently.

Gloria acknowledged his contribution with a perfunctory smile. "We love our children," she continued firmly, meeting my eyes. "We can never see too much of them. But if Alison had told us that she wanted to leave home—of course we would have wanted to make sure that she was moving somewhere *suitable*—but we would never have prevented her. Never." She sounded like a president making campaign promises.

"Then why did she run away?"

12

She looked startled, then offended. She was beginning to dislike me.

"Somewhere suitable," I prompted her. "Is it possible that Alison wanted to live somewhere—or with someone—that she knew you would disapprove of? Does she have a boyfriend or a—"

"Oh that's all taken care of," Fred said with satisfaction, rising to his feet and making for the bar again. (He was drinking scotch—on his third double; I was keeping count.) "No, our girlie's been spoken for some time ago. She's engaged—fine young man." He filled his glass, judiciously.

"Engaged?" I looked at Gloria. She immediately dropped her eyes. "So what does her fiancé say? Doesn't he know where she is?" Gloria seemed preoccupied with the ice cube in her glass, so I turned back to Fred.

"Well, that's what makes it all a bit—ah—" He licked his lips. "A bit difficult, you see. We haven't wanted—we'd hoped—"

"We haven't told Danny yet," Gloria said crisply. "Alison's fiancé," she explained, when I looked at her. "Danny Haswell. We didn't want to worry him."

I stared at them, drained my glass. In my estimation, the plot was deteriorating. I'd been talking to them for over an hour and I hadn't reached first base. I looked from one to the other. "Don't you think she might have told him herself?"

"Not necessarily. You see, it's not quite—"

"He phones us—asking for her!" Fred was indignant. "What are we supposed to say? He phoned last weekend I think it was. Wanted her to go sailing. Wasn't that it, honey? Or was it wind-surfing?"

He looked at his wife, but she was again inspecting her ice cube.

I was inspecting her. "What were you going to say? It's not quite—what?"

"It's not quite—how can I explain it? It's a somewhat unusual—maybe old-fashioned—yes, that's the word." She looked relieved. "It's a rather old-fashioned engagement. You see Danny's been a friend of ours—" she glanced at her husband, "a family friend, you might say, for several years

13

now and the engagement," she gave a fluttery smile, "it just *grew*. It seemed inevitable."

I was losing patience. "Inevitable to Alison? Or to you?"

"Why to—to all of us."

"I see." I did; my vision was improving considerably. "Now would you mind telling me why you're so sure that Alison wouldn't have confided in her fiance?"

"We never said *that*—"

"You certainly implied it."

They both stared at me blankly.

"Look," I said, putting my glass on the table. Fred leapt up to refill it, but I placed my hand over it, shook my head. "If you want me to find your daughter, I'm going to have to make inquiries. I'm going to have to visit her sister, her friends, her teachers, and yes—even her fiance. I have to find out what the situation is; I have to talk to everyone she knows. If you suspect that your daughter is running away from her fiance—then tell me so. It'll save me a lot of work which in turn will save you a lot of money. Make sense?"

Fred was blustering again, incoherent with protests. "No, that's certainly not—quite the wrong impress—don't know how you could have—"

"Yes," said Gloria.

"Yes what?" Fred roared.

Gloria looked at him defiantly. "Yes, I think that Alison is running away from Danny."

"That's nonsense, damn nonsense. I won't hear another—"

"You don't know Alison as well as I do, and for some time now I've suspected that she was having second thoughts about it all. I know that Danny's doing very well for himself and I know how much you like him but—"

"*I* like him! What about you? So did you! So did Alison!"

"I'm not so sure about that."

"Since when?" Fred bellowed. Gloria's lips crimped.

"May I interrupt?" I asked. Fred glared at me balefully, crossed his arms, compressed his lips.

I turned to Gloria. "You're sure that—" I consulted my notes, "Mr. Haswell knows nothing of her whereabouts."

"Yes."

"And doesn't even know that she's moved out?"

"That is correct."

"Do you mind if I tell him?" I saw Fred scowl at me. "I think I'm going to have to."

"It's time he knew anyway," Gloria admitted.

"Good."

I asked her for the fiance's address and phone numbers; she gave them to me. I wrote down other addresses and phone numbers: relatives, friends, anyone and everyone that might know something about Alison that her parents didn't know. I named a retainer fee, quoted my rates, outlined my usual procedure. Gloria wrote out a check.

"Now," I closed my notebook, "let's just make sure that we understand each other. You're hiring me to find Alison and learn something of her circumstances. You want to assure yourselves that she's safe. Right?"

Gloria nodded. Her husband just glared at me.

"She's not attending school, we know that," Gloria said. "We don't really think she's been run over or kidnapped—but one worries, you know? Of course she's of legal age and everything—but what do we tell Danny? We feel it's up to her to get in touch with him because—well, we don't know, do we? We don't know what's going on. We don't know what she wants. But we're not asking you to drag her home by the hair or anything. Are we, dear?"

She looked at her husband, who was watching us morosely. "I just want to know if she's in the morgue," he said thickly (he was now on his fourth). "If it's not too much to ask."

"Fine." I got up. "If I find out anything, I'll phone you. If not, you'll get a report from me next Friday—just to keep you up to date on what I'm doing."

Gloria accompanied me to the door; the chihuahuas snapped at my ankles. And as I drove back down the mountainside I reflected that—again—my sympathies were with the runaway. You'd think, being a parent, I'd have more sympathy for my own side. But I've also been a daughter. I too was once engaged to the man of my parents' choice, and I know that once you've got yourself into that situation, there's no diplomatic way out of it. I suspected that Fred and Gloria Chase had brought this upon themselves.

CHAPTER THREE

I'VE BEEN pretty lucky with my kids. Maybe too lucky with Katie, who is most parents' ideal: attractive, polite, studious, responsible—too good to be true. I've been worrying about her ever since she was born. She's very different from me; I have a hard time understanding her and an even worse time living with her, trying to measure up to her standards. She's had an equally hard time lowering herself to mine. I'm always doing things that Katie disapproves of: divorcing her father (though that was his idea, not mine), carrying cases of beer in public (how else am I supposed to get them from the liquor store to my house?), giving martial arts demonstrations in high schools, "carrying on" with Tom (she adores Tom, but that doesn't mean I'm allowed to sleep with him), being a private eye. "There's absolutely nothing wrong with a mother being a private detective," she used to say (I would hear her practicing it in her bedroom, saying it over and over, trying out different tones of voice). But since she's moved out of home we've been getting along a lot better. That happened a couple of months ago, but I'm still adjusting to her absence. Every so often, usually around bedtime, I get compulsions to phone her—much as I used to peek into her bedroom in the middle of the night to make sure she was still breathing. She feigns exasperation, but I don't think she really minds.

She's a university student now, shares an apartment with a girlfriend—and I'm hoping that, now that I'm out of her life, she'll loosen up a bit. Not that I want her to get into trouble, but she could do with a few less prunes and prisms—and maybe a boyfriend I could tolerate? One who didn't give me lectures on my eating habits and promise to take good care of her? Who didn't *insist* upon coming to tea every Sunday afternoon and regaling me with platitudes until I'm so bored I could scream. Normally, I don't drink tea and I'm sure Rick (that's the boyfriend) doesn't either—but our whole relationship is like that, has nothing to do with who he is or who I am, but is an enactment of some cliche that he's got stuck in his head. Katie sits between us, her eyes going from one face to the other—and it's for her sake that I don't just get up and walk out. For her sake I endure his advice and paternalistic smiles; for her sake I sip my tea and keep my ankles neatly crossed. When she told me she was thinking about moving out, that was my first thought: "No more Rick—what heaven!" She's been dating him now for more than two years, has almost never gone out with anyone else. At the rate she's going she'll end up marrying him. In which case I'll—suffer, to put it mildly. And when they buy their house in suburbia and have three kids in as many years, I'll commit hara-kiri. Yes, I know I'm exaggerating. But when you've spent your whole life climbing out of a pigeonhole, it's pretty hard to watch your daughter burrowing herself back in. And I've never been philosophical, especially about my kids.

Ben, on the other hand, has hardly caused me a day's anxiety in his life. At seventeen years old he's still underfoot, but more helpful than he used to be: he vacuums the house once a week and can cook spaghetti and hamburgers. Unlike Katie, he has never felt the need to defend me, says: "My mum's a private eye!" as if it were something to be proud of. He's an easy-going kid, "idle but bright," according to his teachers, popular with his peers; in school he'd been called up before the principal for various misdemeanors—none of them serious. I know some of my friends considered him cheeky, and probably thought I should have started worrying about him a long time ago—but I figure that if kids let it out in cheekiness they won't go in for full-scale rebellions: stealing cars and looting vacation homes. When dealing with teenagers, one should have a sense of proportion.

But of late, I admit, I'd been a bit concerned about him. He'd just graduated from high school and seemed to think that the be-all and end-all of existence. He had no plans for further education, no thought of how he would earn a living, no desire to leave home even—he seemed perfectly content. He got up around noon, spent the rest of the day with this friend or that, sitting around the beach, the ice cream parlors and fish-and-chip joints, complaining only that he needed more money. "Who doesn't?" I'd retort.

I told myself that this was the first open-ended holiday of his life, that he'd tire of it after a while and start making more realistic plans. He was too poor to drink or buy drugs; I worried sometimes that he'd steal the money he couldn't get from me, but there'd been no indications of this, so I figured that, at worst, he mooched off his friends. Most of whom were as penniless as he was. I tried to talk to him about jobs or training programs or whatever, but he mocked my efforts, protesting that it was unmotherly on my part to be in such a hurry to get rid of him. Which I'm not. As a housemate he's not bad; he's out most evenings and looks after his own meals, and now that he's got more time than I do, I make him do the laundry. We have the same taste in people. People were the major bone of contention between Katie and myself; she never approved of my friends (except Tom); I never approved of hers. I'd clean the house, make cookies, try to dress like the mothers in *Chatelaine* magazine—but still her friends would eye me like I was some kind of exhibit: curious, but not nice.

"Just make yourself scarce!" Katie once yelled at me. "That's what other mothers do. Stop trying to be one of us!"

"I don't!"

"Yes, you do. You show off." It was the most damning accusation she could have made; in her eyes, a despicable fault. And I was left thinking: But I *like* people that show off—as long as they don't overdo it. But in Katie's eyes I was always overdoing it.

And yet—as I started working on my new case, going round making my initial inquiries about Alison Chase, visiting her relatives and old school friends, hanging out at the art school and taking advantage of their subsidized food prices, I realized that I should be counting my blessings. I spent a lot of time watching young people that month, art students for the most part, many of whom affected the most bizarre costumes imaginable—1940 lingerie, day-glo hair-dyes, black lipstick, bikers' chains—and in comparison with my kids they seemed very vulnerable. They were like tightrope walkers with no net—daring all—making a virtue of the situation in which they found themselves, but resenting the necessity to do so. My kids look far less sophisticated, but considerably more secure. When they get into a mess, they still find it possible to talk to me. And surely that's necessary—that a young person can lean, however temporarily, on the experience of someone older, can take their advice—if only until they regain confidence in their own capabilities. Watching many of the students, I felt a kind of hopelessness. There's something wrong with a society that so alienates its young, that can't shelter them, can't make a place for them to fall without killing themselves. Like Lillian Kubicek. And Alison Chase?

But I was beginning to suspect that Alison didn't fall into this category. As I talked to friends that Alison's parents knew about, who referred me to other friends that Alison's parents certainly didn't know about, Alison was revealing herself as a person of many layers. Her old high school friends, like her parents, her sister and other relatives, knew her as a quiet, rather intense person; "still waters" said an aunt; "always finding fault" said her sister: fastidious, serious, critical. They were all impressed by her fiance (apparently a crowd-pleaser) and assumed that Alison was equally pleased with him, though none of them, I discovered, ever actually heard her say so. But then Alison, I was learning, wasn't the type to wear her heart on her sleeve.

One of these high school friends was enrolled in the same art school, and it was she that told me that Alison had, of late, been "getting involved with some people you wouldn't believe." Which meant, I discovered, the students with the day-glo hair and candy-colored running shoes. Finally I succeeded in striking up a conversation with one of them:

"Alison's missing? Oh wow! I wondered why I hadn't seen her around."

"When did you last see her?"

"Not for *weeks*—no, really. I was wondering."

"Any idea why she might have left home?"

"It was *obvious*, wasn't it? What with those chihuahuas and that fiance—straight out of the Mafia, he was—and her father getting too friendly with her girlfriends and all—"

"Pardon?"

"Her dad. Always trying to feel up her friends. *Not* in good taste."

"You've been to her house?"

"Once. To a party. I've never met so many nauseating people in my life."

I studied her, speculatively. "Her parents are pretty worried. Any idea where she might have gone?"

My informant's eyes, circled fluorescent green, narrowed. "They're paying you, right?"

"Only to find out if she's O.K. I won't be betraying any secrets."

She didn't look convinced.

"Alison could be dead for all we know. Or hurt."

She glanced over my head at someone behind me, beckoned. When another student with spiky hair (greased to stand up like porcupine quills) and barber pole striped tights arrived at our table, my informant got up. "Meet Janis," she said to me. "I'm sorry, I don't remember your name."

"Margaret Lacey," I said, and produced a business card.

She passed it to Janis, saying: "She's looking for Alison." Then she left us together.

I had many conversations with Janis. By the end of the first, I was pretty sure that Alison was alive and well and that Janis knew where—but getting that information out of her obviously wasn't going to be easy. I continued to follow up other leads on Alison, but became increasingly convinced that only Janis really knew what I wanted to know. Unfortunately, Janis was a clam (a rarer breed than many might suppose). But she loved to lecture, and allowed me to buy her many coffees on condition that I let her question me about my job and berate me for my iniquities. So I got to know her pretty well—always hoping that one day she'd take me into her confidence.

"You're no better than a cop. In fact, you're worse."

"At least I pick and choose my jobs; cops have no choice. Regardless of the circumstances, if the law has been broken, they have to make an arrest."

"But you're like a sneak."

I shrugged. "Some sneaks are useful. Some people have secrets they don't deserve to keep." I cited Mike Talney as an example. Janis told me he should be shot.

"By whom?" I protested.

"By his wife, if she'd like first crack at it. If not, you could do it for her. You know how to shoot, don't you?"

I agreed that I did. "You think that would be better than what I'm doing now?"

"It'd sure be a lot *cleaner*." (She made me feel like a chimney sweep.) "At least you'd be performing a useful service."

"Tell me—does Alison share these views?"

"Oh Alison!" She exhaled cigarette smoke in disgust. "She's just an idealist. She doesn't understand the importance of shock."

"Shock?"

"Yeah—you gotta make people sit up; you gotta make them *see*, for Chrissakes! Isn't that what art's all about? But Alison won't let go of her—" She stopped. She stuffed her lighter and cigarette package into her purse, stood up with such vehemence that she knocked the chair over behind her. "Oh very clever," she sneered, stooping to pick it up again. "Can't leave it alone, can you?"

"I've got to make a living."

"Then *wash floors!*" she spat, and marched away through the tables. Which gives you an idea of what I was up against.

*

For some time I'd been putting off my visit to the fiance. Given that he was probably Alison's reason for running away, I'd decided that he was the person least likely to be able to help me. But after I'd exhausted the art school scene, he was all I had left. So I figured I might as well pay him a call.

Danny Haswell owned a night club, a place called "Kinky's" on Hastings Street. The entrance itself was discreet, and it wasn't until you got inside that you realized what a big place it was, with a long bar and many levels of tables, leather booths along the walls, a sizeable dance floor and beside it, a stage. It was designed to be disorienting. I felt seasick as soon as I walked in, and became almost immediately lost in the maze of levels and ramps, in the writhing, plunging colors on the walls, in the mirrors—which were everywhere—elongating, segmenting, distorting; set at every angle so that one was constantly catching unexpected views of oneself—almost none of them whole. By the time I made it to the cashier's desk I felt like the victim of an axe murderer. I was told that Mr. Haswell's office was upstairs; a waiter escorted me to the appropriate door. Behind it the walls were a smooth, calm cream and the stairs were carpeted in thick grey pile. It was like stepping back onto land.

The stairs opened onto a small lobby, simply but expensively furnished: a massive receptionist's desk in one corner flanked by ornamental figs, crushed leather couches for the guests. A slight draft from the air-conditioning stirred the fig leaves, the grained wood of the coffee table was like velvet to the touch. The receptionist's desk was empty. I selected a magazine from the table and was enveloped by an armchair; as if I'd sat on a button, the receptionist appeared, closing a solid oak door silently behind her.

At first I thought she was Chinese. But as soon as she lifted her head I realized that she was native Indian, from one of the Coast bands—with a face as closed and beautiful as a sea shell: long eyelids, high cheekbones, broad, slanting nostrils. She was very slim—not tall—but carried herself as if her life depended upon it, as if, at the slightest touch, her defenses would disintegrate. She was undoubtedly very young—seventeen at a guess. When she looked at me it was without friendliness; instead I received what I can only describe as a visual frisk—expert, anonymous. A moment later her eyes dropped, and I had the impression I'd been dismissed.

I walked up to her desk, handed her my card, told her my business. She didn't appear too interested so I further explained that it was about Mr. Haswell's fiance and he'd probably like to hear what I had to say. This didn't impress her either, but she decided she'd better check. Again she slipped through the door, returned in less than a minute, holding it open. "This way, please," she directed me.

As far as I knew Danny Haswell was now the only person in Alison's life who didn't know she'd disappeared. Gloria and Fred Chase still hadn't hit upon a socially acceptable way to tell him, and no one else I'd talked to knew him well enough to have got in touch with him. So I was wondering if my news would come as a surprise to him, or if he had sources of information that I didn't know about. It was one of the many things he never let me find out.

Danny Haswell was tall, dark and handsome—a three-piece executive in an office as sleek and bland as he was. He looked like one of those male models that gets posed behind the blonde or the bourbon bottle (or both) in glossy advertisements; he had no edges, no idiosyncracies, no identifying marks. Masterful eyebrows, a square chin, a few wrinkles ingrained in his forehead. Sanitized good looks.

When I walked into his office he was perusing my business card with an expression of distaste, but rose immediately upon seeing me and professed himself delighted to make my acquaintance. Since my manners were no match for his, I got straight down to business. "I've been hired by Gloria and Fred Chase to make some inquiries about their daughter, Alison," I explained, subsiding into another armchair.

His eyebrows rose, his forehead furrowed; he waited to hear more.

"I understand you and Alison are engaged. Is that right?"

He placed my business card upon his desk. "We've been engaged for more than a year."

"Alison has left home. Did you know that?"

"Ah!" said Danny Haswell, and tipped back in his chair.

"Were you aware that she'd disappeared?"

He made a face. "I suspected as much."

"What made you suspicious?"

"She hasn't been at home for some time. Her parents are running out of explanations."

"Did Alison tell you she was planning to leave home?"

"Wait." He lifted a hand, gave me a conspiratorial smile, the kind a man uses to disarm a bossy lady. "You mean Alison has moved out? Packed her bags? Not been kidnapped or run over by a bus." His eyes twinkled engagingly.

"We don't think she's been kidnapped or run over by a bus," I agreed—but didn't twinkle back. "She's taken some of her personal belongings with her, and I understand that she has an independent income—modest, but adequate."

"And no one knows where she went?"

"That's right."

"Her friends, her sister—"

I shook my head.

He gave an appreciative grimace; apparently he was intrigued.

I returned to my questions. "Did Alison ever say anything to you about moving out of her home?"

He hesitated for a moment. "No."

"Has she been in touch with you—recently?"

He picked up a pen from his desk, twirled it thoughtfully. "How recently?"

"Since June 16th."

He reached for his calendar, flipped a couple of pages. "According to this thing—which may or may not be accurate—" another conspiratorial gleam; he'd win me over if it killed him, "I last saw her on June 12th. We went to a party together."

"That was a long time ago." It was now July 10th.

He shrugged. "Like I said, she hasn't been home since."

"Where was this party?"

"At the house of a friend of mine, Larry Joven. He lives down by False Creek."

"When you went to this party, did you get the impression that Alison was in any way disturbed? Excited?"

He abandoned the desk calendar. "She was quiet—but she's always quiet. I didn't notice anything."

I decided to stop beating about the bush. "Mr. Haswell, would you mind explaining to me why you and Alison got engaged in the first place?"

He feigned surprise at such a question. "We wanted to get married."

"But if you don't mind me saying so, you don't seem to be exactly—intimate? I mean, you haven't seen her for a month, but you're not too upset about it. And why would she leave home without telling you where she was going?"

He regarded me steadily, considering his answer. "Alison's a very private person," he said at last. "I respect that. Even after a year, I don't feel that I know her very well. But I don't want to push. You know?" He quirked an eyebrow. "To me Alison is—" he pursed his lips, placed his fingertips together, "like a present, unopened. She's still got her wrappings on. Mysterious. I like that," he confessed, as it were, man to man.

"Doesn't sound like much to base a marriage on," I said tartly.

Again he crooked an eyebrow; he was surprised to find me so unaccommodating. "It's romantic, perhaps—but then I *am* romantic." He looked at me defiantly. "And maybe old-fashioned." (I wondered if he'd been coached.) He gave me a furtive glance. "Her mother told me that she's quite inexperienced."

The man made me sick. "But mothers don't know everything," I reminded him, archly.

He wasn't stupid, and he finally understood that I didn't like him and that he wasn't going to like me.

"I fail to understand why she hasn't been in touch with you. Did you have a fight, Mr. Haswell? After that party, perhaps?"

"No." He wasn't going to offer me any more confidences.

"Then how do you explain it? You haven't seen her for a month. Don't you wonder what she's thinking?"

He shifted his weight in his chair, as if trying to get more comfortable. "No. I don't. Although *you* don't understand our relationship, Alison does. She knows I'm not going anywhere, and that I'm not going to push her into anything she doesn't like. We're a modern couple; we live independent lives. I trust her."

I must have looked dubious. "So you think she's just taking—time out, as it were."

"I don't know what she's doing!" he snapped, then added, with labored patience, "But I do know that we're engaged and that she's not the kind of girl to throw me over without telling me."

The phone rang. He snatched it up. "O.K., Sally. Tell him I'll be right out." He put down the receiver, regarded me with hostility. "Any more questions?"

I knew I wouldn't get anything else out of him. The man was so fake he probably didn't tell himself the truth, never mind anyone else. So I rose to my feet and thanked him politely; he held the door open while I preceded him through it.

The scene that met our eyes as we entered the lobby was interrupted by our entrance. I only caught a glimpse—but an impression so vivid, that I remembered it for a long time afterwards. The receptionist, that terrifyingly self-possessed young woman, was sitting at her desk, hands clasped, eyes lowered, and towering over her was what I can only describe as a hulk—a man well over six feet tall and muscled like Mr. Universe. He was leaning both arms on the edge of her desk, whispering something, peering into her averted face—which was stiff with some emotion that I couldn't immediately identify. The man was smiling, his fair skin flushed; the girl he was teasing was white about the lips. When we walked in he abruptly straightened, left the desk and strode over to greet Haswell. I noticed then that he was wearing gloves—expensive ones, kid (but surely eccentric, for July?)—one of which he peeled off before shaking Haswell's hand. I suddenly realized that I'd seen him before. I couldn't remember where, but one doesn't forget a man like that: stud stock, the product of a diet of red meat and cholesterol, exuding self-satisfaction from every well-oiled sinew. He greeted Danny with great heartiness, clapped him on the shoulder, beamed at me too while he was at it—as if we were about to become good friends. But behind him I could see the receptionist, who hadn't flickered an eyelid, who sat perfectly still—like a mouse that's been temporarily abandoned by a cat.

Danny gave me a loveless smile and wished me luck with my investigations, told the receptionist to take his calls for the next half hour. "See ya later, Hiawatha," Mr. Universe called over to the receptionist; she pretended she hadn't heard him. Again he smiled at me, but I didn't get the joke. As they stepped into Haswell's office, I heard Danny say: "Christ, Caesar, give her a break," before the door swung shut between us.

Caesar, I thought—yes, even the name rang a bell. Caesar.... But no last name came to accompany it. I looked at the receptionist. She was still staring at her typewriter, erect, clenched. I walked over to her desk.

"That man," I said, indicating the office door. "I'm sure I know him from somewhere. What's his name?"

Only her eyes moved—lifted to meet mine. They were anything but friendly. "Charles Grice."

"Charles?" I said doubtfully—but something was beginning to surface.

"Also known as Caesar," she prompted, as if reading my mind. Our eyes locked.

"Yes," I said slowly. I was mesmerized by her eyes, which seemed to be forcing my mind open, making me remember. "Yes." I nodded at her. Immediately her gaze dropped. "Charles Grice," I murmured—but she didn't look at me again. What a strange girl she was! But I now knew very well where I'd seen Grice before—on the front page of a newspaper; I'd never met him at all. I'd only seen his photograph: one arm flung around his lawyer, who had just successfully defended him against charges of.... But I couldn't remember the charges. Only that he'd made a great deal of money, and the Crown hadn't liked the way he'd made it. But they'd lacked sufficient evidence to convict him.

Yet I'd also heard of Caesar, from an old friend of mine. "Charles" in the newspapers, but "Caesar" on the streets. As I walked back down the grey-carpeted stairway, I decided to visit that friend; I hadn't seen her in some time. "The biggest crook in town," that's what she'd told me, "the slipperiest and the meanest. I wish the cops would get their act together and get that bastard off the streets." I remembered being surprised. It was not like Johanna to come down on the side of the law.

Yet Danny Haswell knew him well. (So did his receptionist.) They did business with him? If so, Mr. Haswell might be more interesting than I'd thought.

CHAPTER FOUR

I wasn't born a private eye. And on bad days I can't believe that I am one; I feel like a fraud, or a little girl playing dress-ups. Not helped by the fact that my mother, my aunts, uncles, siblings, cousins—even some of my friends—are waiting for me to "grow up," as one of my least favorite aunts so kindly put it. It seems one can't be different without being accused of immaturity. Unfortunately, such attitudes rub off on their recipients (as indeed they are intended to), and I'm often tempted to give up—not because it's particularly difficult to be a private investigator, but because it's an exhausting business continually pretending to be one in the face of so much skepticism.

Which is why I still spend as much as ten hours a week on the mats. There, under the critical eye of my Aikido teacher, I become what my relatives keep insisting I can't be—a woman that can take care of herself. It's symbolic, rather than practical. I don't need such skills; most of the male operatives I've met couldn't run a quarter of a mile without succumbing to a heart attack, and no amount of "chi" is defense against a gun. But it's a psychological weapon and, if you believe my Aikido teacher, a spiritual one. It teaches you to be aware of the bodies and minds around you; it trains your sixth sense (and for all their pride in their great deductive powers, private detectives swear by their sixth sense); it gives you an aura that others respect. Even my mother acknowledges that I look elegant on the

Aikido mats. "Very nice, dear," she says, smoothing the gloves in her lap. "Impressive," says Tom, meaning that it makes him uncomfortable. He's been involved with me for many years—but my job still distresses him.

It's a subject Tom avoids—unless we're having a fight. At first I thought he disliked my profession because "like *all* men," I would have said (I've mellowed a bit since), he feels uncomfortable with a woman that doesn't need physical protection. But lately I've realized that he's trying to protect himself; he feels defenseless against the ugliness of many people's lives; he finds the realities of human experience unbearable. So he focuses on the lives of algae and plankton, inhabits dream worlds where he and I walk down woodland trails, calling the dogs to heel; where we toast our slippers in front of the fire, listening to Brahms quintets. We do these things sometimes. But when the record stops, or when we finish examining a frost-furred leaf, I start talking about...Lily Kubicek, for example. At which point Tom whitens around the edges and shrivels like a slug. He never interrupts me, never tries to change the subject—but he looks like he's swallowing arsenic. And for years—well, even now—I've taken his squeamishness personally, and have been extra careful *not* to avoid the subject of what I do for a living. Which usually means that I'm throwing it in his face.

Summers are our nadir. Tom is a biologist, and spends most of his summer months out of town doing fieldwork, only popping in for the occasional few days to submit samples and statistics, then flitting off again to the bug-ridden tundra that he loves. Which is hard on me. When Tom is doing fieldwork he's not there when I want him and I have the added consolation of knowing that he's probably forgotten my existence. I'm very lucky if I get a postcard. I guess for some women, such absences would fan the flames of their affection—but they have the opposite effect on me. I become irritable, resentful, and ultimately, rebellious.

A few days after my visit to Danny Haswell, Tom flew into town and stayed for a whole night. The following afternoon, I escorted him back to the airport, watched him as far as the metal detectors, then went and bought myself a drink in the airport bar. I felt awkward, sitting there; I worried that others would think I was a bar-fly, a divorcee on the make. Maybe that's what I was? Tom had spent our night together telling me all about a new growth that was reproducing itself in undesirable quantities in some watershed in the Northwest Territories; I'd retaliated by telling him all about the Chases, Danny Haswell and Janis. If there was common ground between these subjects, we never discovered it.

I remembered my decision to go look up Johanna. Perfect, I thought—she'll cheer me up. I phoned her from the airport and suggested that we go out to dinner together, but she told me that Margot was in the middle of preparing some Indonesian dish and why didn't I come to her place and reap the results. I readily agreed. Margot is an excellent cook, and I was in need of rehabilitation.

I've known Johanna for many years now, but I've never really become accustomed to her. Our backgrounds are too different; our present lives are too different; our friendship spans chasms of class and culture; sometimes, it seems, we don't even speak the same language. I don't see her very often—but I know that if something irrevocable ever happened to me or my kids, she'd be one of the first people I'd phone. I trust her. I also respect her. She makes me face facts, and she doesn't let me lie. She's also the only person I know (apart from my son, Ben, who's only being filial) that doesn't question my right, my ability to be a private detective. Her support for my career is absolutely unqualified. Sometimes I think I wouldn't have made it without her.

Johanna is a lesbian. She is also a prostitute. Some people think that a surprising combination, but it's actually quite common, and makes sense if you think about it. Prostitutes have reason to be alienated from men, and they're a lot better off if they look for love elsewhere. Margot is Johanna's lover. As a couple they're like the long and the short of it: Johanna is six feet tall and built like the Statue of Liberty—not fat, but large—wide shoulders, big breasts, broad hips, long legs. She belongs to one of those fitness gyms and pumps a lot of iron. Going out with Johanna, I always feel like I'm invisible; she attracts every eye in the vicinity. Margot, on the other hand, works as a legal secretary and dresses more conservatively than the most trusted of family solicitors: feminine, and very proper. She stands five-foot-two in her heels, has a slight French accent and a cocker spaniel, sings soprano in a church choir. I have a feeling that she's religious, though she's never given me any proof of it. Every so often I get nervous about Margot, and think: she knows far more about me than I'll ever know about her. But because she's always been there, I've become used to talking in front of her. I'd actually like to get to know her better, but I don't know how to begin (having already known her for years), and whenever Johanna's in the room I tend to neglect anyone else.

When I first met Johanna she was still working the streets. But being such a phenomenon, both physically and psychologically, she has succeeded, over the years, in establishing a personal following of men who prefer the security of going to the same woman every time. I know the appreciation is not always mutual, but for her too there is security in only seeing men that she knows; she can pick and choose her customers the same way they pick and choose her. It's also a lot safer; she never found it easy to remain inconspicuous on the streets. But her loyalties haven't changed; in her heart she's still standing on the corner, shivering in the wind—and she still spends a lot a time there, talking to her friends. She a natural ringleader, Johanna, and there's nothing she likes better than giving pep talks to the troops. Like many "criminals" I've met, her sense of morality is much more highly developed than that of the average citizen; having discarded conventional definitions of right and wrong, she's come to her own conclusions. The results can be disturbing. Talking to Johanna, I often feel like a child being taught how to swim; I keep wanting to touch bottom to make sure it's still there.

"So what are you up to?" she asked, handing me a gin and tonic.

I told her about Kinky's, about Alison and Danny Haswell. "Ever heard of the place?"

"Kinky's." She frowned. "I've seen it, of course—but I've never been in there. I could ask around."

"Reason is—I saw someone you know there. Or maybe

you only knew of him, I can't remember. Caesar Grice."

The bottle of gin, en route to the kitchen cupboard, stopped in mid-air. Johanna looked at me, her eyes narrowing.

"He seemed to know Danny Haswell pretty well."

She placed the bottle on the shelf, gently closed the cupboard door. She poured tonic water into Margot's drink. "That's bad, Maggie. That stinks. You'd better find out a bit more about this fiance."

"That's why I'm here," I agreed. "I thought I'd start by finding out a little more about Caesar."

Johanna gave me a glance—a look I'd seen before—that always serves to remind me that I'm on the other side of the fence. I like to think that Johanna trusts me—but the truth of the matter is that Johanna trusts no one. In the last analysis, she relies only upon herself. I don't blame her for this; no matter how empathetic I am I'll never stand in her shoes. I've learned to accept small rebuffs.

She finished mixing Margot's drink, put it down on the counter where Margot was chopping chicken, peered into one of the pots on the stove. "You want me to stir this?"

Margot glanced up. "Is it simmering?"

"Boiling."

"Then give it a stir, and turn it down a bit."

Johanna picked up the wooden spoon, stirred the sauce, finally decided to resume our conversation.

"I'll tell you, Maggie—and don't you go repeating it— but that guy gives me nightmares. All the other pimps and pushers I know—they're human, right? You can get to know their weaknesses; you can bargain; you can manipulate. You can make them respect you. But Caesar—I don't know what it is about that man—he's like an armored tank; he doesn't *have* fears. His confidence is staggering. Sometimes I think he's been lobotomized or something. He trashes people the way most people squash bugs. I guess he doesn't know that he is human; he doesn't see any connection between his victims and himself. He's a monster—really."

"What do you mean—he trashes people?"

"I mean that he kills them."

She met my eyes, read my incredulity. "Oh, it's well known in my part of the world. Too many people that have worked for him have died—of overdoses, automobile accidents—you name it. He probably runs a close third to heart attacks and cancer. People don't cross him. They just don't."

I didn't want to believe her. I don't put much stock in talk of this kind—villains of unmitigated evil—but I knew Johanna didn't either. And I had absolutely no desire to pursue Alison Chase if her trail was going to lead me into such treacherous social strata. I took a gulp of my gin and tonic.

"How does he make his money?"

"Pimping, drug-pushing and gambling—all on a big scale. He imports heroin in large quantities, runs gambling rackets out at the race track; is particularly partial to minors—male and female both. He's got high-up business connections, supplies whole conventions at a time. He must be worth millions."

"Couple of years ago he was in court. Isn't that right?"

"Oh they've had him up lots of times." Johanna shrugged. "He's probably on a first-name basis with the judges by now."

Margot's chicken hit the frying pan; there was a wonderful smell of garlic and lemons and God knows what else. Margot, stirring briskly, glanced up at me and smiled. "I don't want to get killed," I found myself confiding in her.

"Of course not," she said, so sympathetically that I felt like a toddler that has been brushed off and stood on its feet, resurrected as a viable human being.

"Look," Johanna said, sitting down across the table from me. "How be we go down there one night, have a drink or two, see if I recognize anybody else?"

"Would you? I know I should go back there—not because I think Danny Haswell is going to lead me to Alison—but I *do* get the feeling that the whole story starts with him. But I should warn you about the decor. It's absolutely stomach-turning. We mustn't get drunk."

"We won't," Johanna agreed. "And I probably won't recognize anyone. But it doesn't hurt to try."

We happened to choose a Tuesday—which was unfortunate. But if we'd chosen any other night, I probably wouldn't be telling this story. Because Tuesday, as we discovered when we arrived at the door, was "Ladies' Night."

"What's that supposed to mean?" I asked Johanna.

"Different things, different places."

At Kinky's it meant that there was no cover charge, and no men on the premises apart from the staff and the stripper. We walked into bedlam—a mass of pubescent femininity chattering, giggling, screaming above the music, glowing lime-green and gold beneath the revolving stage-lights. And I mean pubescent. As my eyes adjusted to the dimness, I concluded that most of the customers should have been at home preparing tomorrow's homework. Instead they were drunk. Uproarious and silly, hysterical with giggles, in paroxysms of embarrassment at the antics of the stripper. Who was singularly untalented. I looked at Johanna. She was towering beside me in three-inch heels, at least a foot taller than anyone else around. "Charming," she murmured, becoming aware of my gaze. She continued surveying the scene with vigilant, hooded eyes.

We circulated warily, trying to find a place to sit down. I swear I walked into six mirrors in the process; in the noise and wheeling spotlights the place was more disorienting than ever. I clung to Johanna's elbow. As we moved among the tables I picked out some groups of what looked like clerical workers or housewives, even some knots of middle-aged women (looking a little flustered), and others that might have been university students. But at least half the customers were simply not of legal age. Finally Johanna led me to a tiny table against a wall, with a view of the bar, the stage and the cashier's desk. We sat down.

"What happened to the law about minors?" I yelled.

"What?"

I put my mouth to her ear, repeated my question.

"He must be greasing a lot of palms; I've never seen anything like it."

The two women nearest us were certainly in their twenties, aware of no one outside of themselves, getting drunk enough to exchange intimate and indiscreet jokes about their husbands, doubling up with laughter, mopping the tears from their eyes. But beyond them, in a corner, was what appeared to be a high school volleyball team; they didn't even look as if they were trying to pass for nineteen. And none of them would have made it down a corridor without the support of the walls. How did Haswell get away with it?

The stripper was downright embarrassing. I've seen erotic dancers before, and know for a fact that there is nothing in the male physique that prohibits the expression of grace and sensuality—but this man had all the finesse of a rapist. He ground and thrust and bared his upper teeth, gripped a knife between his thighs, flexed his biceps, clenched his buttocks. He looked about as appetizing as a dog trying to hump a human leg. Was this what teenage girls fantasized when they climbed into bed at night? I remembered my own adolescent fantasies of brusque, commanding strangers that fell in love with me against their will, challenged by my wit, my daring and independence. If, at fifteen or sixteen, I had witnessed a performance like this, would I have been attracted? Fascinated—yes. Fascinated but revolted.

And when I looked carefully at some of the faces around me, I saw that my adolescent reactions were not yet extinct. Less squeamish girls shrieked and guffawed, cheered and threw pennies, swooned into each other's laps. More sophisticated ones succeeded in ignoring the stripper altogether, conversed laconically, their eyes flickering disdainfully over the antics of their neighbors. But here and there among the crowd I spied a pale, stiff face; a pair of eyes that followed the stripper as if asking: "Is this what I'm in for?" And I wished I could have, with one wave of my wand, scooped them collectively into my shopping bag and deposited them in an ice cream parlor, where I could buy them all milkshakes and restore them to their fantasies of a boyfriend who was also a comrade, a fellow-fighter against enemies and injustice—because girls also dream of this, before the pulp romances get them. I guess I'm sentimental. But it sickened me to think that these girls were preparing themselves to accept this—were being *conditioned* to accept this? Or was Haswell just too cheap to pay for someone that could actually dance? And too lazy to ask for I.D. from his customers?

There was an orgasmic drum roll; the lights blacked out. In the succeeding strobe one could see the stripper sprawled on the stage, pelvis arched, penis bulging—in a crash of cymbals he was obliterated. The house lights came up. And a squadron of staff issued from behind the bar, each bearing a tray loaded with drinks—which they proceeded to distribute. I looked at Johanna. "What's this in aid of?"

Two drinks were set down in front of us. "On the house," the waiter said.

"You make a habit of this?" I asked him.

"Sure do."

Johanna picked up her drink, which looked like some kind of vodka sling, handed it back. "Scotch," she said brusquely. "Ice—no water. And I'll pay for it."

"No problem," he said obligingly, moving on to the next table.

I picked up my glass, examined its contents. "Funny way to run a business."

"On the contrary," Johanna answered. She got up from her chair, walked away through the tables—left me staring after her. She disappeared around a divider and out of sight. I tasted my drink; it was much too sweet. A minute later I saw Johanna coming back.

She sat down. "Go take a look at the front entrance."

"I'll never find it," I objected, but got up obediently and began edging my way through the tables. Around a divider I found some washrooms, then a ticket booth I hadn't noticed before, now occupied and lit. The front door was beyond it. I pushed it open.

Outside on the sidewalk the entrance was cordoned off and policed by bouncers. Behind the big placard announcing

"Ladies' Night" was what looked like a movie line-up, maybe half a block long. Beyond the line-up was Hastings Street, streaming with headlights and neon signs, beneath which its pedestrians strutted or shambled, depending upon their alcohol content and walk of life. Again I surveyed the line-up. It didn't seem to be moving. It was twitchy, talkative, emitted spirals of cigarette smoke and loud gusts of laughter. And finally I noticed that it was composed entirely of men.

"What are they waiting for?" I asked one of the bouncers.

He glanced at his watch. "Ten o'clock."

"What happens then?"

He jerked his head. "The ticket booth opens."

The ticket booth? But Johanna and I hadn't paid to get in. "I thought this was Ladies' Night."

"Yeah—ladies get in free. But the men have to pay."

"I thought the men weren't allowed in at all."

He gave me an exasperated glance; my ignorance irritated him. "At ten o'clock Ladies' Night is over. The placard comes down."

I looked at the sidewalk placard with its luminous pink script, stared again at the line-up. One of the men in the front whistled and beckoned to me. Abruptly I plunged back into the murky interior.

On my way back I got lost. I got trapped between chair legs, behind barricades of bodies—had ample time to observe the condition of the customers. They were riotous, reckless, sloppy with drink. Eyes glazed, cheeks glowed, limbs gestured wildly; beer got splashed down my pant-leg; I trod on broken glass. They can't let those men in here, I said to myself. Could they? A girl reared in front of me. "Give us more!" she bellowed at the workers behind the bar. Her companions hauled at her elbows, tried to make her sit down. "We want more!" she shouted, holding up three fingers—and others took up her call: "More! More!"

I grabbed her shoulder. She had smooth, freckled face, a pair of mischievous eyes; she reminded me of Lily Kubicek. "How many times have they served drinks on the house?" I asked her.

"Twice." She pouted. "But sometimes we get more."

"Three free drinks?"

She nodded.

I stared into her frantic and greedy eyes, and felt a kind of helplessness. Was I so sure that she was worth saving? (Are any of us worth saving?) I looked at her companions in the booth. "Don't you know that it's against the law to serve alcohol to minors?"

"Who says we're minors?" one of them promptly retorted.

"What's it to you—you old bag!" yelled the girl I'd waylaid. "Let go of me!" She tried to twist out of my grip, lost her balance and ended up clutching me.

"Get lost, lady," one of her friends chipped in.

I turned on her. "How old are you?"

"None of your business," she answered saucily.

"Doesn't anybody ever ask for I.D. in this place?"

Her eyes met me head-on. "Get lost or I call the bouncer."

I came to my senses.

I finally found Johanna, hunched over her scotch, glaring at the tables around her. She looked dangerous. I sat down, noticed that I was sweating, reached for my napkin and wiped my face. "You really think they'll let them in here?"

She didn't even look at me. "You know a law against it?"

It seemed to me that there were at least laws affecting it, but with Johanna in this mood, I wasn't going to argue about it.

"There's one over there," she said, aiming her thumb in the direction of the bar.

"One what?

"Someone I recognize."

"Who?" I searched the figures behind the counter, saw Haswell's receptionist.

She looked just as before—tight-lipped, efficient—her profile as indifferent as the figure-head on a ship's prow, her thick black hair encompassing her like a shield. She had a clipboard in her arms and what looked like a stack of bar receipts on the counter in front of her. She was talking to the cashier.

"The native girl?"

"Her name's Salal."

"Salal? Like the plant? He called her Sally."

"Who did?"

"Haswell. I've seen her before myself. When I went to see him upstairs, she was working as his receptionist."

"Keeps herself busy."

"She also seemed to know Caesar."

"Yep. He killed her brother."

"What!"

"I can't prove it," Johanna said blandly. "But I don't know anyone that doesn't say so. Including her."

"*How* did he kill her brother?"

"Very easy. Just a little too much smack. It's so easy to die on smack."

I was silenced. I was remembering Lily's inquest; I'd said exactly the same to her father. Again I looked at Haswell's receptionist (or whatever she was). She was standing beside one of the bartenders, writing something on her clipboard. Doing inventory?

"Why do they say Caesar killed him?"

"Well, Bobby—that's her brother—used to work for him. On the gambling end of it, I think. He started out as a prostitute—his sister did too. They were good-lookers, both of them; no more than thirteen years old but they must have raked in more money than the rest of us combined. Not that they saw too much of the profits after Caesar took his cut. But when Bobby got older he started helping out with the gambling racket—at least that was the rumor. Anyway I don't know what happened; people say it had to do with one of Caesar's trials; Bobby was getting uppity and he knew too much. So he conveniently O.D.'d. I met him once or twice. He was a nice kid. He was smart and witty and real charming besides—much more lively than his sister. But the two of them were thick as thieves. This is the first time I've seen her since her brother died. People said she went home to wherever it was they came from. But I guess she came back."

"How long ago did all this happen?"

"Mmm—maybe two years ago—something like that."

"She's not on the streets now."

"Doesn't look like it. I wonder what she's doing here?"

"Making a living?" I suggested.

I sensed a change in the room. I looked round and saw the men—approaching like a wave, dispersing outward as they came. Then they were everywhere, and the noise mounted to new dimensions.

One of them plopped into a chair right beside us.

Johanna looked him over. "Sorry, Bud, the table's taken."

He met her eyes—decided not to argue—got up and went away. Johanna has that effect on people. She was dressed to kill, with a skirt at mid-thigh and oceans of cleavage—but she looked about as approachable as the Titanic viewed from the waterline.

"I don't think I want to watch this," I said miserably. The volleyball team across the way was swarming with suitors, who were squeezing themselves into the booths, pulling up chairs between friends. I watched some of the girls start to get up, amid clutches and protests, against which they struggled like flies trapped in jam. I wanted to stand up and start screaming: "Go home! Get the hell out of here!"

Then I saw the receptionist. She'd stopped invoicing or whatever, was staring out across the room, her face like a carving—absolutely expressionless. And yet, like the last time, I received an impression of incredible tension, of a person strung to the highest pitch.

Abruptly, she turned her back. She spoke a few words to the bartender, gathered up her clipboard and slips of paper, disappeared through a staff door.

We were now in the middle of a free-for-all. Men grasping, girls squealing, couples grappling and scuffling—while the bouncers prowled like cats. At what point did they intervene? Would they prohibit gang-rape? "I want to go home," I said firmly, just as Johanna muttered a curse, flung back her chair and strode across the room.

Her object was an older woman that was standing by one of the dividers, like a guard, silently watching, wearing the red vest that denoted a member of the staff. Johanna walked straight up to her, grabbed her by the hand and dragged her, literally, back to our table.

"Sit down," Johanna ordered, pushing the empty chair towards her.

"I can't stay a minute," the woman protested, sitting.

"Another one," Johanna said to me. "Her name's Deanne. We used to work the same street corner."

"How do you do," I said.

Staring at Johanna as if hypnotized, Deanne barely acknowledged me. "I'm supposed to be working," she said to Johanna.

"As what?"

"I'm a hostess." Deanne straightened her back, folded her hands primly on the table in front of her.

"Now isn't that nice," Johanna drawled. "I'm real impressed by your hospitality."

"It's just a job, Johanna."

"It certainly is. What happened to the movie business?"

"Oh—" The woman simpered. "I'm past that now. We don't stay young forever."

"They prefer ten-year-olds, eh?"

"Well not quite that—"

"Don't you think some of these *ladies*," Johanna said it with a sneer, "are a little young for this treatment?"

"It's just a job," the woman repeated, her voice rising to a whine. "I gotta think of my old age, Johanna; I got nothing saved. You know what happens."

"It's not a very nice job," Johanna said softly. "Is it!" she shouted, making both of us jump. Deanne glanced wildly around the room. "So what does a *hostess* do?" Johanna continued remorselessly. "I hear Caesar hangs out here—that got something to do with it?"

Deanne was shaking her head, but like a child caught out in a lie.

"No?" Johanna's eyebrows lifted. "Well that's not hard to find out." Her arm shot out; she gripped Deanne by the

43

wrist, pushed up her sleeve, bared a white forearm. Deanne began to struggle. Johanna gave her wrist an expert twist, pinning Deanne's forearm across the table in front of me, inner side up. I gave Deanne an apologetic glance, examined the evidence. Her inner arm was an angry pink, raddled with scars, the veins at the elbow protruding like ulcerated wires.

"That's her salary," Johanna said contemptuously. "Do you get anything left over for groceries?"

Deanne, half-twisted across the table-top, winced, but said nothing. She was looking at something beyond Johanna's head. Just as Johanna glanced up to see what she was looking at, two hands descended, one on either of her shoulders. Two bouncers loomed over her, their faces like wax.

"Let's go, ladies," one of them said.

Johanna let go of Deanne's arm; Deanne grimaced and sat up, hastily pushing down her sleeve. Johanna's eyes met mine; she rose slowly to her feet. "Time to go, Maggie," she said to me, as if there were no bouncers ensuring our exit. I willingly got up. We were escorted through the tables, past the ticket booth and out the door.

"She should have known better," Johanna said sadly, as the doors of Kinky's closed themselves behind us. "Has she no self-respect?"

"I thought she was scared."

"Damn right she was scared. And her with kids of her own. She should be ashamed of herself."

"I think she is." I felt compelled to defend her. "But she did have her reasons. What *do* prostitutes do when they're too old to attract business?"

If looks could kill, my life would have ended at that moment. "*I'm* planning to eat babies," Johanna hissed, venomously, and strode down the sidewalk. I hurried after her, mumbling apologies.

But she stopped again almost immediately, stood staring into the windows of a decrepit hotel lobby, one of the many in that part of town. I came to a halt beside her. Through the glass I could see a weedy dieffenbachia, a few shabby leather chairs, a T.V. flickering in the corner, nobody watching it.

The door was to our left, an old sign lit up over it with two letters burnt out: "N-w Brighto- Hotel." And lower, unlit: "Rooms by Day or Week." Then, as we stood there, staring at it (for reasons that had not yet revealed themselves to me), two couples reeled out of Kinky's, passed by us on the sidewalk and entered the door of the New Brighton Hotel. One of the girls was being practically supported by her escort—the same girl that had been lobbying for a third drink on the house.

"This place has been used by hookers for years." Johanna gave me a sideways glance. "Maybe your friend Haswell has shares in it."

"Wouldn't hurt," I agreed. I knew that this was not the moment to disclaim friendship with Haswell. Another couple staggered out of Kinky's, weaved down the sidewalk, stumbled through the hotel door.

"They make it that easy, do they?" I asked.

"Uh-huh." Johanna nodded. "If you close down the flophouses, where will the businessmen take their whores? Let's be reasonable."

"I'm being reasonable," I answered humbly.

"About time," Johanna said, but now I knew that she'd forgiven me.

We drove home in silence.

CHAPTER FIVE

"Harry," I said, pushing the telephone harder against my ear. The connection was lousy. "It's Meg Lacey. I'm hoping to pick your brains again."

"Christ, Meg, I haven't got many left. What can I do for you this time?"

"I want you to tell me anything and everything you know about a nightclub called Kinky's."

Harry is one of my few lucky breaks. Generally speaking, private detectives are not too popular with police officers and don't get much cooperation out of them. But every so often one manages to strike up a personal acquaintance—in which case one nurses it like the fussiest of plants. Harry, by now, is becoming pretty hardy; I can ask him almost anything. As a cop he has his idiosyncrasies: in his back yard he keeps a coop full of homing pigeons, and he paints landscapes in his spare time. He has a kid with cerebral palsy whom he'd carry in his arms from morning till night if the kid would let him get away with it. He used to be in Narcotics, but in the recent hiring cutbacks, he got transferred to the Vice Squad. He's a credit to the force; I only wish they had more of them.

"Kinky's, eh? Well we've heard of it, of course. Owned by a fellow called Haswell, I believe. Who's got a finger in the blue movie business."

"Blue movies?" Here was a new angle altogether. I reached for my pen.

"We've no proof, Meg. Might be just our dirty minds working overtime."

"He makes them, distributes them—what?"

"I don't know much more about it. I can check. But we can't find out a whole lot without a search warrant and he's given us no excuse to get one. You know the situation."

I could provide you with an excuse, I thought grimly. But I needed to give the matter more thought. "What about Kinky's itself?"

"There've been complaints about minors from time to time."

"Anyone ever follow them up?"

"I'm not too sure—you know what a rat's nest that can be. Unlikely, I'd think. They've been short-staffed in that department for quite some time."

I decided to let that drop. "What about a fellow named Caesar Grice?"

"You mean our one-man-Mafia?"

"Is that what you call him?"

"That—and worse. We've been trying to nail him for years. But everyone's in his pocket. Maybe we are too."

"You think that might be why you can't get him?"

Harry sighed—audibly. "Let's hope not, O.K.? I mean one reason we can't get him is that no one will talk. No one. We've got a guy in the Pen right now; he's worked for Caesar for years. But he'd rather sit in jail for life than act as a witness against him."

"Wow." I was impressed. "He's loyal?"

"No, ma'am. He's scared shitless. He told us he hoped to God we got him, but he wasn't going to have any part of it."

"I've heard that he kills his enemies with a little more junk than they're accustomed to."

"We've heard those rumors too."

"Does that mean he only employs junkies?"

"If they're not junkies when he hires them, they're junkies by the time he's through with them."

"I guess that's one way to keep your employees punching the clock."

"Sure is. But what are you doing, Meg? You're not moving into Caesar's territory, are you?"

"I hope not. I kind of stumbled into it. I've been hired to find a friend of Haswell's. Visiting Haswell, I met Grice."

"Now that's interesting. You get the impression they were acquainted?"

"Well acquainted."

"Hmm." There was a pause. "Tell you what, Meg. I'm going to do a little digging at this end, see if I can come up with anything more about Haswell and his operations. I'll get in touch with you if I find anything. And if you learn anything more about Haswell and Caesar, tell me about it. O.K.?"

"It's a deal," I agreed.

But in fact I was learning nothing—at least nothing to the purpose. Days had passed since my night out at Kinky's and I'd spent them dithering. I'd been hired, after all, to find Alison Chase—and I wasn't expecting to find her on Haswell's property. Yet Kinky's, in my view, cried out for retribution. I couldn't stop thinking about it. I even talked to my daughter about it, asked her if she thought I was being sentimental or naive about adolescent girls. I know I embarrassed her. But she listened, dutifully, as she's been listening to me all her life, wishing we could find something *nicer* to talk about—but prepared to hear me out.

"I think those girls were being taken advantage of," she pronounced finally, with an effort. Coming from Katie, this was a statement of some import; she was attempting to meet me on my own ground. "And besides," she added, "it's illegal. Isn't it?"

I suppressed a sigh. How like Katie to want to talk about the rules! "Serving alcohol to minors is illegal," I agreed, "but for all I know every one of those kids was carrying false I.D. I'm not sure who gets arrested in that case. And there are laws about having sexual intercourse with minors, but I doubt that they're very effective. They're full of clauses about the minors being of 'good reputation' and that kind of stuff." I paused, considered. "But Katie, even if it's legal, it's not right! The guy that owns that place is a pimp! He serves drinks on the house so that all the girls get plastered and then he charges men so that they can get in there to seduce them! And some of these kids are fourteen, fifteen years old! Never mind if it's legal—it's immoral! Doesn't anybody talk about right and wrong anymore?"

I looked at my daughter, and by the expression on her face, saw that she'd turned me off. ("There goes mother again.") She would now keep her eyes lowered and proceed to think her own thoughts until I had finished. There are times when I almost feel sorry for her boyfriend.

Blue movies, Harry had said. And remembering that Johanna had asked the hostess, Deanne, about the movie business, I phoned Johanna to find out a bit more. Sure enough, Deanne was an ex-porno queen, but Johanna didn't know if she'd ever worked for Haswell in that capacity. "I never heard of Haswell till you mentioned him," she reminded me. "As for Deanne—I believed her. She's probably too old. My theory is that she's scouting for new blood for Caesar's prostitute rings. I mean, what else would a *hostess* do?" Mulling this over, I remembered Lily Kubicek, and the friend who'd reported that someone had offered Lily a screen test. Mightn't Deanne also scout for Haswell's movies? And Lily too had died of just a little too much smack.

It was at this point that I decided that I was going ahead with it—Alison Chase or no Alison Chase, regardless of who was paying me and why. After all, I argued, I can say that I thought Alison might have patronized Kinky's; I've no proof that she didn't. And I'll tell her dad about Haswell—that should shut him up. Then I dug through my files until I found the name of the girl that had told me that Lily was too fat to get into movies.

I drove out to see her. Yes, she'd heard of Kinky's, though she herself had never been there. Who'd told her about it? Well, she couldn't exactly remember. Did she know if Lily had ever gone there? She couldn't say for sure, but she thought maybe she had. I thanked her for very little—but it was enough to go on with.

Then Fred Chase got hold of me and suggested that since his wife was out of town, I might as well see him at his office and save myself the drive to North Vancouver. "See you?" I said, wondering why on earth I'd want to see him. Then I remembered—I'd promised him a weekly report. So I agreed to get it over with.

His office was downtown, above one of his biggest stores. I had a minute to spare before our appointment, so I dropped into the store to look around. There were video monitors stacked in towers and pyramids, swinging from the ceiling, lining the aisles—and every one of them was on. The world in all its diversity revealed itself in video. I watched home movies, computer games, golf tournaments, last night's news, nature documentaries, a ballet, a weather report, and had the dubious pleasure of seeing myself on television every time I turned around. All around the walls the video tapes were displayed, arranged by subject matter, like library books: "Horror," "General," "Comedy," "Westerns," "Drama," "Children's." And in the far wall there was a closed door with a sign on it: "Adult XXX." I headed straight for it.

The room was bigger than I'd anticipated, its aisles well-stocked. Apparently pornography was Fred's specialty. There were as many customers in here as in the rest of the store put together. All men. I was careful not to look at them (since some of them were looking at me), and I kept my visit short. I scanned the titles of the tapes, the pictures that illustrated them. "Pussies Can't Be Choosy," "Sex-Starved," "Little Sister" (revealing a bare ass beneath her skirt), "The Naughty Niece" (sidling provocatively against a bedroom door with her thumb in her mouth). Glancing down the aisle, I saw that the really hardcore stuff was against the end wall. But I didn't have the stomach for it. As I returned through the closed door and re-entered the main store, it occurred to me that Fred Chase and Danny Haswell might have something in common.

As soon as I walked into his office, Fred offered me a drink.

"No thanks," I said, "I'm going to be brief."

He poured himself a scotch. "Not bad news?"

"No—very little news at all. I told you about Janis. Well, she still isn't talking. And I don't think anybody else knows what you want to know."

"I'd like to have a word with that young lady," Fred said darkly.

I didn't think he would—but decided not to say so.

"Why don't you tail her?"

"I considered that," I admitted. "But unfortunately, she already knows what I look like. That makes it difficult. Also—I think she'll talk—if I wait long enough."

Fred looked irritated, and I knew he was thinking that he wasn't paying me to sit on my butt. So I decided to launch my offensive.

"You know," I said, "I've been looking into this Haswell fellow, and I'm beginning to think your daughter had good reasons for walking out on him."

"Now look," he said. "I know my wife told you some cock-and-bull story about—"

"What I want to know," I interrupted him forcibly, "is what kind of a father tries to shack up his daughter with a man that makes porno movies?"

"I—I—" he spluttered—literally—his mouth full of scotch. "I don't—

"*Don't* tell me you don't know anything about it!" I thundered. (I love playing the part of God.) "You yourself told me that he was a personal friend. Well I've seen some of his businesses and believe me, if I were Alison—"

"I assure you—"

"You know damn well how he makes his money!"

His lips pursed. "I wasn't going to deny it." He held one arm across his paunch like an offended opera star.

"Oh." I was taken aback.

"And I assure you," he continued huffily, "that Alison is completely ignorant of Haswell's—er—activities. As a family man I can tell you that it is often necessary to keep family and business separate and in fact, Danny and I have had several discussion—"

"But don't you know," I said sweetly, "that evil people smell?"

His mouth dropped. Then he recovered himself. "I've had enough of your insolence!" He quivered with indignation, slopped scotch onto the carpet.

"But it's true!" I protested. "Just because you and Haswell made a gentleman's agreement to keep your business practices to yourselves doesn't mean your womenfolk don't know it, don't sense what goes on—even if they can't put a name to it. And so far nobody has told me that Alison was stupid."

"You don't know what you're talking about," he said haughtily.

"No," I corrected him. "You don't know what *I'm* talking about."

"It's simply a question of good business," he said primly. "Danny gives people what they want, what they'll pay for."

"Including children?" I asked gently.

His head shot up. "Children?"

"I know for a fact that he serves alcohol to minors."

"Oh. Well, I wouldn't know anything about that. But it's the parents' job to keep their children where they belong, and it's asking too much of the businessmen of the community to do that job for them. I'm sure Danny does his best but I know every liquor establishment is pestered by these damn kids that sneak in with fake I.D. and—"

"Get served drinks on the house with—" But then I stopped, remembering that I didn't necessarily want Fred to know how much I knew, nor what I intended to do about it. In fact I'd already said too much.

I rose to my feet. "Let's put it this way. I'm satisfied that I know why your daughter walked out on you. And I think that if you want her back, you're going to have to let her choose her own friends." I thought of Janis. "Even if they do wear funny clothes."

He looked up; his forehead creased. "Who wears funny clothes?"

"Oh, some of her friends from the art school. You know, safety-pins in their ears and purple stripes in their hair and T-shirts with the arms ripped out and deaths-heads tattooed—"

"Alison has friends like that!"

I was tempted to giggle—but having managed to hang onto my job up to this point in the interview, I wanted to keep it. "It's just costume," I said reassuringly.

"Punk?" he asked weakly. He actually looked ill.

The man was too much for me. "You still want me to find her?"

He managed to get me in focus. "You don't think she's got one of those hair-do's, do you?"

"If she does, I'll take a photograph of her and show it to you first, so you can decide whether you want her back or not."

He thought I was serious, and nodded, doubtfully.

I realized I'd better get out. "So I'll drop by again next week," I said brightly, putting my hand on the doorknob.

"Oh—allow me!" He put down his drink, bustled me out of the way, opened the door and then stood, blocking my exit. His eyes were pleading, wet. "We'll just hope for the best." He held out his hand; reluctantly, I took it. He shook my hand as if placing his life savings in it.

"Let's," I agreed. I insisted I could find my own way out.

I sat on a bus stop bench on Hastings Street, staring at the building across the street. It was typical of downtown buildings of that era, built sometime around the First World War, four stories high. At some point, for some reason, the windows of the third and fourth floors had been cemented over. I'd already been to City Hall and found out that Haswell owned it—the whole thing—yet Kinky's, its storerooms, kitchens and offices, couldn't have taken up more than one and a half stories. What did he do with the rest of it? I scanned the ground floor for entrances to other businesses that might have leased office space above the pub, but there was only the entrance to Kinky's and a blank door twenty yards further along the sidewalk, which was undoubtedly a fire exit. Of course there could have been any number of stairways leading up from the interior of the pub; if they'd concealed a dinosaur in that place I'm sure no one would have noticed it. Yet there were no signs advertising other businesses in the second floor windows, no secretaries on coffee break peering down into the street. Every window was identical, shaded by a venetian blind, discreet, respectable. I decided to walk round to the alley and check out the back.

In the alley I found a loading dock with a door at street level on either side of it. Again the second floor windows were hung with venetian blinds, again the third and fourth floor windows cemented in. Glancing around to make sure there was no one watching me, I tried each side door in turn. They were locked. I moved to a comparatively inconspicuous spot, a three-by-four-foot gap between the Smithrite garbage container and the cement wall that divided Haswell's property from the parking spaces at the back of the hotel next door. The sun pressed hot against the back of my neck; my stomach rebelled against the odors of the Smithrite beside me. Then just when I'd decided to give up, a truck turned into the alley and rumbled towards me, veered right, braked, started backing into the loading dock. As it did so, the loading door rolled open. The truck driver hopped out of the cab, heaved himself up onto the loading platform, handed an invoice to the man standing in the doorway. They exchanged a few words, then turned and disappeared into the interior of the building.

Cautiously, I approached. At the edge of the open loading door I stopped and found myself peering into a storeroom, cool and dim after the glare of the alleyway, cases of beer stacked along one wall, a mountain of boxes in the center, a freight elevator beyond them, a passsageway to the right of it, which probably led to the kitchens and back rooms of the pub. The shipper and truck driver were nowhere to be seen. There was a dolly parked against a wall, a janitor's cart abandoned by the freight elevator. I could hear, faintly, the clatter of cutlery from the kitchen, doors banging, water running. But my end of the building appeared deserted, quiet. I could conceal myself behind the boxes? Again I looked at the pile of boxes that were stacked in front of the freight elevator, presumably waiting to be taken upstairs. There was something familiar about them. What did they contain? Typewriters? Appliances? What kind of appliances? I could almost make out the letters printed on the cardboard. "Z-E-N-I-." Zenith. Another read: "SONY." "Goddamn!" I whispered. I scrambled up onto the platform—strode across the storeroom. I peered over and around the boxes, inspecting their labels. They contained audiotapes, recorders, cameras, editing monitors. Haswell was going into video. And guess who was supplying the hardware? The name was right there on the shipping invoice: "Fred's VideoMart." In return for which Haswell would send him pornographic videotapes? They could keep it all in the family if only Alison would cooperate.

I unclenched my hands; my palms were slick with sweat. I glanced around the storeroom, noticed, for the first time, a passageway on my left. From a room at the far end of it issued the low rumble of male voices. What would I say if I got caught? That I was applying for a job and trying to find the manager's office? I looked out the open loading door, at the cracked, smoke-greased facades of the buildings on the other side of the alley, at the truck baking in the sun, exuding visible waves of heat. I heard a car turn into the alley.

I couldn't see it, but it was approaching fast, gravel crunching beneath its wheels. Then it came into view, pulled into the loading bay right beside the truck. The engine shuddered, quit. About a hundred feet to my right was an open doorway, through which I could see the bottom of a flight of stairs. I decided to go that way. I ran to the doorway, nipped through it and found myself standing in a stairwell. A short flight of stairs led down to one of the street level doors, another flight ascended, presumably to the floors above. A car door slammed. The male voices were getting louder; there were footsteps crossing the cement storeroom floor. For an interminable moment, I hesitated. Escape? Or grab this chance to find out more? I plunged up the stairs.

Don't get the wrong impression—I am not brave. But I am sometimes reckless. And danger induces in me a kind of schizophrenia. I split into two selves: a sensible, safe self, which keeps up a litany of moans and groans and regrets and "I told you so's"; and an adventurous self, which talks me through the experience as if it were ground control and I a pilot in the air above, trying to land my plane in a blizzard: "...Good, good...that's one flight of stairs, now the next one...You're doing just fine. And since you don't want to run into Haswell or his receptionist, pass on the second floor and go up to the third, or even the fourth...." On the second-floor landing I arrived at an olive-green door, tested the knob and found it locked. "You see?" said my other, my less intrepid self. "All the doors will be locked and you'll be trapped in this stairwell until someone discovers you." But it seemed silly to have come this far only to give up, so I ignored these premonitions and started climbing again.

At the third-floor landing the stairway stopped. That's odd, I thought; what happened to the fourth floor? Another olive-green door confronted me; as I'd predicted, it too was locked. I surveyed the light panel above my head, the walls on every side of me, the stairs leading down. "Congratulations, Mr. Haswell," I muttered beneath my breath, "you run a tight ship." Back down to the bottom? I turned to descend, suddenly heard footsteps and voices on the other side of the olive door. A key scratched in the lock; the doorknob turned. Having nowhere else to conceal myself I flung myself against the wall and prepared to meet my fate.

The door slammed into me; three girls rushed out—laughing, hurrying. They clattered down the stairs without once glancing back. The door started to close. Unable to believe my luck, I grabbed the knob before it latched, stood, holding it, listening to the footsteps descend, one flight after another, till they came to a stop at the alley door at the bottom. "Come on, come on!" one of the girls commanded, giggling. "I'm trying!" The bolt clicked; their voices dispersed, faded from the stairwell.

I was still holding the door. For maybe half a minute I continued standing there, tempted to let go of it—did I want to get any deeper into this predicament than I already was? Finally I opened it about an inch, peered through the crack, saw a long linoleum-tattered corridor with rooms opening off at regular intervals on either side of it. Offices? I could hear a radio playing from somewhere down the end, and what sounded like a washing machine from one of the rooms close by. There was no one in sight. So I opened the door a little wider and edged through it, surveyed the chipped and grimy walls (which looked as if they hadn't been painted since the Second World War), the stained ceiling, heard the thing that sounded like a washing machine move on to its next cycle. (A *washing* machine?) I let the door slip shut behind me. The radio started playing one of the hit tunes of that summer, a song one heard everywhere ("...hands off, for better or worse, she's my private proper*tee*..."), so that even I couldn't help knowing it, in spite of my aversion to popular music. Yet it seemed strange to hear it here—so familiar, so banal— while my mind was void with terror and sweat seeped from my armpits. Then my "ground control" took charge again: "Well, Meg, you're obviously going to get caught any minute now, so let's see how much you can find out before that happens." And I pushed off the door behind me as if stepping off a plank.

First on my left was a washroom-cum-laundry room which did indeed contain a washing machine (currently on rinse) and numerous washing lines which had been suspended from one end of the room to the other, so that one had to fight one's way through the brassieres, panties, nylons and T-shirts in order to get to the toilets. There were two battered toilet cubicles (one of the toilets was plugged), as well as a makeshift shower stall with a ripped, plastic curtain, a couple of towel racks, a cracked mirror, and a sink that looked like it was about to fall off the wall. All these appurtenances were filthy.

I returned to the corridor and tried the next room down which, like the washroom, was lit—but contained nothing but an ashtray and two dirty cups. I stepped back into the hallway and, since no one was stopping me, peered into the room across the hall, which was pitch dark inside and, as far as I could tell, empty. I remembered then that all the windows on this floor had been cemented in; there was no natural light. The corridor was (ill) lit by a row of fluorescent tubes; the rooms contained bare light bulbs or, alternatively, empty sockets. This lighting, combined with the chipped and flaking beige paint, the discolored ceilings, the cobwebs and greasy smears along the walls, produced a grisly effect. The place looked like a ghetto housing project that was scheduled for demolition—except that there were no windows to smash.

The next room I came to showed evidence of occupation. It contained a soiled mattress, a few blankets, magazines, comic books, clothes strewn across the floor (and others folded in a cardboard box), a broken bedside lamp, a one-eyed teddy bear, a shoe-box full of cheap jewellery, a saucer of cigarette butts, and other miscellaneous items: bobby-pins, various bottles of make-up, smeared tissues, a pair of shoes, a teaspoon, a hairbrush, a box of matches, a hand mirror. What is this place? I wondered, newly alarmed. I stared at the teddy bear. What's going on here? Abruptly I returned to the corridor.

The rooms further down the corridor were variations on this theme, most of them bedrooms, some better lived-in than others. Their furnishings were minimal: one contained an armchair, another a metal spring bed, one had sofa cushions instead of a mattress, one had a bit of carpet. Boxes generally substituted for chests-of-drawers, several had posters or pictures cut from magazines tacked on the walls. In one room five Barbie-dolls (each in a different outfit) had been lined up against a wall; in another china animals had been arranged on the ledge that had once served as a windowsill, like the figures in a nativity scene. All the rooms were dirty (but some much dirtier than others), all stood in need of renovation: dry-walling, repapering, new flooring, paint. Plaster was crumbling from the walls, revealing the lathe-boards beneath; the linoleum had been reduced to patches, like continents on a map. There were dirty dishes and ashtrays everywhere, and dust defined the range of the inhabitants' activities.

I finally found the radio and beside it, a pair of girls, talking and painting their fingernails. They glanced up as I peered in at them. They looked about fourteen years old, unkempt and a bit wan, but otherwise unremarkable. I immediately withdrew and continued down the corridor, attempting to look as if I had legitimate business to conduct at the other end of it. To my surprise, I was not pursued; they raised no alarm. Ten seconds later another girl stepped into the hallway, right into my path, and stared at me, startled. Again I swept right on by (but not before I'd got a good look at her: bangs that dipped over her eyes, thin shoulders, no breasts yet to speak of and no hips either) and then the corridor ended, opened into a larger room, with a couple of doorways opening off it to my right. This larger room (once warehouse or factory space?) was mostly unused, abandoned to dust, paint chips, yellowed newspapers, junk. But one corner of it accommodated a kitchen of sorts: an electric stove, a fridge, a sink, a counter, a garbage can, cupboards, an old formica table and several rickety chairs. Beside the kitchen, shoved up against a wall, was a huge decrepit sofa, a large television perched on a coffee table in front of it. There was a picture on the screen, but the sound was turned off. Three girls were sprawled on the sofa; one of them appeared to be asleep, the other two were staring at the screen. When I appeared they looked up. I stopped in the doorway, not knowing which way to proceed next.

"Sally's in there—talking to Debbie," one of the girls said to me. She indicated the doorway ahead of me, to my right.

I moved into the large room and as I came opposite the doorway indicated, I heard female voices issuing from it. But now I could see that further ahead, on the other side of the big room, the corridor resumed. Ignoring the two girls who were watching me, I crossed the room, re-entered the corridor. It didn't go far. There was another dark, apparently empty room and then, at the end of the corridor, another locked door, like the one that I'd entered from the other side of the building. But this door contained a window. Peering through the dirty, paint-smeared glass, I could just make out another stairway, this one leading upwards as well as downwards, providing access to the missing fourth floor.

Reluctantly, I turned back and saw, without surprise, that I'd been caught. Salal was standing outside the doorway that I'd passed by, and one of the girls from the sofa (who had fetched her to deal with me?) was beside her. Salal held the same clipboard in her arms; when she saw that I'd seen her, she made no move to approach me, but continued standing there, watching me.

"I guess I'm lost," I confessed, re-entering the room. "I'm looking for Mr. Haswell."

"He's out of town," she said, flatly.

"Oh?" This was news. "When will he be back?"

"Tomorrow."

I could see she wasn't overly impressed by my abilities as an actress, but as they say in the business, the show must go on.

"Then I'll drop by again in a couple of days. It was nothing urgent." I glanced around the room, at the girl beside Salal (who had a pretty, pointed face and bare feet), at the other two on the sofa, both of whom were now awake and listening, ears pricked for every word. "I don't know how I got up here. I thought I came through the same door, but—" I gestured, helplessly.

Salal's face was deadpan, her eyes the color of dates, the pupils almost invisible. "I'll show you the way out."

She preceded me back through the corridor, the same way that I'd come, till we reached the door at the top of the stairs. "I know where I am now," I said, as she unlocked it. But she opened it and followed me down. When we reached the bottom door, the one that opened onto the alley, she stepped in front of me, unlocked it, pulled the door open and stood with her back against it, like a guard ensuring my exit.

It was an impulse, a last grasping at straws, that made me stop in the doorway, fish through my wallet, produce my old photo of Lily Kubicek, considerably worse for the wear. "You know her?"

Salal took the photograph, studied it carefully, looked up at me. Holding my gaze, she handed it back. "Sure. I seen her picture in the paper. She died a couple of months ago."

"Maybe one day you'd like to visit me and tell me what happened to her." This time I found a business card, held it out to her.

She refused to take it. "Danny already has one."

"I'd rather talk to you."

"It isn't mutual," Salal replied, and closed the door in my face.

CHAPTER SIX

ONCE I was a suburban housewife, washing diapers and chasing the neighbors' dogs out of my azalea bed, reading murder stories with my ears plugged so I wouldn't hear my kids screaming at each other. I had a model husband, a week's worth of casseroles in the freezer—and one evening as I was pushing a cart full of groceries across a supermarket parking lot, I got yanked into a car and raped at knife-point. Surprise. My husband accompanied me to the police station, where I got poked at, interrogated. Two weeks later they caught the guy, in the same car, the same parking lot—and they chauffeured me down to the police station to identify him. That was the worst part. As our eyes met, I realized that he was a good two inches shorter than me and probably weighed twenty pounds less. My mortification was complete. For weeks I remained buried beneath the bedclothes burning with shame, refusing to answer the telephone or leave the house. Even now the memory pains me, though I know I'm being foolish. Where I'd had curves, he'd had muscles, and I was probably able to wield a bread knife just as professionally as he'd wielded that switchblade. But he wasn't a loaf of bread.

That rape marked a turning point, but it couldn't have been the beginning. Yet when people ask me to explain myself I always start there because up to that time, I'd raised no eyebrows, rocked no boats. Like everyone, I had my peculiarities; like everyone, I'd harbored rebellious thoughts. More than most people? If so, I wasn't aware of it. Overall my life afforded me certain satisfactions; I took an interest in my house, my garden and my neighborhood, rarely tired of the clutch of small arms about my neck. But the rape tipped the balance, was like a rock thrown through my window. It let the rest of the world in.

First I joined a judo club; a year later I switched to Aikido. I learned how to duck and evade, how to slither out from under, how to fly through the air and roll onto my feet. How to disarm a man with a knife. I lost fifteen pounds in the first six months; I got injured three times in the first year. But by then I was addicted. Not to the Aikido so much, but to my new sense of power and freedom, to the feeling that next time I'd be able to take care of myself. By then my kids were in school; I was free to attend classes every day. By the end of six years I had my black belt.

Many different kinds of people take lessons in martial arts: war veterans, religious fanatics, Japanese housewives, accountants, social misfits. I met some interesting people; "weirdos," my husband called them, meaning neither WASP nor middle-class. Of course there were plenty of middle-class WASPs in my Aikido class, but they weren't the ones I got to know. I'd been brought up in a "nice" middle-class family, I'd married into a "nice" middle-class family; I felt that the time had come to talk to somebody else.

To my family and friends this change, when they became aware of it, seemed both irrational and inexplicable; to me it was neither. Women are taught that the world is dangerous, that to fear it is only common sense. They are encouraged to keep their interests confined to their family and immediate neighborhood; they are encouraged to be unadventurous, both physically and psychologically. Therefore, as I became better able to defend myself physically, I changed psychologically; I became braver, more outward-looking. I began wanting to know about things that had never interested me before.

It still embarrasses me to admit this, but I was thirty-five years old before I found out that the rules and sensibilities that ordered my existence were, in many circles, completely unheard of; I was thirty-five years old before I understood that, globally-speaking, I was a member of a minority. A very privileged, powerful minority—but a minority nonetheless. For the first time, I was getting to know people that did not share my assumptions and values, was seeing my class, my culture, my race from the point of view of those outside it. It was disturbing, fascinating, a literally enlightening experience. It made me question everything that I'd always taken for granted, made me feel alive in a way that I'd never felt before. I developed a terror of complacency. I began, purposefully, to choose new experiences, embraced all sorts of situations that I would have formerly avoided: communist rallies, lesbian dances, demolition derbies, zen meditation groups. I talked to anyone who seemed "different," and since babysitters cost money, I invited some of these new acquaintances home.

My children took these visitors for granted; my husband did not. He said I was behaving irresponsibly in bringing home people "we knew nothing about." "But I know all sorts of things about them," I objected. And I'd proceed to tell him where they were from, where they worked, where they lived, who they were married to, how many kids they had. But that wasn't what he meant. At first we argued—but when it became apparent that neither of us was going to yield, it became a cold war.

I'd changed? Yes. But so had he. His changes had been more subtle, occurring over a period of many years, and because they'd seemed like small things at the time, I'd accommodated to almost all of them. So that by the time I changed, when it finally became important to me not to accommodate anymore, he was not the man I'd married. Childless, Brian had been a tolerant, easy-going man, but our establishment as a family, with a mortgage and dentist's bills, brought out a very different side of his character. As a father he felt he stood for something, felt obliged to do all sorts of things that he would never have done for himself. Before we had children, we used to eat when we got hungry, clean the house when we expected company, spend each paycheck as it came in. But parenthood, in Brian's mind, obliged us not only to look after our children, but to buy an expensive house in suburbia, take out pension plans and life insurance, provide dinner every night at six, mow the lawn every Saturday, become block parents, Brownie leaders and hockey coaches. We never did anything because we felt like it anymore, never went to a restaurant except on Mother's Day, never ate french fries with our fingers, never stayed up all night arguing, never retreated into bed on rainy Sunday afternoons. In Brian's mind whatever was good for the children was good enough for us; the only fun we were allowed was the pleasure of watching our children enjoy themselves. Perhaps if he hadn't been so adamant in this respect (perhaps if I hadn't let him become so?), I wouldn't have found it so necessary to rebel. But at some point I realized that I didn't want to live that way anymore, and I didn't want my children to choose that way of life for no better reason than that they'd never known anything else. Especially after I found out that there was a whole world out there that had never heard of Brian's rules. I began to feel that if I didn't show my children that there were other attitudes, other lifestyles, I'd be guilty of raising dinosaurs, incapable of adapting to a multicultural world. Nor did I fancy myself as an aging representative of an endangered species, a daughter of the British Empire with flowers bobbing in my hat.

Our cold war never thawed. In time I became less avid for new experiences, less a collector of human types, but I continued to know people that Brian considered unsuitable. Yet the people I associated with were decent, law-abiding citizens—not wife-beaters, not child-molesters—which was more than I could have said for some of Brian's acquaintances. Brian was curt, but civil to my friends; I was curt, but civil to his. We were curt, but civil to each other. Brian continued to be a model parent and neighbor; I quit being a Brownie leader, but joined a group that worked with new immigrants, helping them get acclimatized. I learned to cook moussaka, falafel, samosas, enchiladas, canneloni and gado-gado; Brian learned to look after a pot-roast. And the children discovered that for many questions, there were two right answers.

But the divorce was not my idea. I don't think I've ever

forgiven Brian for that, for taking me so much by surprise. Divorce had never occurred to me; I believed, still, that the purpose of a marriage was to create a secure place for growing children. When they're grown up, I'd say to myself. I had never been unfaithful; I was sure that Brian had never been unfaithful to me. And of course I was dead wrong.

It took me years to recover from the shock. Once I got used to the idea of divorce, I accepted it with a measure of relief—but I never understood how a man like Brian could, while on the one hand berating me for irresponsible conduct, be carrying on an illicit affair with somebody else. Nor could I make him see it from my point of view. As far as he was concerned, his affair with Barbara was the inevitable and justifiable consequence of having a wife like me. He'd given up hope of making me see sense, and he'd found another woman that he wanted to marry, a woman that didn't demonstrate wrist-holds in bed, that didn't haunt pool rooms, race tracks and gay bars. He made it clear, in other words, that a woman of my stamp could not reasonably expect anything else. And as soon as our plans to separate became known, our neighbors began inviting Brian and Barbara to their bridge parties and barbecues, as if they'd been doing it all along, as if I'd never even existed. I wondered if they were right.

The subsequent years were difficult for me. Despite my rebellions I'd had a place with Brian, a societal status, a community. Without him, I had none. I had miscellaneous friends and family (those that were still speaking to me), but the network of connections that had supported me all my life was no longer there, and I felt the draft down my neck. I felt newly vulnerable—to poverty, disease, death—afraid for my children as I'd never been before. What if Brian stopped supporting them? How would I support myself? Obviously, I'd have to get a job. But where? Doing what?

Like most mothers, my vocational skills consisted of ironing, cooking, laundering, childcare—all of which I wanted to avoid. What I wanted—once I'd recovered sufficiently to take an interest in my fate—was to continue my forays into foreign territories: the stock markets, the Masonic halls, the back rooms above Chinese restaurants where the regulars play mahjong, the press bars and drunk tanks. I considered training to become a journalist, but I've never been able to spell, and "news" has always depressed me. I perused college calendars. I figured out that I didn't want to be a teacher, a nurse, a pharmacist, a forestry management consultant, a lab technician, a social worker, a dentist or an architect. Nor, it seemed to me, had I any aptitude for these professions. Finally, I met George, and the problem solved itself.

Explaining George isn't easy. He was...a friend, I guess, occasionally a lover—but primarily an education. He was an unsuccessful private eye; he was also an alcoholic. When I met him he was in the process of dying. But it took him several years to do this, years in which I learned, finally, to get used to that draft down my neck, to accept the loss of my past. Up to that time, though I'd learned to be tolerant of a multitude of philosophies, attitudes and beliefs, I'd never really let go of the ones I'd been brought up with. Watching George die, I made that transition.

He was one of those people who never really fits anywhere, who rolls around the world like an upset marble on a Chinese checkerboard. Like Johanna he'd evolved a belief system of his own. In many ways he was a mess, a shipwrecked human being, but he'd come to terms with his condition and took full responsibility for it; he required no one to feel sorry for him. He was eccentric, unpredictable and wise about many things. He was also very good to me. He kept me company many a sleepless night and persuaded me to accept insecurity as an unalterable fact of life. He was of no religious persuasion, but he was a very religious man.

In return, I helped him maintain what little material protection he had left in the world. At first, this involved covering for him on his "bad" days, going into his hole-in-the-wall, storefront office to answer his phone, write his invoices, pay his bills. But as his condition deteriorated I took on more and more, began screening prospective clients, and eventually, working on the cases themselves. He introduced me to his contacts, taught me everything he knew. He began talking about it as "our" business and when he went into hospital, made it legally so. "I know it's not quite what you had in mind as a career," he said to me on one of my last visits to the hospital, "but George Sully Investigations would have gone under long ago if you hadn't insisted upon keeping it going. So I'm not giving you anything; I'm just telling you what you've got."

But even after George died, I couldn't think of the business as mine, and continued running it "for his sake," because it was all I had left of him, because I hadn't wanted him to die. And the clients kept coming. I wasn't getting rich, but I was paying the rent. I went down to the office each morning in the same spirit that people make daily visits to a cemetery to lay flowers on a grave; I even advertised a little and drummed up more business, thus giving myself an excuse to work longer hours. Increasingly, I didn't want to leave the office, didn't want to go home—would phone up my kids and tell them to meet me at work, where we'd sit around George's desk and eat take-out pizza for supper.

Then came the day that my kids went on holiday with their father for two weeks, and I stopped going home at all. I sat in that office night after night, remembering the many nights that George had been there beside me, reviewing my past, my present, my future, and feeling...suicidal. On the third night I started crying. But by the time my kids came home again, the wake was over; I'd ordered new letterhead and business cards, changed the name on the office door, made the business mine. But it still comforts me sometimes to find George's handwriting in my files, to finger his cigarette burns on the desk. And I like to remind myself that I'm no more unsuccessful than he was. It's my rightful inheritance.

For years I got by because I had capital in the bank, my share of the house that Brian and I sold when we divorced. It wasn't a fortune, but it covered the "extras," the things I forgot to budget for: car repairs, vacations, Halloween costumes, Christmas presents. I knew it wouldn't last forever, but I thought it would tide me over until either the private eye business became more lucrative or I found something else to do for a living. Neither of which came to pass.

So like most single mothers, I live below the statistical poverty line. But in my neighborhood that's not uncommon and when I hear about conditions in China, Ethiopia, or even England, for God's sake, I can't really think myself particularly underprivileged. When my kids get cravings for the luxuries of suburbia, they go to their father's house and babysit their half-siblings. When I get cravings...I phone Tom and ask him to take me out for dinner. Which pleases him. Not that he wants me to be poor—but he likes to give me things. Which is why I don't marry him. He's a paragon among men, a good companion, a good homemaker; my kids love him, my mother loves him, I'm pretty fond of him myself. But when my job gets me down—when I'm stuck, when I'm broke, when I hate the people I'm working for—he begs me to quit. He can't stand not being able to rescue me. And I don't want to be rescued.

So it was fortunate for both of us that he was still out of town the week I got stuck, the week after Salal shut that door in my face. I've been stuck many times; I know that getting stuck is an inevitable part of the process—but it's definitely the worst part. When police detectives get stuck, they resort to routine, and I've always believed that I should emulate them. I'm not very good at it. What I wanted was to get back into Haswell's building, up to the fourth floor if possible. But I was going to have to be more careful. If those girls were Haswell's actresses, I was dangerous enough to get him put away for years. And what else could they be? His harem? His hostages? He ran a shelter for runaway girls? Of course I could trot on down to the police station and persuade them to investigate—but I didn't want to do that until I had so much proof that they'd have no choice. What I didn't need, at this stage, was for someone to tip off Haswell that he was getting too conspicuous. And I know how easily that happens.

I'd learned that Haswell owned the building that housed Kinky's; it took me another morning at the Deeds Office to learn that the New Brighton Hotel next door was the property of a local realty conglomerate by the name of City-Centre Enterprises—which meant nothing to me—and it took me the rest of the afternoon to discover that City-Centre Enterprises was listed in no business directories or telephone books and had neglected to register with either the Lower Mainland Realtors' Association or the B.C. Realty Board. They did have a post office box, but the receptionist at the post office informed me that the names of persons renting post office boxes are confidential. When I compared myself to police detectives with their armies of paid staff and access to filing cabinets across the country, I felt sorry for myself. Which didn't help.

Nor did Sammy—who'd been caught in a brief, but vigorous summer shower, and whom I found cowering on the stoop outside my office door. He was drenched. In his lap he was cradling a soggy case of empty beer bottles. "What good is it people phoning you when you're never here?" he welcomed me.

"There's an answering machine," I explained. "A tape recorder tells them to leave a message, then I listen to the messages when I get here."

"Let's go hear the messages then." He leapt up, slung the beer case under one arm, stared impatiently at my office door. I pulled out the key.

"There've been no messages, Sammy. I listen to them every day."

"You already heard them today?"

"I heard them this morning. It's been a couple of weeks now. I'm afraid your dog's gone." I unlocked the door.

He pushed into my office in front of me, crouched and peered into every corner, as if expecting to find his dog hiding beneath a piece of my furniture. When he straightened, his shoes squelched. "You gotta *look*, you know," he informed me disdainfully. "Things don't find themselves." This sounded like his parents, second-hand.

"Have you been looking?"

"I've looked everywhere!" he cried, clenching his fists. "And if you were a real detective, you'd have found clues by now."

70

I raised my hands helplessly. "What kind of clues? The pound, the S.P.C.A.—I don't think there's anywhere else I can look."

"Someone probably stole him!" Sammy shouted at me. "Can't you even catch a thief!"

I sighed, flicked the switch on my answering machine; together we listened to my son tell me there was no ketchup in the house and I'd left him no money to buy any. There were no other messages.

"I'm sorry, Sammy. But I think you should give up."

He glared at me—fully conscious of his impotence and determined to make me pay for it. "I should have known," he said, dumping the case of beer bottles on my sofa. His voice was eloquent with bitterness. "I should have known no *lady* detective was gonna find my dog." He stomped towards the door.

"Then hire a man," I retorted. "And take your beer bottles with you."

He gave his bottles a covetous glance. "All right," he sneered, raising himself to his full height, "I will." He marched back to the sofa, picked up the case of beer bottles, slammed out my door.

There were wet footprints on the carpet; one of the sofa cushions was smeared with mud. It wasn't my day.

But the next was little better; I did almost nothing at all. I sat in my office wondering why Harry had never called me back; I wrote Tom a long letter, detailing the reasons for my depression. I knew I'd never mail it. I was supposed to be looking for Alison Chase, and though I wanted to talk to her (how much did she know about Danny Haswell?), I was beginning to think that she was better off lost. I'd given Janis my card; I'd suggested that she ask Alison to phone me. "She can give me a message for her parents," I'd said. "I'll tape it and deliver to them as proof of her continuing existence. If she does that, I'll resign from the case." However Alison hadn't phoned.

I decided to resign anyway. I'd done no work on the case for over a week, and I couldn't persuade myself to do any more. I wrote the Chases a report, detailing my activities to date; I told them that, in my opinion, Alison was safe and sound and only expressing (albeit forcefully) a determination to be independent. I enclosed an invoice.

The next day I accepted the inevitable—prepared to undertake the one routine task that I can carry out as effectively as any police officer, and with just as little enthusiasm. Keeping watch on a building is something I only do when I don't know what else to do, when it's either that or sit in my office feeling like a failure. And this time I had the added inducement of knowing that I was going to have to assume a camouflage. In that part of town, respectable, middle-aged women neither window-shop nor walk dogs; I wasn't going to get away with a pair of sunglasses and a baby carriage. In order to pass among the inhabitants of the area—the rubbies, junkies, crazies and whores—I would have to become one of them. As an indigent I'd be able to sit in full view of Haswell's doors, and people would step right over me.

Some people call them bag ladies, those women of indisputable poverty, usually middle-aged or older, who nose through the alleys of the city, looking for leftovers. Like mailcarriers they follow designated routes and carry a large bag over their shoulder, along with a stout stick with which they root through garbage cans, fend off antagonists and take some of the weight from their aching, arthritic feet. They wear their wardrobes on their backs; even in July the Skid Road regulars don't abandon their overcoats, whether to conceal their clothing (or lack thereof), their sweat stains, food spills, body odors, or the bottles in their back pockets— I don't know. I only mimic their behavior; I don't pretend to be an authority.

So I prepared to sweat it out, spent the morning assembling my disguise: frayed stockings, a shapeless sweater, a pair of gum boots, a plastic rain hat. I took my time, still hoping that someone would phone and provide me with an excuse to pursue some equally productive but less unsavory activity. Nobody did. I splashed the dregs of some cooking wine over my coat, rubbed dirt and ashes on my face and in my hair, stuffed a bottle of unpalatable, homemade wine that my uncle Donny had once donated to me in one of my coat pockets, a couple of sandwiches in the other; secreted a pad, a pen and a pair of binoculars about my person. I found an old pair of rhinestone glasses with one lens missing, dug our ancient beach-bag out of the closet and slung it over my shoulder. I was ready, disguised—not by wigs or false moustaches—but by my fall from social grace.

Bag ladies shuffle, and mutter to themselves as they walk. Some are curious, approach strangers without fear and stare intently at their features—but most act as if they were alone in the world, ignoring the existence of anyone else. I prefer the latter option. As I shuffled, muttering, through the neighborhoods between my home and Kinky's, I added details to my outfit—found two pop bottles, a nickel, half a paperback book, a kleenex (unused—only slightly muddied around the edges), a pencil stub, an orange, a family of rats inside a garbage can (these I left where they were; even the babies weren't cute). By the time I reached Hastings Street, I was safely inside my part: I hobbled and spat, stabbed viciously into litter baskets—no longer worried that I'd be recognized as Meg Lacey. I *wasn't* Meg Lacey; it was as simple as that. I'm always amazed—alarmed—to discover how quickly this happens.

For example. Respectable, middle-aged women don't pick at their teeth, scratch their crotches, spit out orange pits on the sidewalk, clean their ears with their fingertips, wipe their noses on their sleeves, adjust brassiere straps in public. They keep their knees together. They do not sit on curbs, sidewalks, or even the cement steps in front of downtown office buildings; they stay on their feet regardless of faintness or fatigue until they encounter an authorized bench. (And even then they don't sit down if the company's unsuitable.) They don't skip (outside of exercise class); they don't pick up objects that others have discarded or scramble after pennies or allow themselves to be caught looking at anything that is not in the best taste—be it corpses or erotic underwear displays. All my life I've obeyed these dictums, but the moment I assume the character of a social outcast, they slough off me like snakeskin.

But there is something about pretending to be one of the

dregs of society that gets under my skin. It's scary. When I become an inhabitant—however temporarily—of the Skid Road community, I realize how easy it is to become nobody, a person without credit, references, credentials; as faceless as a beggar on a Calcutta street. Of course there's truth to this experience—death teaches us the same lesson—but it's a truth that we avoid. For the inhabitants of Skid Road, avoidance isn't so easy (at least not within the realms of sanity), which is why we're afraid of them, which is why everyone averts their eyes and no one wants to know them; which is why there is no better disguise for a detective in that part of town. By one's very nature, one becomes invisible.

By the time I entered the alley behind Kinky's I was sticky and footsore, more than willing to take advantage of the shade behind the Smithrite. I subsided onto the asphalt, pushed some sharp stones out from under me, pulled out my wine bottle and my package of sandwiches. The loading door was shut; there was no one in sight. I ate one of the sandwiches, pocketed the other for future use, unfolded the newspaper I'd picked up en route, settled in for a good read. Two hours later I'd finished it, and exchanged it for my paperback.

I spent three days in that alley, staying one night till eleven; I read a lot of news. I watched staff arriving and leaving; food and alcohol being trundled in, garbage being trundled out; teenage girls, in couples and trios, entering and exiting through the locked alley door. They were all equipped with keys. I observed these girls closely, sometimes followed them—but their destinations were unremarkable. They didn't go far; they bought cigarettes, pop and sometimes groceries at a corner store; they visited department stores, drug stores, movie theaters, video arcades—much what you'd expect of girls of their age. I considered changing my outfit and accosting them, asking them outright who they were and how they came to be living on Haswell's third floor. But unless their reasons for living there were legitimate and above-board (which I didn't believe), they weren't going to answer my questions.

Once I saw Salal. She appeared in the open loading door,

squinted up at the sun, glanced about the alley, then stared straight at me. I'm sure she couldn't have recognized me but she watched me for some time—and I was reminded of that moment when I'd seen her behind the bar, staring out across the night club at the inebriates of Ladies' Night. She makes herself watch, I thought, and wondered, once again, if she'd informed Haswell of my trespasses. I knew I should have assumed she had—but it was then that I realized (taking a pull at my wine bottle for her benefit), that I believed that she'd kept quiet about my unauthorized visit. An alarm bell went off in my brain. Like everyone else, detectives are susceptible. They have biases and hopes that color their perceptions. I've learned from experience to be particularly wary of people that succeed in gaining my sympathy; it's only too easy to romanticize a chance acquaintance, to flatter oneself into believing that the romanticization is mutual. I don't know why I was thinking that Salal would protect me, but I realized that I was doing so that day in the alley, when I watched her watching me—a filthy, drunken crone—stoically digesting another facet of the human condition. She met your eyes, Salal, no matter who you were. That may be an admirable quality—I happen to think it is—but it was no reason to think that she would be on my side.

I accomplished next to nothing those three days in the alley. I became familiar with the routines of the establishment: opening and closing hours, shift changes, deliveries; I began to recognize the faces of the staff. The girls remained as much a mystery as ever. Every time one of them appeared, I experienced a jolt of incredulity. I remembered that god-awful third floor corridor, the filthy toilets, the teddy-bear with the missing eye. None of the girls looked older than fifteen; none of them were visited by parents or social workers. Who were they? Why weren't they in school? Why wasn't anyone looking after them? They weren't dressed like prostitutes, nor like...my daughter Katie, for example. But Katie is not typical, and these girls looked no more or less—how shall I say it?—"of moral and respectable character" (to quote the law books) than most teenagers you see. On the night I kept watch in the alley until eleven, they were all in by ten p.m. By choice or regulation? The more I examined the scant facts I'd accumulated, the more I chafed and fretted—knowing I was onto something, but unable to figure out how to discover what it was. I had to, somehow, get up to that fourth floor to find out what was hidden behind those blank, cemented windows. Without getting caught.

On the morning of the fourth day I abandoned the alley, had an appointment with a man that said he might have a job for me. I didn't want the job—I had enough on my plate—but I needed his money.

I met him in my office. He was a brisk, dapper little man, crisp as a new dollar bill—but with dark circles beneath his eyes. His name was Joau Goncalves (he made me say it until I could pronounce it correctly), and he'd flown out from Montreal in search of his twin brother, Victor, who'd set out for the West Coast thirty years ago and hadn't been heard from since. "Thirty years?" I repeated, with an inward groan. "Why did he leave?"

Joau made a sound of impatience, tossed whatever it was aside, cleared out a space between us with his hands. "Nothing—a little argument—an excuse, that's all it was. He wanted an excuse to travel, to be a man of the world. I know him."

"An argument with you?"

"Ah—" he screwed up his face, "always we argue. It means nothing. I never worried about it."

"But maybe he did?"

He looked at me intently. "I know what it is you are saying to me; I understand. But this is not how it was. We fight a lot but also we are true brothers; he knew that as much as me. No, he left because he wanted to see somewhere new and to be away from the family. The mother, the father—you know."

I thought I did. "But you don't know that he ever arrived here—and you've no proof that he stayed."

He scowled, didn't appreciate this summation of the facts he'd laid before me. He brought his face close to mine; the whites of his eyes were slightly bloodshot. "All these years—I have known he was here. I have felt it. He said he would get work in the lumber camps and I am sure that he did so. I have been so busy; I have a big family; I was not worried about him. Never." He sat back with an air of finality.

"And now?"

"And now something is wrong. Something is gone wrong for him. I feel this. So I write letters, I phone relatives and friends of relatives—but nobody knows anything. But the feeling is like—" he raised his hands, looked round my office as if for inspiration, "is like big dark clouds coming in my heart. A storm. You understand?"

I nodded.

"So finally I come. I must find him. As soon as possible. I must find out what is wrong. He is my brother—what can I do?"

I picked up my pen. "What have you done so far?"

He'd combed the Portuguese community. He'd visited every church, social club, coffee bar and restaurant owned and/or frequented by Portuguese Canadians—in our city, throughout the Lower Mainland, even on the Island. He'd had no success whatsoever.

"Maybe he avoided the Portuguese community," I suggested. "Maybe that's what he was trying to get away from. Maybe he wanted to strike out on his own."

Joau Goncalves frowned. "This is possible. But you know, for us—family, neighbors, relatives, friends—these things are very important. We feel so lonely sometimes in this country—everywhere strangers. It is hard to imagine that he did not once go to the homes of his countrymen, eat Portuguese food, get news of home. Not once?"

"Describe him. What does he look like?"

"He looks exactly like me."

"Exactly?"

"We are twins, I told you. People cannot tell us apart."

"You mean they couldn't—thirty years ago."

He yielded the point. "But still," he argued, "the resemblance will be striking."

I placed my pen on the desk. "And you went everywhere in the Portuguese community and nobody once mistook you for somebody else."

"Yes." He began nodding at me, continued for some time. "This is important. I know." We gazed at each other. I interlaced my fingers.

"Mr. Goncalves -"

He held up his hands. "Joau—please—you call me Joau."

"But I can't say it," I protested.

"Practice, practice—you will learn very quickly."

"O.K. Joau?"

He bowed his head gravely.

"Why do you persist in believing that your brother is here? He could be in South America for all you know."

Again he looked surprised. "But I *feel* him!"

"You *feel* him?"

"Of course! Even in Montreal I knew he was here. And now that I come here, it is like he is just around the corner. I look at everyone that goes by; I am so surprised I can't see him." His eyes held mine; I tried not to look as skeptical as I felt. "And at night—ai me!" He smacked his palm against his forehead. "I can't sleep I feel so bad. Such a pain in my head—and fear—it is terrible!"

"You mean literally—your head hurts?"

His forehead furrowed; again he was searching for words. "It is like pain—yes. And a darkness, growing. I feel afraid for him."

I decided to take his word for it. After all, I've read the literature; some identical twins blink at the same second, die within minutes of each other—even when thousands of miles apart. I told him what I could do for him; he added suggestions of his own. I wrote them down. He said he'd phone me tomorrow.

"Tomorrow?"

"To see if you have found anything."

I stared at my list. "But I'm not going to have all this done by tomorrow."

"Of course not. But I am impatient, you know; I have

nothing else to do here. Only to worry. So every day I will like to find out what you have learned."

"All right," I said, unwillingly.

"Good." He stood up, sketched a bow. At the door, he turned. "Use the intuition." He tapped his finger against his skull. "This is why I have hired you. It will be much faster."

"I don't quite understand."

"Because you are a *woman*," he explained.

I looked doubtful. "You think I'm going to be able to find him because I am a woman?"

"Exactly." His eyes sparkled with triumph. "I have faith," he proclaimed as he stepped out my door.

I wondered if I was going to live up to it.

CHAPTER SEVEN

W HEN you phone government ministries with unortho-
dox requests, such as, "Do you have any record of a Victor
Goncalves applying for assistance from your department?"
you spend a lot of time on hold. So that's where I was the
morning Sammy showed up again, half-carrying, half-
dragging a moth-eaten brown dog through my office door. I
put my hand over the mouthpiece.

"What's that?"

"I told you I'd find him!" Sammy got the door shut behind him, let go of the dog, which immediately trotted up to
my desk, sniffed at my ankles. Sammy regarded it admiringly.
"I just knew it would come back." The dog abandoned my
ankles, turned its attention to the legs of my sofa. I noticed
that it had a collar.

"Sammy, I thought you said your dog had patches.
Where did you get this one?"

"He was *exactly* where I left him." Sammy's eyes
widened with amazement. "I bet he was waiting for me to
show up again. He's really a smart dog."

"And what happened to the patches?"

The operator came on the line. "I'm sorry, ma'am; the
line is still busy. Will you continue to hold?"

"I'll call back," I said to her, and hung up.

"They dyed him," Sammy said. "They do that, you
know. I saw it on T.V. They dye the dog a different color so
you won't recognize him."

I got up from my desk, walked round to the dog, crouched and inspected its collar. But there was no tag. I examined its ears, peered between its legs.

"See?" Sammy explained. "I never got him a tag yet. That's how come no one could bring him home to me."

I sat down on the sofa. "It's female."

"Huh?"

"This dog is female," I repeated. "It has no bitten ear, no patches, and its eyes are the same color. Amber," I pronounced.

"So?" Sammy thrust out his chin, shoved his hands in his pockets.

"So it's not yours."

"Who says?"

"*I* say."

"Prove it!"

The phone rang. "Sorry," I said, getting up to answer it, "but you're the one that has to do the proving. You described your dog to me; I wrote it down; I phoned in that description to the S.P.C.A. and the pound. You were right here, listening, making sure I got it right. And that is not the dog you described." I pointed at it—vindictively—and picked up the phone. "Margaret Lacey speaking."

"Mrs. Lacey?" The voice was so soft that I could hardly hear it.

"It is so my dog!"

I put a hand over my other ear. "Yes—can I help you?"

There was silence.

"Hello?"

Then suddenly the voice returned, still speaking softly, but enunciating every word. "If you want to know more about Lily Kubicek's death, go to the Bloedel Conservatory at 2:30 this afternoon. Wait beside the eucalyptus."

"Who is this? Who's calling?"

"You never even seen my dog—how do you know what he looks like! And how come he was sitting *exactly* where I—"

"Hello? Hello?"

But she'd hung up.

81

I replaced the receiver, feeling suddenly short of breath. Salal? Was it possible? Or was it a trap? She'd told Haswell she'd found me snooping? But no one was going to mug me in the Bloedel Conservatory. Meanwhile Sammy was still arguing.

"He even smells like my dog! And he knows his name—see?" He turned to the dog. "Here, Radar, here fella." He crouched and snapped his fingers. The dog pricked its ears, cocked its head inquiringly.

"It's female," I reminded him. But I was mentally reviewing the sound of that voice, trying in vain to identify it. If not Salal, who else? One of Lily's friends, the one I'd been out to speak to? Or someone else entirely?

"Well, maybe my other dog was female. How'm I supposed to know?"

I glanced at him. "Your other dog?"

"I mean this dog—my dog! I can't tell the difference!"

"Apparently."

"I mean I don't *know* if it's a boy or a girl!" he roared in exasperation.

"Well, this one's female," I said coldly. "And it probably has a home somewhere. I suggest you take it back to where you found it and leave it there."

"And let it starve, I suppose. If it's got a home, how come it's got no tag?"

"If it's got no home, why does it have a collar?" I just wished the hell he'd leave. "Look, Sammy, it's none of my business. But as far as I'm concerned, that's not your dog. If you can't find its owner, you should take it to the S.P.C.A."

"They'll *kill* it!"

I rolled my eyes heavenward. "Ask them how long they'll keep it before they dispose of it. Tell them that if nobody else wants the dog, you do. Ask them to write down your name and phone number."

"Your phone number."

Not this again. "Sammy," I said wearily, "you can't keep a dog without your parents' permission. How will you feed it? How will you pay for its registration? And rabies shots? What will you do with it while you're in school all day?"

"Your phone number," he repeated, stubbornly.

"No." I was equally firm, tired of playing along with him. "You can't have a dog if your parents are opposed to it."

I was getting the full treatment; his eyes glinted like razor blades.

"If your parents won't let you, I'm sorry, but that's the breaks. When you grow up you can have as many dogs as you like."

He continued to glare at me, willing my imminent death.

"Have you even asked them?" I inquired.

For a moment he didn't answer, then stepped closer, threatening me. "Cantonese people *eat* dogs," he hissed. "Maybe I'll take him home and we'll cut him up with flied lice."

I sat, open-mouthed, shocked by his hatred—against me? against himself? Why had he even brought the dog to my office? Just so we could get into an argument about it? "All right." I washed my hands of him. "Do what you like. Just leave me out of it."

"I can keep him?" His face lit up.

"Sammy!" I cried. "*I'm* not your parent. Go talk to your mum or your grandma or whoever. It's their decision, not mine."

He gazed at me for a moment; I could see his thoughts ticking over. He finally turned, looked at the dog that was still waiting by the door. "Come on, Radar," he said. "Let's go." The dog wagged its tail.

"What are you going to do with it?" I asked, as he moved toward the door.

He lifted his chin, looked at me defiantly. "If he follows me home, I ain't stopping him. If he don't, he don't. It's *his* decision," he announced, as if proclaiming a new charter of canine rights. He opened the door; the dog pressed against his calves.

"Hers," I reminded him.

"So *you* say," he retorted, and closed the door behind them.

*

I've always liked the Conservatory. Being a person of limited means, I don't travel much, so the Conservatory's about as close to foreign climates as I can get. As I entered the hushed, steaming atmosphere of the dome, I realized why whoever it was had chosen this place to meet. There was only one entrance: a turnstile, and you had to pay to get through it. You had only to sit within sight of the turnstile to make sure you weren't followed.

I paid my fee, started along the white, pebbled pathway, edging around groups that had stopped to sniff flowers, read the inscriptions to one another and compare the live specimens with the sketches in their botany books. As I passed them, I noticed the way their voices evaporated into the gurgle of running water, the hiss of humidifiers—so that it was almost impossible to overhear someone else's conversation. I was beginning to get nervous. But there were no dark corners; the sunlight penetrated everywhere—fractured, dispersed, as if viewed from under water. A tiny, bright orange bird flickered over my head, an orchid glowed in a hollow of dense foliage. I rounded a stand of Norfolk pine, descended the path toward a foot bridge, heard a footstep crunch in the pebbles behind me. Before I had time to look around, I found myself accompanied; our feet echoed dully over the curved, wooden bridge. We passed on to the rhododendrons.

She was wearing a navy-blue scarf, tied bandanna style, and a large pair of sunglasses that almost completely concealed her eyes. It was the first time I'd seen her off-duty, so to speak, and I was surprised by the change. It wasn't just her clothes—though these were certainly more casual—her whole manner seemed different. The stiffness was gone. She was still wary and tense, but also graceful, fluid; she looked muscular and lithe. Her clothes were downright shabby: tight blue jeans, a wine-red blouse (both faded and trailing threads from the seams), running shoes on her feet that were barely in one piece, revealing numerous glimpses of metatarsal and toe. But she wore an exquisite pair of earrings of native design, two silver whales, leaping. She fingered them often, as if afraid she was going to lose them.

When we got off the bridge we slowed down a bit, but neither of us spoke. Prayer plants crouched beneath festoons of trailing vine; we passed beneath the trunk of a soaring banana tree. I was conscious, for the first time, of the difference in our ages. Perhaps because of the clothes, I was finally seeing her as an adolescent: ill-at-ease with the older generation, struggling to appear more competent than she felt. By contrast, I felt experienced, a socially competent adult. I relaxed a little.

To the left of the path was an impenetrable, waist-high tangle of dark, glossy leaves, as familiar a sight in our part of the world as sand in the Sahara. I stopped. "That looks like your namesake," I commented, pointing at it. "You wouldn't think they'd let it in here." I fingered one of the thick, green leaves; Salal had come to a halt beside me.

"What do you think?" I asked, for the first time looking at her directly.

Her eyes surveyed the extent of the salal patch; she lifted a branch, peered underneath it. "But it's got no berries or flowers," she commented. "In summer there should be one or the other."

"If it's salal, it'll take over."

"Kill it in the garden, it'll come up through the floorboards. That's what my granny used to say." She was looking at me, but I couldn't make out the expression of her eyes through the sunglasses. "She named me."

"Did she want you to emulate it?"

A single crease divided her eyebrows. "What's emulate mean?"

"Did she want you to follow its example?"

Salal suppressed a sigh. "Yes. That's what she wanted, I guess." The thought seemed to depress her. She moved on.

Again we fell silent. And I remembered that, in effect, I'd requested this meeting—but I was in no hurry to start talking about Lily or Danny Haswell. I needed, more than anything else, to get to know this girl better.

"What made you decide to see me?"

She kept her eyes on the path ahead. "Someone told me I could trust you."

I stared at her. Whatever answer I'd expected, it certainly wasn't that one. "Who?"

She just shook her head.

I couldn't believe it. Who could Salal know that knew me? Who would tell her to trust me? Not Haswell. Alison? But Alison didn't trust me herself. A friend of Lily's? Fred Chase? None of these answers seemed plausible. But as far as I was aware, we had no other acquaintance in common. "Who?" I asked again, my curiosity getting the better of me.

But she wasn't going to tell me. She reached up, removed her sunglasses and as her eyes surveyed me, my pose of adulthood crumpled. Under the scrutiny of this cool, hard-bitten teenager, I felt bumbling and naive. "Are you sure you weren't followed here?" she asked me.

"Why would anyone be following me?"

She looked over at the turnstile on the far side of the dome; my gaze followed hers. A group of women were paying for postcards; a family with two children were entering the turnstile, an elderly couple was leaving. My eyes returned to Salal's profile. "There's nobody following me," I said.

"I know. I was watching." She glanced back at me.

Then why ask? I wondered—not without resentment.

"Lily was murdered—remember?"

I refused to be intimidated. "By whom?"

"By Caesar—or someone he paid to do it."

"Why?" I asked—but she abruptly began walking again, and I had to hurry to catch up. When I came abreast of her she slowed down, gave me a sideways glance. "Lily was real dumb," she said quietly. "I told her so to her face. We all did. She never shut up; she never figured out that she wasn't in high school anymore."

"Wait," I said. "Start from the beginning. How did you get to know her?"

"The usual way." She said it with distaste.

"Yes, but I don't know what that is."

"Ladies' Night. You were there; you saw how it works."

So she'd seen us! At what point? I could have sworn she'd never even looked our way. But if she'd—*Johanna*!

That's who'd told her to trust me. Who else could it have been? Yet I hadn't realized that they knew each other that well.

"Lily went to Ladies' Night," I said. "But explain the process—where does she go from there? I'm sure you're not personally acquainted with every girl that shows up at Ladies' Night."

She sighed. "Deanne brought her up. Stupid cow."

I flinched, but forbore to comment. "Who's stupid—Deanne?"

"Yeah. The moment they walked in I took one look at Lily and said: What are you bringing her up here for? But Deanne gives me the big hush-hush look, right, and takes Lily off to one of the rooms and I think: Now what's she pulling? She makes me sick."

I saw that I wasn't the only one to experience Salal's contempt. "I don't quite understand. Why shouldn't she have chosen Lily?"

"For *porno* movies?" Salal looked at me incredulously, saw that I still didn't get it. "Look—the ones for the porno movies are supposed to look like the nice little girl door next door. You know, ten-year-old Alice-in-Wonderland types. WASPs," she added. "Lily doesn't make it. No, it wasn't Haswell she was picked for."

I waited, but nothing more was forthcoming. "Salal," I said patiently, "I don't know as much as you think I do. You have to explain. Who was Lily picked for?"

"Caesar," she answered. "Deanne is always sucking up to him. She told Lily she'd get a screen test but she knew Danny would never touch her."

"Caesar's a pimp, right?"

"That's right," she drawled.

"You used to work for him."

She gave me a look like a barbed wire fence. Then she glanced upwards, just as a spray of tiny birds erupted from a nearby bush. Our eyes followed them across the dome. When I looked back at Salal I saw that she was still staring upwards; following her gaze I saw the round, bluish leaves of the eucalyptus shimmering over our heads.

"Compared to me and my brother," she continued, lowering her eyes back to me, "Lily was real sophisticated. But she thought she had rights—I don't know who taught her that. My brother and I were a little more perceptive."

"She made trouble, did she?"

"It was partly Deanne's fault. Deanne told her she was going to be a movie star and of course Lily never got near a camera. But she started working for Caesar and seemed to take it in her stride; she got her benefits regular and the pay was pretty good compared to waiting on tables or something like that. But it was like—she thought she was a member of the Teamsters or something. She never shut up. She'd say things like: 'You give me more money or I'll report you to the police.' To Caesar, she'd say it! I tell you she gave the rest of us something to talk about."

"What did he do?"

"He beat her up, of course. But you can only beat up someone for so long, especially if you want 'em to look pretty for the customers. He cut off her junk supply, stuff like that - locked her in her room. Trouble was she was stupid. Stupid in a way that was dangerous. I figure she was a Daddy's girl, used to getting her own way. She couldn't see what she was up against. The other kids—all of us tried to talk to her one time or another, but—" She shrugged.

We were still standing in the middle of the grove of eucalyptus, bathed in a mottled, watery light that made our faces look green, Salal's lips purplish-black. A couple of yards to our right was an empty bench. I looked at it; together we walked over to it and sat down.

"Who do you work for?" I asked her.

"Haswell."

"Not Caesar."

"Never."

"You mean never again?"

She lowered her eyelids, but didn't deny it.

"What's the connection between Haswell and Caesar? How does Caesar fit in with the movie business and Kinky's?"

"He doesn't."

"Really? But then why—"

"He's the banker, that's all."

"The banker?"

"You know—the dealer. He supplies the benefits."

"You mean the—"

"The junk. That's what we call it. Like medical benefits."

"So then why is Deanne pulling up kids for Caesar?"

Salal puffed out her cheeks, exhaled—loudly. "Well that's it—she's not supposed to. Danny does give Caesar girls, but only the ones that don't work out or that get too old—"

"How old is too old?"

Salal made a face. "Depends. Depends what they look like. Jeannie, she was still making kiddie porn when she was sixteen years old. But most of them don't last beyond fifteen."

"Did you used to make movies?"

Her gaze was level and hard. "I told you, they want WASPs."

Yes, she'd told me. "So what do you do?"

She looked out across the dome. "Secretarial stuff. Correspondence, typing, payroll, bookkeeping—except I got some extra responsibilities. I'm also supposed to look out for the girls, make sure they don't make themselves too conspicuous—stuff like that."

"Then why work for Haswell?"

She gave me a puzzled look.

"Secretarial jobs aren't that hard to find, are they? Couldn't you work for someone else?"

She had a trick of lowering her eyelids so that her eyes seemed to flicker beneath them, an expression that was somehow both bitter and mocking. "You think my salary would pay for the habit?"

"Oh." I hadn't thought of that. "You're a junkie."

"Ever since I was thirteen." She spoke almost proudly. "Even Haswell is. We all are. We're all in the same boat."

"Keeps you where he wants you."

Her eyebrows lifted. "You think we don't know that?"

All right, I thought; I took a deep breath. "So what are

you going to do about it?"

To my surprise she didn't react, but continued to watch me, attentively. "I thought you might have some suggestions."

I stared at her—but she was serious. She meant it? She was willing to inform against them?

"How about some stills—or I could get you some film scraps?"

I didn't understand. "Scraps of what?"

"You know, the stuff they edit out. And there's always extra stills kicking around. All I have to do is get to the garbage before they burn it."

"Stills.... You mean you could get photographs from the— "

"Kiddie porn movies," she prompted me, nodding. "And scraps of film, you know?" She decided to spell it out for me. "For you to take to the cops."

"For *me* to take?"

She was getting irritated. "Well, why else are you here? Why am I talking to you?"

"You don't think you could go yourself? And testify against them?"

"I know I couldn't."

Why not? I wondered, and debated whether to voice the question. But she read it in my eyes.

"Lily was murdered. I'm going to get out of this alive."

"So am I," I said immediately.

"But Haswell doesn't *know* you. At least, he won't if you stop advertising yourself. When he's trying to figure out who informed on him, he won't think of you. And if he asks the cops, they won't be able to tell him."

"I don't understand," I said—but now knew why it was important that our meeting be kept secret.

"*You'll* know who squealed on Haswell—but the cops won't."

It was becoming apparent to me that she had this whole thing planned, was just waiting for me to figure out what she had in mind. "Why are you willing to do this? Why now? I don't get it."

"I've been waiting for the right opportunity."

"What's in it for you?"

Her eyelids drooped, then widened again. "What's in it for you?"

I was taken aback. "Why I—I—" I glanced at her, became indignant. "I don't like kiddie porn and I don't like men that turn children into junkies and prostitutes."

Again those eyes flickered. "Maybe I don't either," she suggested, softly.

I felt like I'd been slapped. I stared at her but couldn't interpret the expression on her face; I turned abruptly away, lifted my eyes and feigned an interest in the structural components of the dome.

"Can't see much danger in this for you," she pointed out.

"That's nice," I answered coolly, and gave her a look.

We sat in silence for some time. From the path behind us on the other side of the eucalyptus grove, voices wafted and blurred in the damp, hissing air. A fat parrot, green and gold, perched momentarily on a branch, then took off again, squawking.

"But if Haswell's in the Pen, where will you get your benefits?" Formulating the question, I'd thought it reasonable enough, but when it came out of my mouth, it sounded vindictive and prim.

"I guess that's my problem."

By now I was getting used to this treatment; she was turning out to be less likeable than I'd thought. "I'm only trying to understand you," I defended myself. "I need to know where you're coming from."

"Since there's no risk to you, why worry about it?"

I sighed. "There's my credibility. It's me that's going to have to talk the cops into investigating Haswell."

"With the evidence I'm giving you, that shouldn't be so hard."

"But how are you going to get hold of this evidence? Where will you hide it? How will you deliver it to me?"

Her shoulders lifted. "I told you—I just have to root through the garbage and wait for the right stuff to turn up. Might take a couple of weeks. And getting it to you is no problem. He gives me a fair amount of rope. I been with him a while now."

"He trusts you?"

Her eyes met mine. "As much as he trusts anyone. I'm a nice efficient machine; I get everything done. I don't think Danny's ever wondered why I should be loyal to him. Except for the smack, of course. Maybe he figures that's all the loyalty he needs."

And is it? I wondered—but kept the question to myself. How far could one trust a junkie, especially when their supply was involved?

A child approached, half-hopping, half-skipping, a girl of about five or six, dressed to the nines and already fully conscious of her charms. As she passed in front of our bench, she slowed to an idle, dragged a patent leather shoe in the gravel behind her. She simpered at us. I glanced at Salal. She was watching the child as if assessing an equal; there was no indulgence in her eyes. The little girl's smirk faded, altered to a pout. "Gillian!" a woman called, from the direction of the banana trees. A spark of complicity lit the child's eyes; she ran away in the opposite direction.

"We'll aim for a shoot," Salal said, watching the child disappear around the bend.

"A shoot?"

She turned back to me. "You know—when they're filming. For the raid. We'll tell the cops when to come, unlock the doors—make it easy for them."

"We're going to tell the police when to stage their raid?"

"Yes." Again she looked irritated; she seemed to assume that I could read her mind. "I'll choose a good time, draw a map—and one night when they're all up there, shooting a big scene— "

"They make them upstairs, do they?"

She glanced at me. "Wasn't that where you were going, that day I found you snooping?"

"The fourth floor?"

Again she didn't bother to answer me, was gazing through me, past me—preoccupied by her thoughts. Despite her belligerence and bad manners I couldn't help but be

92

moved—by her youth, by her courage, by the very real dangers of what she was proposing. "You'll be careful?"

Unexpectedly, she put a hand on my arm. "Don't worry," she said kindly. "I know what I'm doing."

This didn't reassure me—but there wasn't much I could do about it. Something else was bothering me though, and I decided to bring it up. "How about Caesar?"

"Caesar?" She looked startled.

I was surprised that she hadn't found some way to include him in her plans. "Wouldn't you like to turn him in too?"

She gave me a sharp glance. "How?"

"I got the impression you don't much like him."

"I'm not alone in that."

"Cops tell me they can't get anyone to testify against him."

Her upper lip curled. "Including themselves."

Three elderly women, pink-powdered and permed, strolled down the path towards us. Their eyes rested curiously on Salal; then they glanced at me and smiled—with practiced warmth. They made gestures at the eucalyptus, exclaimed at a parrot, slowly moved on, leaving a scent of lavender behind them.

"It's not that easy," Salal explained, when the women were out of earshot. "He's very, very careful. Even I've never seen him with any junk in his hands and I've been watching him for years. All I can tell you is that if Caesar doesn't visit, we don't get our benefits. And sometimes he makes us wait—which we don't exactly appreciate. But there isn't one of us—except maybe Haswell—that could testify against him in court. You saw the gloves?"

"The gloves?" Then I remembered: Caesar's gloves. "Oh yes. I wondered about those."

"He treats our place like home, but I don't think you could find one fingerprint of his on the property. He takes his gloves off to shake hands, then puts them right back on again. And you want me to nail him," she concluded, derisively.

"Maybe when I tell the police—maybe they'll think of

some way they could include him."

"Don't count on it," Salal answered, getting to her feet. "You don't get that far in the world without a little help from the authorities."

This kind of automatic cynicism has always annoyed me. "Are you so sure?"

She stood before me, hands in her jeans pockets. "Look—when my brother died, I was desperate, eh? I phoned them, anonymously. I told them that he'd been working for Caesar, that he'd started doing a little business on his own account, that Caesar had found out about it. I told them everything they needed to know. Result? Zilch."

"You can't use an anonymous phone call as evidence in court."

"So what am I supposed to do? Send them photographs of Caesar in the act?"

"You have to testify in court. They have to have witnesses."

She exhaled—with emphasis. "When you were talking to the cops, did they ever tell you about a woman called Karen Bauer?"

"No."

"Do me a favor. Next time they tell you about how they can't get witnesses, ask them what happened to Karen."

"She agreed to stand as a witness?"

"On condition that she got full police protection—from the moment she walked out of their station to the moment she stood in that witness box."

"What happened?"

"She overdosed. Isn't that a coincidence." She spoke wearily, pushed a hand through her hair, glanced at the turnstile. "Look, I've got to go. I've been away long enough. We'll work out the details next time."

I stood up. "You want to arrange our next meeting now or—"

"I'll be in touch," she said. "One other thing—" Keeping her eyes on my face, she reached into her shirt pocket, pulled out her sunglasses, disappeared behind them, as if cutting the connection between us.

94

"What?" I said. I hate talking to people who wear sunglasses.

"If anyone asks you—" She stepped forward a pace; since I couldn't see her eyes, I found myself staring at her teeth. "You never heard my name, and you couldn't describe me if your life depended upon it."

"Of course."

"We're going to make up a story and as long as you stick to it, we'll both be O.K. You got that?"

I watched her, dubiously, but couldn't read anything through those sunglasses. "I don't see how this is going to work."

"Don't worry. You will. I'll explain it to you next time, when I've got it all figured out."

"All right," I said.

"I'll leave first. You watch."

She turned, started walking briskly away along the path towards the turnstile. As she passed through the exit I saw her glance back—but her eyes passed right through me, scanned the paths and the people behind her. Then she vanished through the glass doors.

For a few minutes longer I stood watching the turnstile; no one followed her out. Fronds stirred, the stream gurgled; the child, Gillian, reappeared, this time complaining fretfully, accompanied by adults. Then I too continued my stroll along the white pebbled pathway, remembering, as I reached the turnstile, to look back.

I was learning.

CHAPTER EIGHT

In the subsequent weeks I was grateful for Joau Goncalves. Without his daily phone calls, his instructions, his demands, his unflagging energy, I might have subsided into a mass of nervous jelly, incapable of coherent thought or productive activity. But Joau didn't let me. After I'd exhausted all the government agencies, searched the files of the major lumber companies and woodworkers' unions, placed ads in every newsletter and newspaper in the province, he set me to work on the smaller logging operations (of which there were hundreds) and the companies that had gone out of business five/ten/fifteen years ago. Then he told me to start on the pulp mills.

Joau was my only client. At least that's what I thought until I received a phone call from a young woman who told me she wanted me to record a message for her.

"Who is this?"

"Alison."

Alison? Oh yeah—Alison Chase. Now that I wasn't looking for her, she'd decided to show up.

"Are you ready?" she asked.

"O.K. You're on." I flicked the switch.

"Hi, Mummy," she said. "And Daddy. This is Alison. I'm fine; I'm well; I'm living in a house with some friends of mine; I've started a tapestry." She had a clear, high voice; she spoke slowly and distinctly, as if to a kindergarten class. "I want you to call off your detective. I have not been kid-napped; I just want to get away for a while. I'm not going to marry Danny—but I've already told him that, so you don't have to get involved. So stop worrying; when I've finished this—phase, you can call it—I'll come and visit. *Please* get rid of the detective. O.K? Bye now." She stopped.

"Is that it?" I asked.

"Isn't that enough?" Her voice had dropped—at least a register—she was no longer playing kindergarten teacher.

"It's up to your parents. I don't know if this will satisfy them or not."

"I thought this was your idea. That's what Janis said."

"Yes. It is. But as a matter of fact, I dropped your case a while ago. Which doesn't mean, of course, that your parents haven't hired somebody else."

"You mean I'm wasting my time? I'm talking to the wrong detective?"

"Not necessarily. This phone call may convince your parents to give up if they haven't already done so. I haven't heard from them since I sent them my last report, so I don't know what they've been doing since. Anyway, I'll take this message to them and we'll see what happens. Tell me—when did you tell Danny Haswell that you weren't going to marry him?"

"Last time I saw him. Ages ago. Why?"

"When I talked to him myself, he led me to believe that the engagement was still on."

"Really?" There was a pause. "I thought I made myself pretty clear."

"Perhaps he's still hoping," I suggested. "People do."

"Maybe." She sounded doubtful.

"Why did you break up with him?"

There was a pause. "I don't think that's any of your business."

"You're right. It isn't." I let the subject drop. "Have you got enough money? I'm asking because that's what your parents will probably be asking me."

"Sufficient."

97

"O.K. I'll see what I can do for you."

We hung up.

Fred and Gloria Chase sat at either end of their chesterfield, my tape recorder on the coffee table between them. Fred was hunched forward, holding his head in his hands; Gloria was sitting back, legs crossed, body slightly averted, as if the tape recorder were something sordid or repellent. Alison's clear, high voice wafted into the room like smoke. "Hi, Mummy. And Daddy. This is Alison...." Neither of them moved. The moment the recording ended, Fred lunged at the tape recorder, stabbed the rewind button, re-played the message. When it stopped for the second time, he hit rewind again.

"That's enough," Gloria said. "I heard it the first time."

Fred ignored her. For the third time Alison—sounding increasingly mechanical—labored through her message. Gloria stared out the window, her crossed leg twitching.

The recording ended; Fred hit rewind once more—like a gambler compulsively losing nickels to a slot machine. "What do you think?" he asked his wife. He looked belligerent, suspicious. "You think it's her?" His thumb pushed the play button. "Hi, Mummy. And Daddy. This is..."

"That's enough!" Gloria cried. Her foot arched in mid-air; her throat was mottled pink. "Turn it off!"

Fred did so, reluctantly. He remained hunched over the tape recorder as if determined to keep his eye on it. "I don't like it," he said.

"You don't like *what*?" Gloria spat at him. Something—her daughter's message?—had clearly upset her.

He looked at her, his lower lip protruding. "You can do anything with these things. That could have been anybody."

Gloria's look was withering. She turned to me.

"That girl you were speaking of."

"Janis?" I suggested.

"Would she meet with us do you think? So that we can make our own— " her lids lowered, "assessment?"

"No," I answered candidly. "I don't think she would."

Gloria's plucked eyebrows furrowed. "Why not?"

"Because she's on your daughter's side. Both of them only want you to call off the search."

"Would you ask?" It was a command.

Fred lurched to his feet, made for the liquor cabinet. "I'm having her tailed," he pronounced. "I've had enough of this pussy-footing around."

I shrugged, reached across the coffee table for my tape recorder. "I believe you've already received my invoice."

"Invoice for what?" Fred roared. His finger quivered at the tape recorder. "For all I know you cooked up that tape yourself. Could have been anybody!" He poured out his scotch.

"Fred—" Gloria warned.

He turned on her. "Well, what did she do? Came up with some cock-and-bull story about a punk friend and three inches of tape. You think I'm paying her for that? I asked her to find my daughter!" He downed half his glass.

"If I remember correctly," I said, putting on my jacket, "all you wanted was to know if your daughter was in the morgue. As soon as I came to the conclusion that she wasn't, I stopped working on the case. I was told, specifically, that I was not being asked to produce your daughter in person, especially if this was not agreeable to her. It's not agreeable to her. I explained to you in the beginning that you pay me a weekly retainer fee and I charge by the hour. We settle the difference at the end of the case. At the moment I'm out about ten hours work."

"I pay for results!" Fred's eyes, red-rimmed, glowered at me over the top of his glass. "I don't pay nothing if I don't get results!"

"Then I'll be seeing you in court," I said sweetly, "for breach of contract." I picked up my bag, tucked the tape recorder under my arm, held my head high as I walked to the door.

"I'll see you in hell!" he bellowed after me.

I opened the door. "My lawyer will be in touch with you." I made a swift—but I hope, dignified—exit.

But I don't have a lawyer. And I don't have the resources to take anyone to court. Up to that point in my career, I'd had clients that argued over the amount of their outstanding expenses—but Fred was the first that actually refused to pay them at all. After my experience with him, I never gave any of my clients credit. I demanded cash on the table before lifting a finger to help them. The world needs people like Fred; without them, people like me would never learn the ropes.

I guess I lasted about a week before my nerves got the better of me, and I dialed Johanna's number.

"She told me someone told her to trust me," I said.

"Hmm," said Johanna. She didn't sound too interested. "You told her that?"

There was a pause—which extended until I decided I'd better fill it up. "See I'm feeling a little out of my depth. I was wondering, for example, if you'd care to reciprocate the recommendation."

"What do you mean?" It sounded like she was chewing gum.

"Would you tell me to trust her?"

Another pause. Goddamn her, I thought.

"Do you have any choice?" she asked me. "I mean, what have you got to lose?"

I gave an exasperated sigh. "That's what she said."

"Well?"

It was definitely one of those days when we stood on opposite sides of the fence.

"Johanna," I pleaded. "I'm nervous. This is the most dangerous thing I've ever done in my life. She could get killed! Or if not her, someone else. I keep worrying that I haven't thought it through enough, or that I've got no right to let her go ahead with it. Do you think she knows what she's doing?"

Another silence—but this one sounded more promising. "Yeah," Johanna said slowly. "And I don't think you could stop her even if you wanted to. I got the impression she'd been planning this for a long time now. Your showing up on the scene was just an opportunity she decided to take advantage of."

"What kind of opportunity?"

"A contact—with the police."

"Oh." I thought about this. "She came and saw you then, did she?"

More gum-chewing. "Yup." She wasn't going to elaborate.

"I didn't know you knew her."

"By sight. And by reputation, a little. She probably knows as much about me."

"I see." It was less than I'd hoped for. "It's just that it all seems so unreal—Ladies' Night, Caesar, Haswell, Salal..."

"And me?"

"Why no, not you so - "

"Because sometimes, some days, you seem unreal to me. Your mother, your ex, your sisters...It's like one of those nice middle-class novels you find in the library. Sometimes I don't believe in you."

I was silenced.

"And sometimes you don't believe in me, right?"

"Right," I said, somewhat unwillingly. I always forget that when I go to Johanna, I get more than I bargained for.

I finally found his name. He'd worked in a pulp mill up near Prince Rupert from 1973 to 1980—until three hundred workers were laid off, him among them. "Victor Goncalves"—employed as a scaler, one of the men that graded the logs. No record of any subsequent applications for unemployment insurance, no address or phone number in Prince Rupert that I could find. I phoned his brother.

"I don't know what to do. I'd go up there myself—but I can't. I've got another case on my hands and it's crucial that I stay around town for a while."

"Don' you worry. I go. I see the country, ehn?"

He came down to my office, looking more drawn than ever, with dark purple patches—like bruises—beneath his eyes. But his manner hadn't changed—he was brisk, even cheerful. I gave him the information he needed, a list of questions he should ask, offices he should visit.

"I hope and pray," he said, holding up his hand, the first two fingers crossed. "I have to go home soon; my family writes me letters. But I get more and more worried about my brother. All the time now—headaches. I feel ver' ver' bad."

"You don't look well," I agreed. "Maybe you should see a doctor."

"No." He was decided. "The doctor will say—too heavy the blood—how you say?"

"High blood pressure?"

"Yes. The blood pressure. He will tell me to take it easy. But how can I take it easy when I am worrying about my brother? No. More important I think," he wagged his finger with emphasis, "is to find my brother. This is my sickness. I know." He prodded his chest.

"I only hope you find something. When are you going?"

"Tonight."

"Tonight?" As usual, I was awed by his efficiency. "Where are you staying? Do you know?" I picked up my pen.

"Sorry." He waved a hand—approximately in the direction of his hotel. "I forget the name. I phone you."

The next week I was on tenterhooks. But I heard nothing from Joau, nothing from Salal. Sometimes I remembered how belligerent she'd been, how unfriendly; sometimes I found myself hoping she'd get caught so that I'd be let off the hook. Why *should* I trust her? Why stick my neck out? Why not, simply, play the good citizen and take my story to the police?

My son, Ben, went camping to Long Beach with some friends; Katie and her boyfriend were vacationing with her father in the Okanagan; Tom was still paddling through Arctic swamps. I had no one to talk to but the cat. The cat's a good listener; it purred sympathetically while I enumerated my problems—some of which were becoming acute. I owed rent on my townhouse and office both; I hadn't paid any bills for over three months; and now something was ailing my clutch or transmission—I couldn't tell which and was afraid to find out. I tried to change gears as seldom as possible. Fred Chase owed me money; Carol Talney owed me money; even Joau owed me money—but I hadn't remembered to ask him for some before he left town. I phoned my least "I-told-you-so" sister, who lent me four hundred bucks—with which I paid off one of my landlords. I considered selling my car—after all, it wasn't working—but a detective needs a car. I'm always driving out to Surrey or Abbotsford or Squamish—and sometimes I have to get somewhere in a hurry and as everybody knows, buses never hurry. I telegraphed Tom. "Flat broke. Lend me a thou?" Two days later the money appeared in my account. But I don't borrow money from Tom without suffering emotional consequences.

The sad fact of the matter was that I wasn't making a living. It was partly that I wasn't getting enough clients, partly that I was choosy—but if I couldn't afford to be choosy, I didn't want to be in the sleuthing business at all. I considered setting myself up as an Aikido teacher, going after the next rank—but there's a limit to how many Aikido teachers one city can support, and my teacher is better than I am. Sell cosmetics, door to door; give Tupperware parties. Start a business. Without capital? Hadn't I already tried that?

I needed a back-up, something else that brought in money, something that could be picked up or dropped at will, so that if I landed a big case, I could put my back-up on hold until the detective business slumped again. I started reading want ads: "Mature, capable woman needed to run household for three school-age children"; "Management trainees wanted for retail outlet of large manufacturing firm; applicants must be go-getters with related business experience." They were hardly inspiring. I went down to the employment center to look at the job board. That was a mistake. There were so few jobs and so many people looking for them; the line-ups were long, the forms incomprehensible, and there was a bad-tempered snot of a clerk that insulted anyone who didn't have the language skills to negotiate the process. Since about two-thirds of the applicants fell into this category, I left in a hurry. I knew that if I had to sit in that crowded waiting room among those bored, forlorn faces, listening to that bloody clerk, I'd get arrested for assault. Which wouldn't have got any of us closer to a job.

I was walking down Hastings Street, by chance (sort of). I do shop in that neighborhood from time to time, and I was on my way from Chinatown to Woodwards—a route that happened to take me right past Kinky's. But my surveillance was discreet; I was on the opposite side of the street and I was walking, briskly, when I glanced across the road and saw two familiar figures emerging from the lobby of the New Brighton Hotel. As they came through the door, the man gave the woman's shoulders a squeeze—and I felt like my stomach had intercepted a football. Automatically I sought the cover of a nearby parked van, but they were quite unaware of anyone but themselves, had started walking, arm in arm, proceeding west, in the same direction I was. I only caught glimpses of them, through the windows of parked cars, through gaps in the traffic that divided us—but there was no mistaking them. They were both tall, both blond; they were talking, animatedly. Johanna and Caesar. When they reached the corner, they turned east, out of sight.

I couldn't believe it. I managed to get myself to the next bus stop bench and sat down, stunned. *Johanna*? But she'd told me that he was a monster! What was she doing? And why? Did this have something to do with the raid, with Salal? But Salal had told me that she was out to get Haswell, not Caesar. Surely Johanna wasn't sleeping with him? Suddenly I was convinced that I'd been lied to—by both of them. I was furious.

I phoned Johanna that night. I told her that if she didn't talk to me, I'd go to the police. I don't know if I meant it—though I was certainly angry enough to say so. She got mad back. She thought I'd been tailing her—and it took me half an hour to convince her that I'd only seen her by chance. Having got that sorted out (and yes, I had to admit that I shouldn't be doing my shopping in Haswell's neighborhood anymore), we proceeded to the problem of her association with Caesar—which proved insuperable.

"I don't have to tell you what I was doing with him," she insisted. "It's none of your business. I've got my reasons, you've got yours. I don't give you a hard time when you hang out with cops."

"I don't hang out with cops!"

"Then who's that guy, Harry, that you're always going to lunch with?"

"That's business, Johanna. He's a connection."

"Well, mine's business too. You think you're the only person who ever does business? Sometimes you work with disgusting people, and sometimes I do too. But I don't tell you I can't trust you because of it."

"Is that what you're saying then? That he's a customer—nothing else? This has nothing to do with Kinky's, nothing to do with Salal, nothing to do with me. He's just one of your johns—is that it?"

"I'm telling you that this is my business, and that you should keep out of it."

"But it's become my business too! Can't you see that?"

"No. Your business is with Salal, and with the cops. You don't need to concern yourself with anything else."

"Now hold on. I'm only as credible as my informants can make me. If you tell me lies, I'll be telling the cops lies—and it'll be me that swings for it."

"I'm not telling you anything. I don't come into this. This is between you and Salal."

"But you're the one that sent her to me. You're the one that told me about Caesar."

"No way. *You're* the one that got me involved! I don't know Haswell from an ash tray. It was you that found Salal, you that asked her to spill the beans about Lily whatever-her-name-was. You started it! Not me!"

For a moment I was silenced. "That's true," I admitted. "I did start it. But I feel like it's already out of my hands. I don't know what's going on; I'm being kept in the dark."

"Of course you're being kept in the dark. You've been told what you need to know, and no more. What you don't know, you can't tell the cops."

"But I didn't know that you were involved at all!"

"And now you're going to forget that I am. I'm just helping out a little, that's all."

"You're casing Caesar?"

She didn't answer. So there it was between us: Was I going to trust her or not?

I didn't feel like I had much choice.

Out of the blue—the Northwest Territories?—Tom phoned.

"Why Tom!" I cried. "You sound so close!"

"I am."

"You are? Where?"

"I'm back."

"What! How nice! For how long?"

"Well, for some time, I suppose. One of us has to do the reporting and compiling—we're already far behind. And I was wor—wanted to see you so I volunteered."

"You mean the others are still up there?"

"Yes, well, it's barely August. They should get another six weeks in yet."

"But you're finished?" I didn't get it; this wasn't making sense. Why had he stopped working in the middle of the season?

"Yes, I'll stay here now and start writing it up. I thought I'd— "

"But that's not your job, is it?"

"I'm perfectly capable of it," he assured me. "And I thought it might be best if there were problems at this end..." He trailed off.

"Problems?" I asked warily.

"Well I thought—I was afraid—It sounded like— " He cleared his throat.

I'm familiar with these throat clearings, and the truth began to dawn. "*Not* because I cabled you," I protested, in tones of dread. "I didn't—I'm sorry. But it was only money. Nothing to get alarmed about. Oh dear. Can't you go back?"

There was a moment's silence—in which I realized that I'd been tactless. "I mean, of course I'd love to see you; I hate it when you're away. But I never intended you to make such a sacrifice— "

"There's no sacrifice involved," he said promptly.

"But Tom, I know how much you like fieldwork. And I know you never do reports if you can possibly avoid it. But I wasn't saying that I was in trouble—I was only broke! You know me—I'm always broke! Now I feel terrible!"

"But you've never asked me for money before." He sounded baffled.

"Haven't I?" I said weakly. I wondered how I'd managed it. But searching my memory, I came up with numerous dinners, favors, money for food supposedly eaten, gas supposedly consumed, airline tickets for Christmas, hotel bookings for Easter—but no out and out gratuitous cash. "But I only wanted a loan," I protested.

"I know that. But I assumed some emergency must have come up and...I was worried."

"Tom," I said gently. "I couldn't pay the rent. And my transmission went. That's all."

"Oh—I see." And I could hear that he was trying very hard to do so—as if being unable to pay the rent were something that could happen to anyone. Anyone but Tom, that is, who'd been working at the same job for over twenty-five years, steadily accumulating promotions, raises, benefits and pensions. "Well," he said, attempting to sound more cheerful, "that's good. I was afraid it was ah— " More throat clearing. "Perhaps we could get together, then. Shall we? How's your schedule these days?"

My schedule being as wide open as an Alberta wheat field, we arranged that part without difficulty.

But his return was untimely. I was giving myself ulcers waiting for Salal to show up again, and my fight with Johanna had made things much worse. I felt miserable and paranoid. Tom reaped the results. Everything about him rubbed me the wrong way. I resented his chivalry, his solvency—even his solicitude. I felt that I should have been able to ask for a loan without feeling obliged to him. Being a sensitive man, he was determined to prove to me that there was no obligation involved. But when I'm in a bad temper, I can't stand tact.

We made it through the first weekend, but on the second (still without word from Salal), we were sitting on my patio, sharing the newspaper, grilling ourselves shish-kabobs—when my landlady showed up at the door. Would you believe it, another month had gone by—and I'd spent all of Tom's money on the car, the groceries, the overdue bills, and the office rent. When I told Mrs. Rayburn, trying to keep my voice low so that Tom wouldn't hear, that I couldn't give her a check until the following week (and God knows how I planned to do that), she began to lecture me. Loudly. So of course Tom had to come out to find out what all the commotion was. The landlady, who was well aware of his position in our household, was only too happy to explain it to him. He listened, gravely, then turned to look at me.

"Would it help," he suggested, "if I settled with Mrs.—ah—and then you reimburse me when you—ah— "

"I'd be satisfied with that," Mrs. Rayburn said quickly. But it was my answer he was waiting for.

I didn't want him to do it. I wanted him not to be there so that Mrs. Rayburn would have to work it out with me—but since he'd made the offer—since she knew he'd made the offer—it seemed my bargaining position was hopeless. After all, she wasn't a rich woman—for all I knew she needed my money to pay her own bills. So I agreed, reluctantly, and went straight back out onto the patio so I wouldn't have to witness their mutual satisfaction in resolving my difficulties.

I won't detail the fight. Suffice to say that it started when he said: "Meg, I'm worried. I don't see how you can go on like this." Since I felt the same way, I should have been able to sympathize—but instead I pulled a Johanna and told him to mind his own business. If we couldn't help each other through the bad times, he said, why be together at all? I told him I didn't need a white knight.

Tom and I get angry in different ways. I flare up at trifles, then forget them a moment later, but Tom is like thick stew—he takes a long time to heat up, and just as long to cool down. So when I told him that I thought I should avoid him for a while (meaning, until Danny Haswell had been dealt with), he asked me (naturally enough, since he'd only been back for a week) why I didn't just say that I didn't want to see him at all. We argued that one at some length. But we couldn't or wouldn't understand each other, and the long summer absence had made both of us mistrustful. Finally, when we seemed to have said it all—had proved to our mutual satisfaction that we were utterly incompatible—Tom got up and went home.

When two people live together, it can't stop there; they bump into each other in the bathroom, their eyes meet over the breakfast table. In order to separate, they have to do something, say something, act. Not so with us. In order to *meet* we have to do something; somebody has to make a phone call. Sometimes I like it this way; I like it that we only see each other when we want to. Sometimes I don't. For the first couple of days, I didn't phone because it was me that said that I shouldn't see him for a while, that I wasn't good company, etc. Then, when a week had gone by and he hadn't phoned, I began to get worried. I started wondering if this was serious. After about ten days I couldn't stand the suspense anymore and phoned him at his office.

"Mr. Greenall?" said his secretary, who knows me well by now. "Oh no, dearie, didn't he tell you? He went back up north."

"He did?" But I don't trust Tom's secretary; she takes a vicarious interest in our relationship—so I suppressed my expletives. "When did he leave?"

"Well, it was yesterday—yesterday morning. Didn't he tell you?"

"Oh, yesterday," I said. "That explains it. Thank you, Nancy." I hung up.

Gone—without even phoning to say: "Well, I didn't see too much point in sticking around so...." To which I could have said: "Perhaps you're right, then. And hopefully I'll be in better shape by the time you come down again." Something like that. Something to indicate that...it wasn't over? Or was it?

It was about then that the bad time began to get worse.

CHAPTER NINE

By THE end of the fourth week I was certain that something had gone wrong. Salal had lost her nerve, changed her
mind. Maybe somebody had changed it for her. She'd told me
it might take a while to accumulate the evidence, but I'd
never anticipated this long a wait. I had no resources against
it.

I was still broke. And I now owed Tom $1,575, a debt
that, in the circumstances, I was in no hurry to re-pay. Since it
was all I had left of him, I intended to hang onto it. But I was
hardly going to ask him to lend me more. So I phoned my second least I-told-you-so sister (I've got four of them), who lent
me five hundred dollars. Then, fortunately, Joau phoned me
from Prince Rupert, so I asked him if he'd send me an interim
payment. He said he would. He also told me that he was getting warmer, was now meeting people who said he reminded
them of someone else. But everyone he'd talked to agreed that
Victor Goncalves had left town a year or more ago—to con-
sult a specialist, one source said. Another said: Vernon. So
Joau was going to Vernon and wanted me, in the meantime,
to hunt down specialists.

"What kind of specialists?"

"You know—doctors," he said. "Maybe for the nerves.
This man tell me—you listen to this—he say my brother get
very bad headaches! Like me, hah? You see—I told you!"

"You told me," I agreed. Wrote down "headaches."
Then I phoned my own G.P. and asked her where she'd send

a man that suffered from chronic headaches.

"Where—what part of the head? Migraines? Has he had his eyes checked?"

As I'd suspected, headaches could mean almost anything. But I put in a lot of time, calling up specialists—for the eyes, brain, nerves—and anything else I could think of. Their receptionists didn't appreciate me, and were cagey with their information.

For all of a day I thought I might have a new job—until I met the client. She was an elderly widow who was planning to leave her money to her sole remaining relative, a nephew—but first wanted to inform herself of a few pertinent facts concerning him. She wanted to know if he was attending church regularly and if so, what denomination; if he had a girlfriend and if so, what race, religion and socio-economic background; she wanted to know who his friends were. "You can judge a man by his company," she admonished me, severely. Her nephew was twenty-eight years old and refused, apparently, to answer any of these questions himself.

"Do you like him?" I asked her.

"That has nothing to do with it."

"You want to know if he deserves your money. Is that it?"

She frowned, considered this way of putting it. "Yes...I suppose."

"Hasn't it ever struck you that most people in this world who have a lot of money, don't deserve it? I'm speaking ethically, of course.

"That may be true," she said, "but it doesn't make it right."

"Then I guess I can't help you. You see, I think you should leave your money to whomever you please, regardless of their religion or economic circumstances. On the other hand, if you want your money to do 'good,' give it to an organization: OXFAM, UNICEF, something like that."

"I see," she said. "I never thought of it that way."

Thus I did myself out of a job—and a nephew out of an inheritance?

Katie returned from the Okanagan and invited me over to dinner. Apropos of news of sailing trips and white-water rides and evenings around the campfire, she happened to mention that she and Rick had been talking about getting married. I managed, I think, to receive this news calmly.

"Why the rush?" I asked, finally. "Or why not live together first, see how you get along?"

"I suggested that," said Katie, "but Rick didn't like the idea."

"Why not? Would his family object?"

"I'm not sure." Katie looked puzzled. "I think it's him, really. You know how he likes to do everything properly." She made a woeful face.

I certainly do, I thought, but I never expected to hear *you* say so. "Is he still living at home?"

"Yup." She looked rueful. "I think that's part of the reason that he wants to get married. So that he can move out of home."

"How romantic," I commented. Katie gave me an evil look, but I decided to persist. "Does he pay room and board at home? How is he planning to support himself if he moves out?"

"Well, he'd continue to work at the supermarket in the summertime, just like he does now, and maybe his parents would give him an allowance...." She looked doubtful. "Or something. Or maybe he could work weekends? Though I know he doesn't like to do that because he needs the study time...." She frowned.

"You mean he hasn't figured it out yet."

She gave me a swift, suspicious glance. "I don't know what his plans are. We haven't discussed it." She assembled her cutlery on her plate, screwed the cap onto the bottle of sauce.

"He wasn't thinking that you would support him, was he?" This was sticking my neck out—but in my opinion that boy was straight off the rack and capable of more cliches than a soap opera.

Katie's hands paused on the sauce bottle. Her lips

tightened; she stood up. "And how would I do that?" she inquired haughtily, stacking our supper dishes.

"You couldn't." I handed her my plate. "Not unless you
quit school." I watched her face.

Her eyes narrowed. "Don't worry, Mother." She gave
me a pitying smile. "I won't quit school. I'm not *that* old-
fashioned."

"Good," I murmured as she turned her back on me and
stalked to the sink.

The city sweated under an August heat wave. Lying, sleepless, with a token sheet over my hips, I listened to the sound
of traffic outside and thought of Salal, making furtive visits to
the editing room, digging swiftly through wastebaskets,
hiding crumpled photographs beneath the inventory sheets
on her clipboard. Or sometimes I'd think of Johanna instead;
I'd picture her striding down Hastings Street on Caesar's
arm—and I'd feel sick all over again. I couldn't believe that
Johanna would actually have sex with him; my imagination
balked. It occurred to me that I'd never really faced the fact
that Johanna was a prostitute—never made myself understand exactly what that meant. I had never had sex with a
man I disliked (except the time that I was raped); I avoided
shaking *hands* with a man I disliked. But Johanna did it all
the time. How? And knowing that she not only could, but
did—how did I feel about her? I wasn't sure. Yet nothing had
changed. With me, she was still the same person she'd always
been. But who did she become with other people—with
them?

And sometimes, unsticking one limb from another, I
imagined myself in the tundra with Tom, the sky still blue at
two in the morning, the sound of mosquitoes on the other
side of the tent flap. I wondered if I'd like it. Perhaps, I
thought, if one of my clients ever pays me, I could fly up there
for a week and just hang out for a while, go for walks, get
away from people. Or maybe he could train me as a field as-
sistant; we could become one of those man-and-wife teams.

Man and wife? Now that he was gone, it sounded downright desirable. What, after all, was so wonderful about being an unsuccessful private detective? The independence, I reminded myself; that sense of getting out there, going after it. But...going after what?

The next week at the office Joau phoned again, this time from Vernon.

"Margaret? Big trouble. Very big trouble. Right away you must help."

I got my feet off my desk, searched frantically for my pen beneath the mess of newspaper.

"What is it? What's happened?"

"I don' know. Something terrible. You must phone the hospitals at once."

"Why?" I was now searching through my desk drawers. "What have you found out?"

"Is nothing I find—is the feeling!"

I stopped searching, tipped back in my chair. "What do you mean? What feeling?"

"I have ver' bad pain. Like a knife, Margaret. Is terrible!"

"Joau—for Christ's sake—would you go to a doctor!"

He got mad. "No!" he shouted. "Is no time to be so stupid! You do what I say! You phone the hospitals. Every one!"

"I've phoned the hospitals!"

"Today? Today you phoned?"

"No, of course not today. I phoned them weeks ago!"

"And now you phone them again. Right away. Every hospital in the province!" He was shouting; he meant it.

"Long distance too? You're going to pay for it?"

"Of course I pay! I pay you every penny!"

"All right," I said. "You're the boss."

"And you phone me back right away."

"Even if no one's ever heard of him?"

"Don' matter. You phone." And he gave me his phone number.

Victor Goncalves was in the Vancouver General. He'd

checked in two days ago and was now in the operating room, undergoing surgery.

"What's wrong with him?" I asked, cursing twins and all others of intuitive ilk. "I'm calling for his brother, who's been trying to get in touch with him."

"You're calling for the family?"

There was a knock on my office door.

"Yes—for his brother. Joau Goncalves." I spelled it, began disentangling the telephone cord from the legs of my desk, edging toward my door.

"One moment please," said the nurse. "I'll have to check the records."

But before I got to the door, it opened; a face appeared in the crack. The eyes met mine—adrenalin slivered through my veins like volts of electricity.

I put my hand over the mouthpiece. "No one's here. Come in."

Immediately she slipped in, closed the door behind her. She glanced at me, at the telephone, scanned my office as if casing it for a theft. Then she turned back to the door, inspected the latch, flicked the lock.

I returned to my desk, rewinding the telephone cord before me. I indicated the sofa. "Sorry, it's an important call. Can you wait a minute?"

Again she assessed me, gave the briefest of nods. But she didn't sit down. She began walking around my office, fingering things. Then she noticed the Aikido photographs on the walls and moved closer to inspect them, giving each one its due, as if she were in an art gallery.

The nurse returned to the telephone. "Mr. Goncalves is undergoing surgery."

"Yes—but for what?"

"For a..." The rest was in Latin.

"And what does that mean?"

"He is undergoing surgery for the removal of a brain tumor," she said, as if such plain speaking offended her.

"A brain tumor!" Headaches, I thought. Goddamn him—headaches! I glanced up and found Salal watching me—with a flat, uncurious gaze—and like a young child she continued staring until she lost interest in me, turned back to the photographs. "And what's the prognosis?"

"Pardon?"

"Is he expected to live?"

"It's exploratory surgery," the nurse said stiffly.

"Meaning they won't know until they open him up?"

"In cases of this nature, it varies greatly from person to person."

"I see. Well, if he ever regains consciousness again, would you tell him that his brother Joau will be coming to see him?"

"I'll transfer you to Intensive Care," said the nurse. "That's where he'll be going after the operation. You can give your message to the ward sister there."

"No, just give me the number— " I objected, but the phone was already ringing. Again Salal was staring at me. "Only another second," I apologized to her, but for all the reaction I got, I could have been speaking gibberish. That girl, I thought, is singularly devoid of social graces. Then I got through to Intensive Care.

I explained who I was and why I was calling, finally got off the phone. Salal was still studying the Aikido photographs.

"Hi," I said.

She gave me a glance. "Are these faked or something?"

"No."

She studied me, then one of the photographs, comparing them. "You can really do this stuff? Like in those Chinese kung-fu movies?"

"Sort of like that."

"That right, eh?" She moved on to the next one. "Could you kill someone?"

"It's more a form of self-defense—teaches you how to get away without getting hurt. And, if necessary, how to put your opponent out of commission."

"Whatever that means." She was examining a time-lapse photo of a break-fall.

116

"How to hurt them—badly enough so they won't come after you again."

Again she inspected me, from head to toe. "Doesn't take much strength, eh?"

"Strength helps. But if you know what you're doing you can get by without it."

She moved on to the next set of photos; I felt that she was seeing me for the first time as a person in my own right, as something more than a tool that she'd decided to make use of. "Wasn't it a bit risky," I asked, "to come here?"

She was studying a photograph of my teacher, variously defending herself against three black belts. She ignored my question, pointed at the photograph. "That's a woman, right?"

"Yes, that's my teacher."

"She's better than you?"

"Yes."

"How long would it take—to get really good?"

"Well, you can always get better. But it would take at least five years before your training was of any practical value in a real-life fighting situation. And even then, of course, it depends who you're up against."

She was examining another photograph of my teacher, this time in flight. "But you've never killed anyone."

"I've never been that desperate."

Slowly she turned, gave me a long, intense look—then nodded her head as if I'd just said something profound. Today, it seemed to me, she was behaving more oddly than ever. She rounded the corner, started down the side wall.

"I've killed animals," she said, like a child exchanging boasts, elaborately nonchalant. She began trailing her fingertips over the surface of everything she passed: the radiators, the windowsills, the strip of supposedly decorative molding that ornamented my office walls—again like a child, as if needing to accumulate as much tactile information as possible.

"What kind of animals?"

"Deer, moose, bear, rabbit—anything we could find. My

grandad used to take us hunting—me and my brother. We lived off it."

"Really?" I was impressed. "What did you hunt with?"

She shrugged. "Rifles. We also trapped. And fished, of course. You put me out in the bush with a knife, I'd be able to survive."

"With nothing but a knife?"

Her chin lifted. "He taught us. The old ways and the new ways. Even with arrows and spears. He taught both of us. Usually my people don't teach the girls to hunt—just skinning and cooking and stuff. But my grandad was an oddball. He had his own ideas. He said that nowadays the girls needed to know how to hunt too. I got pretty good. I was better than my brother was."

"Did you live on a reservation?"

"No. We don't have status. Some great-grandmother of mine married a white man. We lived way out in the bush; nearest school was a hundred miles away; no neighbors—nothing."

"So how did you end up here?"

She had now arrived at the opposite side of my desk, and when she raised her eyes I noticed that her pupils were pinpricks, in spite of the fact that I'd drawn my blinds against the sunlight. So that's it, I thought; she's just had an injection. No wonder she's behaving strangely. I kept forgetting that I was dealing with a junkie.

"One winter my grandad was away trapping and my granny fell and broke her hip. They didn't know what to do with us. Then someone remembered we had an uncle in Vancouver, though no one had heard from him in years. Finally a social worker found him and we got shipped down to him. We tried to run away, but the cops kept bringing us back. In the end, we just got used to it."

Used to what? I wondered, but as if seeing the question coming, she dropped her eyes, turned away. She went back to the sofa where she'd deposited her bag, sat down beside it.

She reached into her bag, pulled out a pair of gloves, started putting them on, carefully, finger by finger. She then unzippered a different compartment, extracted a brown, manila envelope. She held it out to me.

"You got it!" I moved round from my desk, stepped forward to take the envelope—but before I could do so she'd withdrawn it again, now held it on the opposite side of her body, as if to prevent me from snatching it.

"Go get another envelope," she ordered. "I'm not giving them this one."

"Why?" I asked, but obligingly returned to my desk and opened the bottom drawer.

"Because this one's from my office."

I selected an envelope that looked about the same size, walked over and handed it to her, watched as she dumped the contents of her own envelope onto the sofa cushion. A pile of crumpled photos, intermixed with curls of filmstrip, slid out into an untidy heap; I bent over them curiously. I put a hand out to straighten one, but Salal's gloved finger intercepted me. She pulled the photo I'd been looking at to the top of the pile, then selected a couple of others, lined them up for my inspection.

"These are recent?" I asked. I thought I recognized some of the girls.

"Yep," she answered. "From the last movie they did. They finished it last week and now Haswell's taking time out to play with his new video equipment." She pointed a finger at the photograph on the end, in which a girl's body was arched over the armrest of a couch, hairless pubes exposed, the ribs clearly visible beneath her pale chest. "That's Laurie," Salal explained. "She's the current star. She's twelve—but she doesn't look it, does she?"

I lifted my eyes. "She's a junkie too?"

"She wouldn't be there if she wasn't. Not that she's got anywhere better to go. She says her home life was no improvement—same story, but no junk."

"Haven't any of you kids ever heard of Children's Aid?"

"Sure. Get shunted from one foster home to another where nobody wants you, only the money you bring in. My cousin went that route. If there was anything left on their plates, they told her she could eat it before she washed the dishes."

"But it's not always like that!" I protested. "One of my friends is a foster parent—and she's crazy about her kids. She never shuts up about them."

"But you don't know who you'll end up with until it's too late. It's not worth the risk."

"It can't be worse than that!" I indicated the photographs.

Salal glanced at them, shrugged. "At least you get paid. And you can do pretty much what you want when you're not working. As for the porno—you just ignore it. You make your mind go somewhere else. I think my cousin had it worse, if you want the truth. Because she was all by herself, and no-body else in her shoes; just a world of strangers all thinking themselves better than her. By the end, she was a real mess."

"Did she complain? Did she tell someone what was hap-pening?"

Salal didn't answer. She continued poking among the photographs, selected one, peered at it, let it fall back into the pile. "Would you complain to a social worker who told you to smarten up or you'd end up like your mother, selling tricks for a bottle of beer?" She looked up, read incredulity in my eyes. "The people she lived with were big shots. They were in with the mayor and people like that. They went to church every Sunday. And out of the good of their hearts they took in a dirty little half-breed." She watched me. "See?"

I saw. Abruptly she dropped her eyes, picked up the en-velope I'd given her, began re-packing the crumpled stills and scraps of film inside it. She handed it back to me. "Put all the fingerprints on it you like," she invited, magnanimously.

"Thank you." I carried it back to my desk, inserted it in the top drawer. I closed the drawer, locked it, pocketed the key. "Now what?" I asked.

She didn't seem to have heard me. She was half-slumped upon the sofa, staring at her feet, which were stuck straight out in front of her. Junk, I thought again. Some accomplice she would turn out to be if she glazed out on smack at the critical moment. Dare I remind her of the danger?

Finally, she looked at me, seemingly unaware that she'd kept me waiting. "So now you go down to the police station, show them what you've got and get yourself a warrant." She inhaled, sat up straighter. "Tell them to raid the downstairs too while they're at it."

"Why?"

"I'm choosing a Tuesday."

"Ladies' Night?" I stared at her. "You want the raid to happen on Ladies' Night?"

"Why not? They don't stop making movies just because it's Tuesday. And that way the cops will get more for their money. Gives us a better bargaining position."

I considered, agreed with her. Our eyes met; for one brief moment we seemed to be on the same wavelength, mutually satisfied at the thought of bringing Ladies' Night to an end. Then she hauled her bag onto her lap, started searching for something else.

"Next Tuesday?" I asked. "That doesn't give us much time."

She pulled out a piece of paper, handed it to me. "No, not next Tuesday. The one after. They've scheduled some big scenes that night; everyone who's anyone is going to be there. It's perfect."

I glanced down at the piece of paper she'd given me, finally realized that it was a map. It looked pretty thorough—with street names and compass points and arrows and Xs—but I couldn't make head nor tail of it. I finally sat down beside her, held it between us.

Her finger traced the lines. "See—two doors—not counting the loading door which we won't bother with. They open onto the alley—and a few minutes before eleven o'clock I'm going to unlock them. Each of the alley doors opens onto a staircase and off the stairways are doors that lead to the first, second and third floors. Only the left-hand stairway, as you found out for yourself, goes all the way up to the fourth floor. When I unlock the alley doors I'll make sure that all those other doors are unlocked as well."

"But you can also get to the fourth floor from the right-hand alley door by cutting through the second and third floors, right?"

"Yes—which is why they have to put guards on both alley doors—because people can get out either way. Same goes for the loading door. I'm not going to unlock it because you can't open it without making a lot of noise, but they should station some cops outside it. Same goes for the staff doors into the pub. Maybe I should mark them all."

She reached behind me for her bag, found a pencil inside it. I passed her a magazine from the coffee table. She placed the magazine on her knees, started drawing in small stick figures in front of the doors.

I tried, mentally, to visualize the raid. One team coming in the front pub doors, another squad entering simultaneously from the alley. But it would take them at least a minute to get up all those stairs. "Is there an intercom?" I asked.

"An intercom?" She stopped drawing, looked at me.

"From the pub to the fourth floor. Or vice versa. Can't you phone Haswell from the pub?"

She watched me, thoughtfully. "I know. I'll take the phone off the hook upstairs on the second floor. The phone on the fourth floor is just an extension of Haswell's office line; if I put the office phone on hold, they won't be able to get through to him. Simple."

"All right. Now what about fire escapes?"

"Fire escapes? Outside, you mean?"

I nodded, trying to remember. After all, I'd checked out the building pretty thoroughly myself.

"I've never seen one. He's got two inside stairways. Maybe he doesn't need an outside fire escape."

"But according to this— " I pointed an accusing finger at the map, "that fourth floor has only one exit. No fire marshal would have passed that."

"I'm sure no fire marshal has ever seen it."

"But they inspect all the buildings—especially the ones that contain a public facility, like a restaurant or a club."

She watched me, her face expressionless. Then she returned to her map, began drawing in stick figures with renewed concentration.

I knew what she was saying—or rather, not saying—but I had a certain amount of faith, unfounded perhaps, in the integrity of fire marshals, and I didn't want to give it up. "Nothing on the outside? No way out through one of the windows?"

"The windows are cemented in."

"So they are." I leaned back against the sofa cushion, envisaged the back of Haswell's building, the hotel on one side of it, a warehouse on the other, the third and fourth floors with their rows of blank, cemented-in windows—and no fire escapes anywhere.

"There's a fire exit down in the pub, opens out onto Hastings Street."

I looked at her. "Yes, I remember that one. Did you put a guard on it?" I followed the point of her pencil to the door in question, noted the stick figure in front of it. "Well then," I suggested, temporarily abandoning the problem of the fire escapes, "what about the roof?"

"The roof?" She met my gaze head-on; again I noticed the size of her pupils. How could she see if her pupils didn't dilate?

"Trap doors," I suggested. "Isn't there a trap door to the roof?"

She shook her head. "Not that I've ever seen." Her eyes lowered to her map; she started drawing hats on the stick figures.

Again my eyes followed her pencil. "That's odd. Most of those old buildings have got some way out onto the roof—especially if the roof is flat. Take another look around; you can walk under a trap door for twenty years and never notice it."

She sat back, regarded her handiwork, saw a figure she'd missed and started drawing again. "He's done some renovating. Maybe he boarded it up." Her hair draped forward concealing her face; a thick black lock spilled over her forearm. "But I'll look."

123

"And check out the fire escapes again because, frankly, I just don't see how he could have got away without one. I'd come down and look myself, but I think I should probably steer clear of the place once I've been to see the cops."

Salal's pencil stopped. She turned her head so that the curtains of hair parted from her face—and it was as if I'd switched television channels—was now confronted by an entirely different character. "Don't you come *near* me!" she hissed. "Once you've gone to the cops your phones will be tapped and you'll be followed—*everywhere*." She spoke as if she, personally, planned to implement these measures against me. "You don't get in touch with me no matter what!"

I watched her, unmoved. I didn't see why the police would go to such lengths against someone working on their own side. "And if it doesn't come off?" I inquired.

"If what doesn't come off?"

"If the cops don't buy it. If they tell me to go to hell. Or if they decide they'll stage their own raid, in their own sweet time, unaided by us. Then wouldn't you like me to get a message to you?"

Chameleon-like, she changed again, now eyeing me like a suspicious old woman, lips puckered over something she didn't much like the taste of. "In that case, you'll get to a phone. Not a pay phone—a phone in a friend's house or in a corner store—somewhere they can't see you and figure out what you're doing. You'll phone this number. Give me a piece of paper and I'll write it down." Again I got up, fetched my memo pad from my desk and handed it to her. She wrote down a telephone number, a 67 exchange: probably downtown. "Memorize it," she instructed me, "and then get rid of it. For sure, they'll search this place." Her eyes scanned my office walls.

I took the number she'd given me. "So I phone this number—and who will I find on the other end?"

"You'll either get a receptionist, or an answering machine. In either case, the message is the same. If the raid isn't going to happen, tell the receptionist that Mrs. Connor won't be able to make it to her Tuesday appointment."

"Mrs. Connor?"

"Yes, Connor." She spelt it. "If the cops can't make it that Tuesday, but want me to find another time, then say that Mrs. Connor can't make it for Tuesday, but she wants to schedule an appointment for a different day."

"What day? How would I arrange that?"

"Don't worry, you won't have to. If you leave that message, then the receptionist will tell you that Mr. Healey will get back to you. He won't—but I will."

"Mr. Healey?"

For a split second she looked uneasy—but recovered immediately. "It's just a name; it doesn't mean anything."

"But whose phone number is this?" I glanced again at my memo pad.

"You don't need to know. But there's another message," she continued hastily, seeing that I was about to argue. "If you've blown my cover; if you've let the cops know who I am— "

"Of if they figure it out for themselves," I interjected.

"Then leave a message saying that Mrs. Connor is *out of town* and won't be able to make it to her Tuesday appointment."

"In which case you'll split?"

She nodded.

I thought for a moment. "And this receptionist—if I get a receptionist—isn't going to ask me any awkward questions? She's been briefed?"

"She'll just take your message."

"And get it to you."

She lowered her chin in agreement.

"But what if a problem comes up? What if I need more information? What if they ask me to get in touch with you?"

"Who? The cops?"

"Yes."

For a moment she just looked at me. Then she tilted her head to one side, surveyed me through her eyelashes. "How are you going to get in touch with me? You don't even know who I am."

I got up from the sofa. I walked over to the window, lifted a corner of the venetian blind, peered out into the street. I don't even like her, I thought. She's a supercilious brat. "Who is it that you don't trust?" I asked her, aloud. "The cops? Haswell?"

"I don't trust either of them."

"You figure the cops will squeal on you. They'll tell Haswell what you're up to. But if they're so chummy with Haswell, why would they agree to raid him at all?"

"No."

I let the corner of the blind drop, turned around to look at her. Again she was shaking her head. "It doesn't work like that. Word just gets around. One cop starts talking to another cop, and my name keeps coming up, and then an informer gets hold of it, and even after the raid has been and gone, the story's still circulating. Everybody talks. And Haswell does have friends."

"Like Caesar?"

Suddenly she looked amused. "No, not him. Not anymore. They had a big fight—did I tell you?"

"A fight?"

"Yeah—because a couple of weeks ago Caesar didn't show—not for *days*. He's been late before, but not that late. So Danny got mad and bought off someone else." Her eyes held mine, as if anticipating a specific response.

"And?" I prompted.

She sniffed, made a face. "Well—*two* days later Caesar shows up and the shit hits the fan. I was right outside the door—heard it all. They yelled at each other for about half an hour, then Caesar stomps out—and ooh, he was mad. When he gets mad he smiles—he smiles and he smiles— " She shivered, involuntarily. "And then Danny comes out all red in the face—but blustering, you know? I could tell he was scared. 'I'm tired of his power-trips,' that's what he said to me. And he's right; Caesar makes us wait on purpose. It's no accident. But what can you do about it?"

"Buy from someone else. Exactly what he did do."

She gave me a patronizing smile. "Sure."

"So who's the dealer now?"

She gave me a puzzled look. "Caesar is."

126

"But I thought you said that—You mean they made it up? Haswell's buying from him again?"

"Of course! He has to! Caesar owns this town. You can't just walk out on him like he was a drugstore or something."

I still didn't get it. "But then why are you saying that Haswell won't get away with it?"

"Because Caesar's going to pay him back." The prospect obviously pleased her. "Right now Caesar's playing it cool, delivering our benefits right on time, being sweet as pie. But when Caesar's being nice, that's a dangerous sign. Danny's days are numbered." She nodded, sagely.

Then why are we doing this? I wondered, irritably.

"All right," I said. "So I don't know who you are, and I can't get in touch with you. Yet I've got these photographs, and I've got a map. Now how did I manage that?"

She held up the map. "You're going to burn this. You're going to copy it into your own hand—make it your map, your way. Then you burn this one." She placed her own map back on her knees. "There's prints on the photos, but none of them are mine. At least a few of them should be Haswell's."

"And these photos came from—?"

She ignored the skepticism in my voice, was now, clearly, at the crux of her plan, and anxious that I should understand it. "After you visited Kinky's asking questions about Danny's fiance, you received an anonymous phone call from someone who seemed to know the inside set-up. Maybe an employee, he wouldn't say. A man, of course. And he offered to blow the joint open for you, mail you the evidence, tell you everything you needed to know. Even about Lily Kubicek, he'll say. Weren't you the lady was interested in Lily?"

"How will he know that?"

Salal's hands lifted expressively. "Beats me. It's a small world, isn't it?"

"And he sends me a map?"

"No. He describes the place—in detail. And then you draw a map from his description." She picked up her map again, held it at arm's length, surveyed it. "You spent a lot of time on the phone with him; you must have. But you also cased the joint yourself—so you had something to go on."

"He's going to mail me the stills and filmstrips?"

"You got a mail slot?" She twisted around in the sofa, peered over the back of it, saw that there was indeed a mail slot in my office door. "There—right there." She pointed at my door mat. "You walked in one morning and there it was—no stamp, no postmark. It got crumpled up a bit coming through." She turned back to me. "Pass the envelope through that slot before you take it to the station."

"Then why are the photos in *my* envelope?"

She cocked her head. "You're right—they shouldn't be. Buy another one somewhere and push the new one through the mail slot."

I looked at my office door, the door mat in front of it, drummed my fingernails on the windowsill. Would it work? "And why is he doing this? Who is this informant? What's he got against Haswell?"

Salal considered. She gave me a sideways glance. "He wouldn't tell you, would he?"

I stared at her—and remembered that I'd asked her that question myself—and been rebuked for it. Again I was getting irritated. Come on, Meg, I chided myself. She's younger than your daughter and she's been living on the streets since she was thirteen years old. Don't expect miracles.

I walked back to the sofa, sat down beside her. Automatically my eyes moved back to the map. If I wasn't going to be able to get in touch with her again, this was our last chance; if there were questions that needed answering, they had to be answered now. What had I missed? Again I envisioned the raid, the squads at front and back, Salal working her way up or down, unlocking the doors as she went. "Sounds almost too easy," I said.

Salal was also contemplating the map. "Well, they'll have to coordinate the two raids. Otherwise someone from downstairs could get a warning up to the top floor before the cops get up there." She thought for a moment, sucking the inside of her cheek. "The cops should be able to take them by surprise. Get everyone covered before they can move.

128

Remind them that some of these people aren't amateurs."

"And some are?"

"And some are," she agreed. "*Real* amateurs. Some of the girls will start bawling for sure."

I gave her a look. "You don't waste much sympathy on them."

"On them?" She seemed surprised. "What good would that do?" Then, seeing my expression, she explained: "I'm not saying anything against them, but they're not my friends or anything."

"So what will you do? Afterwards."

She stared at me, appeared not to understand.

"After the raid. Where will you go?"

She lowered her eyelids and smiled—a genuine, but secretive smile. "Home," she answered.

"Back to the bush?"

She nodded. "Time to go visit my granny again. She needs me. She's getting old."

"What about your grandfather?"

The smile vanished. "He died. Right after my brother did."

"Salal," I asked, with considerable temerity, knowing I was on thin ice, "what are you going to do about the junk?"

She ran the tip of her tongue along her upper teeth. "My granny will help me. She got me through it the last time."

"The last time?"

"I quit once before. After my brother died."

I knew better than to inquire further. I re-folded the map, walked over to my desk, unlocked my drawer again, deposited the map inside it. I re-locked it, slowly, reluctant to say what was on my mind. "Cops don't like anonymous informants."

She didn't look at me, was gazing at her feet again, flexing her toes against the plastic lattice-work of her sandals. "Sometimes that's all they get."

"They're not going to like it."

"They'll grill you, that's for sure." She eyed me, obviously wondering how I was going to stand up to it. "And tell them they take it or leave it—no snooping around on their own. If I catch their detectives on the premises the whole thing's cancelled—I'm not playing."

"Sure," I said. "We can make all the conditions we like. That doesn't mean they'll accept them."

"They've been looking for Danny for a long time now. Even if they don't like your story, they won't be able to pass it up."

She reached across the sofa, pulled her bag towards her, tucked her gloves back inside it. "You've got one thing going for you."

"What's that?"

She hitched the strap of the bag over her shoulder, stood up. "You look so respectable. Like somebody's mother."

"I *am* somebody's mother."

She looked surprised. "You've got kids?"

"Two of them. About your age, as a matter of fact."

She stared at me for a long time; I couldn't tell what she was thinking. Finally she turned away, looked around to make sure that she was leaving nothing behind. "I'm just saying that it's an advantage," she said, off-hand. Then she gave me a sharp glance. "Someone like you could get away with anything!"

"You forget," I said, "that cops have considerable experience of human nature. They've seen a lot of ladies like me; they know what we're capable of."

She made a face—impossible to interpret—started moving towards the door. I suddenly realized that I might never see her again. I'd been thinking about her for so long now that she seemed like a member of my family. I walked over to her and, not knowing how else to express myself, held out my hand. She seemed taken aback.

"Good luck," I said to her. "And do be careful. Send me a postcard if you ever make it to your grandmother's."

"No postcards," she said, but now let go of the doorknob and took my hand. She shook it, with solemnity. Her fingers felt thin and cold. "I'll be counting on you," she said. It came out like a plea. Abruptly she dropped my hand, turned to the door.

130

I edged her out of the doorway and opened the door myself, peered up and down the street. I stepped aside to let her past. Without looking at me again she left, strode purposefully away down the sidewalk. I waited to see that nobody followed her.

Then, when she'd disappeared around the corner, I went back into my office and phoned Joau.

CHAPTER TEN

WHAT one forgets—what I forget—when dealing with police officers, is that they are members of a bureaucracy—and bureaucracies are the same the world over. Bureaucracies don't like dealing with people they've never dealt with before (because they necessitate a new file, and file label, and in extreme cases, even a new filing cabinet); they particularly don't like people that don't have appointments (because they necessitate erasures and ugly scribbles in desk calendars); and more than anything—they hate surprises. Thus, when I arrived at the downtown police station one warm, smoggy August morning, there was a dearth of open arms.

In short, they made me wait. Then they tried to take my envelope away from me (they'll take objects over people if you give them any choice), but I refused to relinquish it to anyone other than a senior officer of the Vice Squad and told them so, firmly. They tried to fob me off with lesser mortals, but fortunately, I knew the difference. Finally, after three hours of waiting, I was escorted into the office of Detective Sergeant Robert Menzies, Vice Squad Division.

He was a pasty-faced man, with a stiff, mouse-coloured brush cut, heavy jowls and watery blue eyes. Right away I decided to mention my good pal, Harry, and credited him with putting me onto the blue movie angle in the first place. (It's my experience that police officers become more cooperative if you can convince them that the information you're giving them is already in their possession.) About halfway through my story, he pushed some buttons on his phone, asked someone on the other end if she could get hold of Harry. Then he told me to continue. Harry arrived just as I was finishing. Menzies asked me to tell my story again. This time he asked questions. At one point Harry turned to him and said: "I think this is it, Bob. You know we've been wondering where those damn things keep coming from." But Menzies only grunted, and asked another question.

Predictably, they weren't happy about the anonymous informant and Menzies tried, several times, to trick me into giving away more information about "him." The first time he nearly succeeded; but after that, I was prepared—and didn't open my mouth until I'd given my answer careful thought. Thus my interview quickly assumed the character of an interrogation, a format with which Detective Sergeant Menzies was obviously more comfortable.

"How can we know this information is reliable if we don't know where it's coming from?"

"Look," I pointed out. "He's already taking a big risk. We can't expect more. And you've got all the proof you need—right here in this envelope." The envelope was still on his desk, unopened, untouched. I gave it a pat. "You yourselves have had your suspicions about Haswell. All I'm doing is giving you the evidence you need to investigate those suspicions."

"How the hell do I know where you got that stuff from?" He gave the envelope a contemptuous glance (but I noticed that he'd been careful not to touch it). "Even if you do have porno stills in there—for all I know you went out and bought them on Davie Street."

"All right," I said amicably. "Forget about the porno for a minute. But I, personally, am willing to promise you that if you raid Kinky's that night, you're going to find enough inebriated minors to fill your cells for weeks. And while you're doing that, no harm in checking out the rest of the building, is there?"

He watched me, jaws working—like a cow chewing a cud.

Harry, still standing behind me, cleared his throat. "I've

known Mrs.—ah— " But he couldn't remember my last name. "Meg here for some time, Bob. And I don't know anything about her informant, but Meg here has given me some good tips in the past."

Only one that I could think of; I gave him a grateful smile. But he didn't so much as look at me, kept his eyes on his superior, and I wondered if I was putting him in a difficult position.

"You say this informant's an employee?" Menzies asked suddenly.

I gave him a dirty look. "I told you I don't know. I'd say he's paying off a grudge—but that's only intuition."

"Fallen out with Haswell, has he?"

"That's what I think—yes—but he's never said so. But he promises me that a week from next Tuesday you'll find them all in the act—and he, personally, is going to be unlocking the doors so that you can get up there."

Again Menzies reached for the map—which I'd reorganized somewhat and copied into my own hand. He studied it, lips pursed. Then he studied me—with exactly the same expression. "This is your work, huh?"

"Like I say, I was in there on a couple of occasions—and I asked the informant every question I could think of. I think we've thought of everything; I went over it with him pretty carefully."

"But you say he's never seen this map?"

With an effort, I kept my temper. "Since I've never seen him, that's the logical conclusion."

Menzies tipped back in his chair, finally looked over at Harry. "Well, I guess the first thing we'd better do is take a look at this here evidence." He reached into the top drawer of his desk, pulled out two pairs of tweezers and a magnifying glass, handed one pair of tweezers to Harry.

"On your mark," Harry said jovially, flourishing his pair of tweezers.

Menzies ignored him. "You open it," he said to me. I obliged. The stills and scraps of filmstrip spilled from the envelope into a heap on Menzies' desk.

They worked in silence, their faces unreadable. At first

they concentrated upon the photographs, then moved on to the filmstrips, holding them up against the light. At the second one, Harry stopped. He whistled.

Menzies glanced up at him. "You got something?"

Harry proffered him the curl of filmstrip. "It's that same girl. She was in that movie—what was it called? *Baby Dolls.* They caught a whole case of them at the border. Remember?"

Menzies took the piece of film, peered at it. His fist slammed the desk; I started, violently. "Where'd you get these things?"

I gazed at him steadily, counting off the seconds. When I could trust myself to speak, I said: "I just finished telling you all about it."

Again he grunted; my answer did not surprise him. He returned his gaze to the piece of filmstrip. "Kids," he snarled.

"Kids," Harry confirmed.

Menzies stood up. "I want you to make a statement."

"My pleasure."

"We'll look into it," he said. He gave Harry a sidelong glance. "If we think it's worth investigating, we'll get in touch with you."

"Fine." I reached for the map.

"We'll keep that," he said and tried, too late, to intercept me—but the map was already in my hand.

"It'll be yours when I see that you intend to use it." For a moment I thought he was going to try and take it away from me—by force, if necessary—but then I watched him, consciously, decide to let me keep it. Even in the police force, senior officers learn diplomacy. I shoved the map back into my purse. "And my informant would really appreciate it if you kept your officers off the premises," I added, getting to my feet. "It's important to his health that no one gets suspicious." I latched my purse, buttoned my sweater.

"One other thing, Meg," Harry said suddenly. I looked at him. "Did you ever find out anything more about Caesar? I remember that you told me you'd seen him with Haswell."

"According to my informant, Haswell's employees are junkies. So's Haswell, himself. Caesar supplies."

Harry swore softly. "No chance he'd be in on this movie business?"

"Not as far as I know—but my knowledge is limited. My understanding is that he's just the dealer—and sometimes gets the kids when Haswell's finished with them."

"Remember what I was telling you about finding witnesses to testify against him?"

I shook my head. "Sorry, Harry. No go."

"You asked, did you?"

I just kept shaking my head.

They took me to another room, where I made my formal statement, signed it. Menzies then disappeared. "There's less than two weeks," I reminded Harry as I was leaving. "If this raid's going to happen, we'll have to move fast."

"You'll be in touch with him? Your informant?"

I gave him a suspicious glance—but his eyes were innocently inquiring. You too? I wondered. "No," I said, "but he might get in touch with me to find out what's going on."

He put a hand on my shoulder. "Don't do anything without our say-so. Bob Menzies doesn't give much away, but I could tell he was interested. And those blue movies have been a thorn in our ass for a long time now. I don't think we can afford to pass up this chance."

"Good," I said, hoping he was right. I hadn't taken to Menzies—and seeing Harry on the job, in uniform, in the presence of his superiors, I wasn't too sure that I trusted him either.

By the time I pushed through the plate-glass doors of the police station, the downtown office workers were pouring out of the buildings, cramming the buses for home. For one sentimental moment I wished I were one of them, with nothing more to worry about than beating the bank line-up at noon hour. But instead I was me—worrying about cops and trying not to think about how much depended upon their honesty and competence. I was also feeling deflated. I'd gone in there prepared for extensive questioning; I'd forgotten that bureaucracies are cautious by nature and addicted to their procedures. Before questioning anyone the detectives would re-read their files, run tests on the "evidence," check out their own sources for verification. And my real test would be—not the interviews with the police—but the days of waiting and uncertainty. I was not looking forward to them.

A day passed. Another. Joau phoned me a couple of times; his brother was not yet conscious, no one knew what to expect. They'd extracted the tumor and pronounced it malignant; they said that might be the end of it. Then again, it might not. Joau visited the hospital every day and sat by the bedside, holding his brother's hand. "I feel much better," he told me. "I sleep much better—everything. I think my brother is O.K. now." Every time he called, after giving me news of his brother, he thanked me profusely for having found him, waxed eloquent on the subject of my powers—but I refused to accept these compliments, insisting that I'd only done the leg-work, following his hunches. But Joau, I discovered, had obliterated these from his memory; intuition, he believed, was the province of womanhood; therefore both the hunches and the credit were all mine. Every time he phoned we got into the same argument. I was reminded of long-married couples that bicker every night over who's hogging the blankets. Perhaps he was missing his wife? Perhaps I was missing Tom.

Nearly a week went by and I heard nothing from the cops. I was trying not to think about them, trying to keep busy—but I felt like I was being gnawed at, internally, by rats. One morning, like an ex-smoker allowing herself to reach for a cigarette, I watched myself pick up the telephone directory, flip the pages to the letter "H." Almost immediately I found what I was looking for: "Healey, Mulligan and Proctor, barristers and solicitors." Their offices were located at 1174 West Pender Street; I knew their phone number by heart. Oh Salal, I thought reproachfully, you're not supposed to make it so easy. As I'd suspected, Healey was more than just a name. He was a lawyer. (But who was his receptionist?) Should I try to find out?

The answer, of course, was no. I was not supposed to be investigating my accomplices—even if they did tell me lies. So for a day or more I did nothing—nothing, that is, except to pay a lot of attention to the people around me: the man working on the cables in the alley behind my townhouse, the woman at the bus stop across the street from my car, the van in my rearview mirror. By the end of the second day, I felt certain that I wasn't being watched. On the third day, I made damn sure of it. I changed buses three times, dived in and out of department stores, ducked into a few elevators, took a taxi to the 900 block West Pender Street. From there I walked. I crossed the street a few times, passed 1174 West Pender going one way, then backtracked back to it. This was the heart of Vancouver's business district; 1174 was a mammoth, black, glass-plated office building, lodged like a tooth in a long row of others. The people, equally uniform—all well-heeled, coiffed and buffed—trickled like ants across the massive cement plazas, past the plashing fountains, up and down the long, wide steps. Even the doorhandles were enormous, proportioned for a race of giants.

I entered the lobby of 1174, consulted the directory. Healey's offices were on the eighth floor. The business day was ending, all the elevators were in use, going up empty, coming down loaded. Now what? An elevator door opened; my eyes searched the faces of the officeworkers getting off. (Was Healey's receptionist one of them?) I moved to a bench that was partially concealed by a large cement buttress, from where I could see without being seen. The elevator doors opened and closed like jaws, disgorging mouthfuls of officeworkers, who swarmed like schools of fish across the wide, echoing lobby.

By five-thirty the rush was over, and the elevators rested on the ground floor, humming. I'd seen no one I recognized. I got up, went out onto the street, joined the line-up at the bus stop. By the time I got on the bus, there was standing room only. I worked my way through the bodies towards the back, found an empty stanchion, appropriated it. The bus rolled a little, lumbered out into the traffic. I glanced down at the woman sitting in the seat to which my stanchion was attached. It was Margot, Johanna's lover.

"Margot!" I cried, pleasantly surprised to see her. She

looked up, smiled. "Are you on your way home from work?"

"Yes. I got on at the last stop."

"But that's where I got on. You must have been at the front of the line."

"I was. I know when the buses come, and I time myself accordingly."

"Oh yeah. You're a— " And then the coin dropped. I stared at her and felt my face flush. She was peering at me, inquiringly. "What—what is it— " I stammered, "I can't remember what you do."

"You probably never knew," she assured me, smiling. (She had a thin, severe face which broke into beautiful, curving creases when she smiled.) "I'm a legal secretary. But it's a small office, so I do everything, really. I run the place. I've been working there for years."

My mouth was hanging open. I managed to close it, blinked, tried to think of something to say while my mind ran around in circles. "Oh yes. A legal secretary. I knew that but...." No, I was thinking. Not you. But of course it was her; she was the obvious choice. Now I needed to find out who she worked for. But she was already telling me.

"...There used to be three of them, but one of them left soon after I started working there and Proctor retired last year. So now there's only me and Bert Healey, and he's past it, really. He's just a family solicitor, doesn't take on anything new. I water his plants and help him keep his files dusted, answer the phone...."

I should have guessed, I thought, watching her face as we chatted about work, about vacations and recipes. But I still didn't want to believe it. I'd always thought of Margot as living in a different world—a *respectable* world. And so she does, I argued with myself. But she's also a lesbian, which gives her a different angle on the so-called respectable world, and she's been Johanna's lover for years. Doesn't that tell you something about her? It should have—yet it hadn't. I glanced at the classic beige purse in her lap, at the brooch on her lapel. She looked like a small town librarian or a Sunday school teacher. But she was neither.

I got off the bus before she did, transferred to another

that took me back to my office. I decided to check my answering machine before going home. As soon as I inserted the key into the lock of my office door, I knew that something was wrong. I stepped back a pace, looked at the door, at the lintel, at the lock—at the venetian blind in my office window, the bottom of it slightly askew, as if someone had been peering out. There was a dead wasp caught between the shades, its body pressed against the glass. I glanced behind me—at my car still parked where I'd left it that morning, then up and down the street. Nothing. Nothing untoward—nothing that could explain my sense of unease. Finally I unlocked the door, stepped into my office. Everything was as I'd left it; nothing had been disturbed. And yet there was *something* foreign in that room, something as tangible as a smell. I went to my desk, squatted by the left-hand bottom drawer, lifted it and pulled it out an inch, peered underneath it, at the narrow ledge over which it slid. Just as I'd suspected, the line of salt was scattered. It had been intact that morning, had been intact ever since I put it there, before taking Salal's evidence to the police station. But today I'd had a visitor and he or she, in opening that bottom drawer, had scraped it over the ledge. I rubbed my fingers into the pile of the carpet beneath the drawer, inspected the white grains that clung to my fingertips. I went through all my other drawers, but nothing had been moved, nothing taken. My visitor was a pro.

It's a funny feeling knowing that you've been searched, knowing that an unknown hand has been rifling through your papers, that unknown eyes have scanned and summed up your possessions, read your appointment book, studied your bitten pencil ends. Even if you have no secrets, it's unpleasant. I wasn't worried about what they'd found; I'd taken Salal's warnings seriously and covered my tracks. But I'd also made quite sure that I wasn't being watched—and if I wasn't being watched, how did they know I'd gone out?

I got up and went to the window, parted the shades of the venetian blind, looked out into the street. I watched the traffic passing, a mother tugging her young son along the sidewalk. There was a black woman sitting in a parked car, filing her fingernails; there was a beaten-looking old man standing at the bus stop; there was a crowd of youths at the corner, outside the billiard hall. Who was watching me? But whoever it was hadn't followed me to West Pender Street; I'd made sure of that. I wondered if Margot would tell Johanna that she'd seen me. Would Johanna think it suspicious? Well, I'm suspicious! I defended myself. This whole set-up stinks. "Call it off," I whispered. "Get yourself out of this." And then what would I say to the cops? "Tell them that your informant phoned you and said he was clearing out." I glanced at my phone, but knew for sure now that it was bugged. "Tell them that he followed you, accosted you in the street." In that case I should be able to describe him to the police. I raised my eyes above the storefronts, the telephone poles and hydro wires, let them rest upon the mountains. They were there, as always, their rocky summits butting the sky, so near and yet so far from the city swarming over their feet.

A bus came and picked up the man at the bus stop; the black woman in the car was joined by an older woman and the two of them drove away. The youths were still cavorting and arguing outside the billiard hall. I looked again at the mountaintops. I wanted to believe in God.

Joau phoned again. Today his brother had been conscious for all of ten minutes, had recognized Joau, had even spoken his name before falling asleep again. Joau was elated. He wanted to take me out to dinner. Even as I accepted I knew I was making a mistake—but the alternatives were so dismal that I felt justified in accepting any diversion that offered. People do dumb things.

He took me to a steak house. A good one. We were two middle-aged adults, off the leash for an evening, thrown together by circumstances as arbitrary and temporary as a shipboard cruise across the Atlantic. He ordered Portuguese wine. In one sense we had nothing in common; in another, we had everything. And to give him his due, he was a person of great energy and charm. He also had intentions.

Dreamy and languorous with wine, satiated with rich food, fascinated, like a child, by the perfect flames of the candles, by the lights starred in the wine glasses, by the solid weight of silver cutlery.... Restaurants, these days, are more sensuous than beds. But it was his eyes that did me in. He had gorgeous eyes—large, black, sparkling with the passions that animated him. When he started telling me about the intuitive powers of womanhood again, I only shook my head smiling and gazed into his eyes, feeling soft and a little weepy, allowing myself to slide, luxuriously, from my reality into his. Sometimes there is nothing more pleasurable than letting one's principles turn to mush.

We sat in the restaurant for three hours, talking. He did most of it. He told me all about his wife, children, siblings, friends; he gave me his views on love, childrearing, politics, Canada, men, women, much more. Occasionally he interrogated me. Why had I married? What was my ex-husband like? How old were my children? Why had I divorced? He told me about myself. He did not approve of my situation; he was sure it was not good for me. He said I was the kind of woman that needed a husband. "But if I had a husband," I pointed out, "I wouldn't be here now." "This is true," he agreed gravely, "and my position would then be unfortunate. But I am talking about what would be the right thing for *you*." And I was tipsy enough to be impressed by his rectitude.

By the time we left the restaurant, walking out arm in arm into the warm summer night, I was waiting to find out what would happen next. The results were predictable.

The next day I woke up with one hell of hangover. Fortunately, Ben was out and I was alone in the house; I sat all morning at the kitchen table, staring stony-eyed out the window, drinking one cup of coffee after another. Reality— my reality, the one I'd reneged on with such willing abandon—had never seemed more uncompromising. No fool like an old fool, I kept saying to myself, until I couldn't bear it anymore and climbed back into bed. Now, looking back, I don't know why I took it so hard; after all, a night spent in bed with an acquaintance is hardly a crime. But I was upset, probably, more about Tom than Joau, and beginning to realize what a mess I was in. I was also getting scared. I had little faith in my abilities as a liar and felt that I'd end up telling the cops the truth in much the same way that I'd ended up sleeping with Joau: I'd run out of energy to resist anymore.

Ben must have come home sometime that night because he was there the next morning when I woke up, and only too willing to put my life back on track. I was his mother, and as such I'd been remiss. No food anywhere—did I intend him to starve? I found him some money, sent him out to buy groceries. Then I collected the morning paper off the porch, picked through its pages. Ben returned with some food; I cooked the eggs while he made toast.

"You still broke, Mum?" he asked, wolfing down half an egg.

"In debt."

"Jamie told me they're looking for a new bus boy in his restaurant. Guess I'd better go apply, eh?"

I stared at him, fork suspended.

"Well?" He stared back. "We're broke, right?"

"I've got ten bucks," I said brightly. He gave me a look, wiped his plate. "Is it night work?"

"About half and half. I'd probably start off in the afternoons." He got up from the table, carried his dishes to the sink.

"How much do they pay?"

"Three-eighty-five an hour."

I grimaced. He looked at me. "Unless you'd rather go apply for welfare."

"Thank you," I said. "But I'm putting that off."

"Well, someone's gotta do something!" He placed both hands on his hips, looked at me with an expression of bewilderment and exasperation—exactly as I'd seen his father do a thousand times before. I was tempted to giggle. He glanced down at his hands as if surprised to find them there, finished clearing the table.

"So when are you going to apply?" I asked.

"Now," he answered, tossing the dishcloth into the sink.

"Now?"

"Yep." He slammed the fridge door with the mandatory

gusto of a man on the way to making his first million, then strode out of the kitchen and up the stairs into his bedroom, where I could hear him banging drawers. Ten minutes later he yelled, "Bye!" from the hall and the front door slammed.

I lingered over my coffee, acutely conscious of the silence of the house, realizing, for the first time, that my days as a parent were finally coming to an end. I wasn't sure I appreciated my impending retirement. It was the one job I'd been good at.

That evening as I was climbing into bed, the telephone rang. I returned to the hallway and picked it up.

"I told you to tell them to stay out of here."

"What? Who is this?"

"I told you to keep them out of here." The voice was muffled, grainy, sexless, unrecognizable. Its owner might have been suffering from laryngitis, throat cancer, emphysema, or all three. Finally I clued in.

"In Kinky's? There's cops in Kinky's?"

"Plainclothes," the voice rasped.

"O.K., just take it— "

"Get them out!" it ordered, and then the line clicked dead.

For a moment I stared at the phone, incredulous, shivering. Surely that couldn't have been Salal! A friend, a cohort? Or just a very good disguise? For at least five minutes I sat there, more unnerved by that scabrous, diseased-sounding voice than by the message it had delivered. But finally, that, too, penetrated. Cops in Kinky's? Those idiots!

First I phoned the police station. Of course Menzies wasn't there that time of night and they didn't give out home phone numbers. I asked them if there was anyone else there on the Vice Squad that I could speak to, and was informed that if I explained my problem to the receptionist or whoever he was, he would transfer my call to the appropriate department. I gave up on him, phoned Harry. I got him out of bed.

"Harry, there's plainclothes officers in Kinky's and my informant is furious. Give me Menzies' home number."

"Now don't jump to conclusions, Meg. They're probably

from Narcotics. I bet it's just a routine check-up. Nothing to get upset about."

"You mean there's no liaison between departments? You couldn't have told them to keep away for a while? Nobody talks to each other or what?" Now I was getting mad.

"Yes, of course, but.... Well, I don't know exactly what stage the whole thing's at right now, but I'm sure— "

"Just give me Menzies' number, would you?"

"I can't give you his number, but I'll phone him myself and ask him to call you back."

Five minutes later, Menzies phoned. "There's plain-clothes officers in Kinky's," I said. "I got a call half an hour ago."

"Yes?" said Menzies.

"I guess you've forgotten. I told you to keep your people off the premises. They're jeopardizing the whole operation, including the safety of my informant."

"Mrs. Lacey, we have our own methods. You can't expect us to organize a raid on respectable premises on the basis of your say-so. It is our responsibility to substantiate all information given to us, to verify our— "

"It was you that sent them!" I couldn't believe it.

"The officers have been advised," he continued evenly, "to act with the utmost discretion; they are men of considerable experience in this work— "

"But they've been recognized! Why do you think my informant phoned me!" I realized I was yelling, tried to lower my voice. "He said he'd pull out if you came snooping on him. Don't you know anything!"

"Mrs. Lacey, it won't help you to— "

"Get them out of there," I threatened, "or the *whole thing's off*. That's straight from the horse's mouth. Got it?" I hung up.

But that was hardly the end of it. I lay awake for hours, chafing, worrying, cursing the cops and myself, feeling that I'd betrayed Salal's confidence in me. But I'd told them to stay away, and didn't they know by now that underworld operators can spot them a mile off, plainclothes or not? Or was this a deliberate tip-off on the part of the police? This was a rough town with a fairly high crime rate—but I'd been told that our cops were, as cops go, tolerably honest. Maybe my information was out of date.

Ben was told that he'd got the job as bus boy, and that if he worked out well, they'd train him to be a waiter. This didn't sound like a whole lot to look forward to, but he seemed pleased enough. At least, I thought, it'll start him learning about money and the charades you have to perform to acquire it.

My daughter Katie phoned; she was gearing up for the new school year. I asked her if she was still planning to get married. There was an ominous pause. "No," she answered finally. "We changed our minds."

"Will you live together?"

"No," she snapped, then added, begrudgingly: "Rick can't afford it."

"Hmm—too bad," I said, trying to sound sympathetic.

"Well, actually, Mum," she said, in her lecturing voice, "I've decided that I'm too young to get seriously involved with anyone. I've got my own career to think of."

"Oh," I said. Statements like this are typical of Katie; she's always been more of a parent than a child, has been making rules for herself since she was three years old: "Now Katie has to clean up *all* the toys. Right, Mum?" She makes me feel redundant.

Then Joau got hold of me. I'd been praying that he might vanish, that he might know, intuitively, that our ship had now docked and we were back to our real lives. Instead he was on the other end of the phone and determined to introduce me to his brother. I refused. "He wants so much to meet you!" Joau insisted. "He has heard so much!"

"Well, that's your doing," I snarled. "So you can un-do it."

"Meg? What has happened? I have done something to make you mad?"

"No, no, it's just— "

"I come over right away," he decided. "There has been a mistake. We must talk."

And before I could object, he was on his way.

Communications of this nature are always fraught with difficulty, even when they're not cross-cultural. One tries to be tactful—but someone's feelings are invariably hurt.

"Joau, I enjoyed my evening with you very much, but I do not wish to repeat it. It is not appropriate to my age and circumstances." Put that way it sounded very pompous, but I thought it was something that he might well say himself, so I was hoping he'd accept it.

Instead he frowned. "Repeat it? No—we have no time! Who talks about this? I want to introduce you to my brother—soon—because I have to go home now."

"You're going?" I was both relieved and deflated.

"Of course I go! I already tell you. My family is waiting and my business runs to pieces—but my brother he would like to see you. I tell him the whole story."

"When are you going?"

"Tomorrow!" He flung his hands up impatiently. "This is why I am phoning you every day, but you do not answer my messages, you— "

"O.K., O.K.!" Now we were both gesturing wildly. "I'm sorry. I didn't understand. So when can we see your brother?"

He glanced at his watch. "Now?"

"Now," I agreed.

As Joau had promised, the two brothers were identical— at least, as identical as two people can get who have completely different personalities. Of course Victor was still recuperating—but even at his best he must have appeared as a softer, more faded version of his brother, like a fabric that has been through the wash many times. But he too had his charm. When Joau introduced us, Victor took my hand, held it in his own. "So here I am, you see? This is the pot of gold." He made a self-deprecatory gesture at his body stretched beneath the bedclothes.

"But more valuable," I replied, affected by the atmosphere in which I found myself. "Your brother has been so worried about you."

Victor gave his brother a glance that was downright resentful. "My brother," he explained, as if Joau were not there to hear us, "makes so much fuss. I am never lost. Only for him."

"Go then—die!" Joau cried, piqued. "Die then by yourself! I don't care anymore. Don't tell me nothing." He turned to me indignantly. "Even he has a wife!"

I looked at Victor; he made a rueful face.

"Never phones, never tells anybody. No invitations to the wedding—nothing!" Joau was launching himself into a tirade. "Now she is dead!"

Again I looked at Victor; he didn't deny it.

"Didn't tell nobody she is alive; didn't tell nobody she is dead. Some brother this is! Twin brother! Born twenty minutes before me! Come home! I tell him. You are too old now for this foolishness!"

"You're going back to Montreal?" I asked Victor.

"I'm thinking about it," he conceded. "Maybe I will visit. But all this yelling makes me tired."

"O.K.—I go! Now!" Joau literally stamped his foot. "On the plane—whsst!" His hand sliced through the air. "Never see me again. No letters. Nothing!"

His brother watched him, unblinking. Was this, I wondered, a typical example of Joau's hospital visits, or were they attempting to entertain me?

"Come on." Joau gestured at me to follow him. "He is right. He is not worth the trouble." He waved his brother away, was actually walking out the door. I glanced at Victor, who was still watching him, without expression.

At the door Joau stopped. "Come on!" he insisted. And I finally understood that our visit was over. I turned to Victor.

"I am very pleased to have met you," I said, ceremoniously. "I hope you will soon be better."

He considered, gave me a conspiratorial look. "Already I am better," he confided. "I am waiting, you know?" He made a gesture in Joau's direction; I wondered if he meant

148

that he was waiting for his brother to be gone. "I just need a little peace and quiet." He nodded, sagely; we shook hands. I looked at the doorway—but Joau was already gone. I found him outside in the hall.

All the way back Joau talked to me about his brother, enumerating his faults, recalling examples of his past iniquities. And even when it came time for us to part, it was his brother that was uppermost in his mind; it was as if our evening had never been, as if we'd never slept together at all. I was almost hurt. It is one thing to be put aside, but quite another to be forgotten entirely. As a result, however, I found it possible to give him his invoice in person, instead of mailing it to him, as I'd planned. "Thank you," he said. "I will mail you a check." More handshaking, then he was gone.

That night I was alone in my house, listening to the ticking of the clock, to the sounds of my appliances—the freezer, the dryer—fulfilling their functions. No children, no lovers— I tried to read, but the silence intruded, made itself felt between paragraphs, at the turning of each page. Finally, I gave up. I held the book in my lap and thought about Salal, about the silence of the forest, the silence of the coastal inlets where the black, silky water slaps against the rocks. I thought about death. And that night I slept well—deeply, dreamlessly—as if the silence had invaded me.

CHAPTER ELEVEN

THE POLICE called me on Monday morning. They wanted me to come down. With my map. Driving down to the station I reviewed my lines and wondered how I'd landed myself with such a implausible script. Did Haswell really make porno movies? With a cast of teenage runaways kept acquiescent with heroin, stashed behind the locked doors of a downtown office building? A likely story. Now that others were prepared to believe this rigmarole, I could no longer believe it myself.

I announced myself to a receptionist, who led me through a maze of long, khaki-colored corridors, past open doors where typewriters clattered and people lined up at counters, arguing over slips of paper. We passed a man in handcuffs, two guards on either side of him, a posse of constables around a coffee machine, guns protruding from their hips. We stopped in front of a closed orange door. The receptionist knocked. "Come in," a voice commanded, and she opened the door upon what looked like a seminar room, blackboards along one wall, venetian blinds on the windows, a screen set up at one end. There was a large table strewn with coffee cups and papers; around it sat five cops—four plainclothes, one in uniform. Four men, one woman. Detective Sergeant Menzies got to his feet.

"Carry on, Jarnell," he ordered, walking towards the door. He backed us out into the corridor, closed the door behind him. "The map," he said, and held out his hand.

I stared at it. "Wait a minute. The raid's going to happen? Tomorrow night, as planned?"

"That's why we're here," he answered, good-humoredly. As if we'd been buddies since the day we met, as if there'd been no telephone calls in the middle of the night.

I watched his face and was not reassured—but finally opened my handbag, produced the map and handed it to him. He unfolded it, studied it for a moment, then turned to the receptionist who was still waiting beside me. "I want six copies and a transparency for the overhead. Pronto. At my office." He gave her the map. "Come on," he said to me and started off down the corridor.

We passed through a door, turned right, then left, climbed a flight of stairs, marched down another corridor, finally arrived at his office door. He gestured me in, by now I knew where to sit. As he walked around to his chair, he punched a button on a cassette tape recorder that was on his desk beside the telephone. Then he seated himself with the visible satisfaction of a man knowing himself on home ground. The tape recorder clicked.

"I told you to tell them to stay out of here."

"What? Who is this?"

"I told you to keep them out of here."

"In Kinky's? There's cops in Kinky's?"

"Plainclothes."

"O.K., just take it— "

Menzies stabbed the stop button, leaned back in his chair and swivelled sideways so he could cross his legs. "That him?"

At first I didn't answer. Even though I'd suspected that my phones were tapped, the proof of it shocked me. I'm naive, that's all there is to it, the product of a sheltered upbringing. And then I remembered Salal's comment—that this naivete was my trump card and I should play it for all it was worth.

"You tapped my phone!" And because this was me—my genuine reaction—I had no need to act. "I come to you—one of those helpful citizens you're always going on about—and get this!"

"How do I know you're helpful?" Menzies retorted. "I don't know the first thing about you. So I make it my business to find out."

"Then do a credit check," I snarled at him, surprising even myself with my vehemence. "Ask for references. No wonder nobody ever trusts a cop."

Menzies shifted in his chair, keeping his eyes lowered. "You never answered my question."

"Because it wasn't a question. It was a threat—gratuitous bullying." I stood up, thrust my handbag under my arm. "All right, have it your own way. You don't trust me; I don't trust you. Rely on no one but yourselves—and I hope you bungle it." I strode to the door.

"Mrs. Lacey— " I looked back, my hand already on the doorknob. "This is standard police procedure. It's not a question of trusting you, it's your informant we're after. We have to know as much about him as possible—too much depends upon him, maybe even our lives. Surely you can see that."

For Menzies this was undoubtedly a magnanimous speech—but his standards weren't mine, and I didn't see why I should accept them. "Then why didn't you *ask* me?"

He honestly didn't know what I was talking about. "Ask you what?"

"Ask for permission to tap my phone? You know—take me into your confidence. Ever thought of doing that?"

Menzies protruded his lower lip. "Because you might have refused—obviously."

"In which case you could have gone ahead and done it anyway."

"In which case we'd be no further ahead than we are now—wasting time we haven't got. So let's get back to business." He pointed his chin at my chair, indicating that I should sit in it. For a moment I debated, my hand still on the doorknob.

"If you're finished," he added.

I decided to sit down. "But *you* wasted the time," I pointed out, settling my handbag back in my lap.

"I'm not going to argue about it." He made this sound like a virtue, folded his hands upon his desk. "Now—tell me—did he always sound like that?" He nodded at the tape recorder.

I looked at it. "No. That's why I didn't know who it was—at first."

"Didn't usually disguise his voice?"

"No. Only that one time."

"Because we ran some tests on that one—could have been a woman, you know."

"It didn't sound like a woman—not to me."

"No—but that would have been the intention, wouldn't it?"

"I thought he was just disguising his voice."

"How would you describe his normal speaking voice?"

I hesitated. "A light voice—but definitely male. A little higher-pitched than average, perhaps. Nothing distinctive about it."

"No accent?"

"The same one you and I have got." For a moment he stared at me. Then he glanced at the tape recorder.

"You sure that was the same guy?"

"Not by the voice. That voice didn't sound like anybody I ever knew. I was only going by the words—and the context, of course."

Menzies nodded, chewing his upper lip. "Has he been in touch with you?"

"You mean, apart from that phone call? No."

"Weren't you expecting him to check up on things?"

I shook my head. "Not necessarily. He never said he would."

"What if something went wrong? What if we didn't buy this story? What were you supposed to do then?"

I held his eyes. "Nothing."

"You mean he's going to go down there tomorrow night and unlock the doors whether we show up or not?"

"I guess so. He never said."

Menzies leaned back, picked up a pencil from his desk, frowned at it, put it down again. "That doesn't sound like very good planning."

I considered. "Well, maybe it's not much of a risk. Opening the doors, I mean. Maybe he thought— "

There was a knock at the door. "Yeah?" called Menzies and the receptionist appeared again, placed the photocopies and a transparency on his desk. "Thanks." Menzies immediately reached for one of the photocopies, scanned it avidly.

"Maybe he thought," I repeated, returning to our conversation, "that his anonymity was more important. After all, if we didn't show up within fifteen minutes or whatever, he could always lock up again. And nobody the wiser."

Menzies wasn't listening to me. He was squinting at the map, and counting under his breath. "...Nine, ten, eleven... Eleven? What the hell does he think we are—an occupying army? Why doesn't he *lock* some of those doors?"

"There are a lot of them," I agreed.

"It's going to be like trying to catch flies in a fishnet!" Abruptly he scooped up the rest of the photocopies, placed the transparency on top of them. "All right." He stood up. "Let's get back."

Again we marched through the corridors, myself in Menzies' wake. So far, so good. I'd had a couple of bad moments, but thought I'd got through them pretty well. After all, the story *was* weak; the anonymity of the informant was a major disadvantage, but it seemed like the evidence was going to be sufficient to carry us through. I wriggled my shoulders, trying to make them relax.

Menzies opened the door to the seminar room; inside it was almost dark, only the screen lit up at the other end of it. "Lights," ordered Menzies and the image cut from the screen; we were flooded in fluorescent light. Everyone stared at us, blinking.

Menzies closed the door behind me, introduced me to each of the officers in turn: Harry Jarnell, whom I knew, Inspector Dikeakos, Sergeants Carruthers and Maschak. He pulled up a chair for me, sat down in his own. "Carry on," he said to Harry.

I sat down, aware that I was being surreptitiously observed. Police officers are clannish, and only work with outsiders under protest. I wondered what Menzies had told them about me.

The overhead lights dimmed; Harry was at the projector. The screen lit up. On it was what appeared to be a map, drawn by hand.

"As you can see, we've been doing some research of our own," Harry explained for my benefit. "This is the outside. Kinky's is here; north is up."

I now had my bearings, and realized that I was looking at a detailed sketch of the area immediately surrounding Kinky's, the buildings on either side of it, the alley, Hastings Street, nearby loading zones, parking spaces, stairwells, fire hydrants, street lights. Even my Smithrite container was marked on it.

"So the first van sits here— " Harry indicated an X that had been drawn in at the west end of the alley, "and the other van parks at this end, behind the hydro pole." With his pencil he marked in a second X, again on the north side of the alley, but this one at the east end of it. "It's less than a hundred yards from here— " he indicated the second X, "to the east side door of the building. If you leave the van at one minute to twenty-three hours— " He was now looking at the woman and the round-faced officer beside her, "that should do it. Move fast. There's good cover all along the north side. Right, Dikeakos?"

The spare, hollow-cheeked man at the end of the table shrugged. "It'll be dark," he said. "You won't be out there for more than a couple of seconds anyway."

"Right." Harry looked back at the others, who were both scribbling busily. "There's no distance involved. Just move. Carruthers and Maschak take the east door, Menzies and I will take the west side. And we'll each need two more— three? Leave that for a moment until we get to the other map. Three or more extra men to stand guard at the exits."

Now Menzies spoke up. "Timing is crucial," he announced, looking at each of the others in turn. "I want us in those back doors by twenty-three hours at the latest, Dikeakos at the front door within fifteen seconds of that. Synchronize your watches. Under no circumstances does Dikeakos go in first—but don't use your hand-sets unless you absolutely have to. Make sure that your guards know exactly where they're going, and see that they get there before you do anything else. It's very important that we take the fourth floor by surprise, before they have time to start destroying their evidence. Let's get an open-and-shut case for once. Everybody got that?" Again he met each officer's eyes, then stood up and walked around the table, passing out the photocopies of my—Salal's—map. When he reached the overhead projector, he handed Harry a map, elbowed him aside, removed the transparency from the projector and replaced it with the new one, reproduced from Salal's map. Harry sat down. Menzies adjusted the focus.

"Now you can see what I'm talking about," he said, and proceeded to explain the layout of the building. He pointed out doors and stairwells, marking in red dots where he wanted to station guards. A discussion ensued about personnel: how many cops could they rope in from other squads, how many officers would Dikeakos need down in the pub, how many guards would be needed to cover the doors, how many detectives would be needed to conduct the interrogations. As Menzies and Dikeakos debated, Harry tallied up numbers on a calculator, and Carruthers and Maschak carefully copied red dots onto their photocopies of Salal's map.

Menzies turned to Harry. "Now what's the total?"

Again Harry counted. "Forty-two."

Everyone looked up. "Jesus!" Maschak said.

Harry looked up from his figures. "But if this pans out as expected, it'll be one of the biggest scoops we've ever made."

"If," said Menzies. Now he was looking at me, and though I knew I shouldn't let him intimidate me, I was feeling intimidated. "Did you speak to Sims about the paddy wagons?" he asked Harry—but without taking his eyes off me.

"Yep," Harry answered. "And the fingerprint and photo crew. Everyone's on standby."

"An intercom," Menzies barked. It took me a moment to realize that this time he was talking to me. "They got no intercom from the pub to the fourth floor?"

"A phone," I said. "The informant is taking care of it."

Menzies gave a dissatisfied grunt. I glanced at the others,

but they were all writing, heads bent, except for Dikeakos—
who was scrutinizing me. "You're telling us," Dikeakos said,
"that there's only one exit to that entire top floor?"

"I went over that point with the informant quite a few
times. That's what he said."

"No trap door, no fire escapes?"

"I suggested those myself. In fact I told him to go up
there and take another look. He said he'd do so."

The woman, Sergeant Carruthers, finally spoke up, thus
assuaging my fear that she was only there to make the coffee.
"And?"

I met her eyes. "He never got back to me. If he'd found
another exit, I'm sure he would have told me. Either that or
he dealt with it himself."

"How is he getting out?" Dikeakos asked.

"I don't know."

"Out a fire escape on the fourth floor," Dikeakos suggested, acidly, "which he didn't want you to know about."

"A *secret* fire escape?" I retorted. "Known only to him?
Why would he do that when he can just walk up one staircase, down the other and then out an alley door?"

Dikeakos flicked his map with the back of his hand. "But
no fire marshal would have passed this building as you've described it."

"I know that. I told him so."

"And what did he say?" asked Carruthers.

"He said, in effect, that fire marshals can be bought."

The silence that followed was distinctly unfriendly. I was
now being openly scrutinized, and the reservations they'd
concealed were plainly written upon their faces. The overhead projector hummed; I became aware that the room was
stuffy, and too hot.

Menzies, who'd been slumped in his seat throughout this
exchange, now lifted his head. "Any more questions?"

No one else produced any, so I decided it was my turn.
"Where am I going to be?" I gestured at the map on the
screen.

This question, for some reason, appeared to put Menzies
in a good humor. "At home, I hope." He looked round at the

others, inviting them to share his amusement. "Where did you want to be?"

I gave him a level stare. "Somewhere where I can see what's going on."

"A tall order." He was still playing indulgent. "Upstairs or down?"

"Up."

Menzies now dispensed with his joke. "I'd rather you stay home." He turned off the overhead projector, terminating our discussion.

"You might find me useful," I argued. "After all, I've been up there before—which no one else has—and I know what some of these characters look like."

"Oh, we don't leave these things to chance," Menzies assured me. "Where's those slides, Harry?"

"Right here," Harry answered, putting his hand over an envelope on the table in front of him.

"Pass 'em over."

Harry shoved the envelope across the table.

"I want to be there," I insisted.

Menzies was opening the envelope. "This is how it'll work," he said, and I couldn't tell if he was speaking to me or to all of us. "Carruthers and Anders will be going up the east-side stairs and cutting through the third floor corridor to pick up any strays. Then they'll join us at the top." He spilled half a dozen slides out of the envelope, tilted his head towards Harry. "Slide projector's in the cupboard behind you, Jarnell. Get it out for me."

Harry did so, carried it over to him. Menzies began unpacking the slide projector from the box. "Maschak and his buddy will be doing the same through the second floor." He passed the cord to Harry, who plugged it in the wall. Now Menzies glanced at me, in such a way that I realized that he'd been talking to me all along. He began inserting slides into the tray.

He inserted the last slide, stood up, lifted the tray and slid it into the projector. "I guess you can tag along with Carruthers," he conceded. "But keep in the middle and don't break rank. If you get hurt it'll be your own fault; in fact we'll make you sign a statement saying so." He adjusted the position of the projector. "That all right with you, Carruthers?"

Sergeant Carruthers looked up from her notebook. She glanced at him, at me—nodded. "Be down here, Room 306, by ten-fifteen tomorrow night," she instructed me. "Wear dark clothes and shoes that you can move in. And if you've got a gun, leave it at home."

"Fine," I agreed, "I'll be there."

"And if you get in the way we'll charge you with obstruction," Menzies added for good measure.

I gave him my sweetest smile.

Menzies turned his attention to the screen. The projector clicked—I found myself looking at the alleyway behind Kinky's. Menzies was getting it into focus.

"O.K.," he said, "we're just about through here—a few things to look for. This is the alley behind the building; the New Brighton is here on your right. This shot is taken from approximately the location of van number two—so we're looking west. Everyone got that?" He glanced round, stepped closer to the screen, pointed with his pen. "This is the loading door; you can just make out the westside alley door; the other is here, out of sight behind the Smithrite. Van number one will be down that end."

"And those doors are going to be unlocked?" asked Maschak.

"So Mrs. Lacey informs us," Menzies said, dryly.

I felt everyone's eyes move to my face.

"What if they're not?" asked Carruthers. "I mean—an awful lot seems to hang on that. What do I do if my door's locked?"

Menzies fixed her with a stare. "If either of those back doors is unlocked," he said to her, "we use it. If they're both locked, we page Dikeakos and get him to send some of his men through to the back so that they can open up for us. Then we proceed as planned. If that happens, Dikeakos, send all your guards straight through to the back—even if they have to fight their way through the staff to get there. Don't let anyone get to those stairs before you."

"Just keep me posted," Dikeakos replied. "I'll do what's necessary."

Menzies changed the slide. We were now looking up Hastings Street; Haswell was in the foreground, climbing out of a taxi-cab. He was carrying an attache case and looked very dashing, a lock of hair blowing over his forehead. "This is number one," Menzies introduced him. "Take a good look; we've got a few more shots of him, eh Harry?"

"Yeah, there's better ones," Harry agreed.

"Name's Danny Haswell, about six-foot-one, dark brown hair. We once had him up for extortion, but they said there wasn't enough evidence and let him off. He keeps his hands pretty clean. Blue eyes, a good looker—wouldn't you say, Mrs. Lacey?"

"Very well dressed," I said, deciding to cooperate. "And conscious of his charms. What is sometimes called a 'ladies' man'—though most ladies have better taste."

"A queer?" Maschak asked.

I looked at him. As I'd feared, he was serious, his eyes protruding earnestly. "I didn't ask him," I answered.

Maschak swelled. "Sometimes you can tell."

"Yeah," I agreed, "and sometimes they wear buttons. I find that makes it easier."

"All right, all right," Menzies protested irritably. He changed the slide. I looked at it, and froze.

It was taken from the interior of Kinky's and showed, clearly, Haswell sitting on one of the bar stools, talking to two men, one seated beside him (whom I didn't recognize), one standing across the counter from him holding a shot glass—presumably the bartender. And beyond the bartender, on the same side of the counter but with her back turned to the camera, stood Salal. There was no mistaking that sheath of glossy, black hair, nor the tense set of the shoulders beneath it. "That's him on the barstool—on the left," Menzies said.

"And the others?" asked Carruthers.

"Bartender," Dikeakos answered. "And I think the guy beside him is one of the cameramen. Name's Larry Joven—

we've got him on file. We questioned him at the time of the porno postcard racket."

"No record?" asked Harry.

Dikeakos shook his head.

"And the girl in the back?"

Dikeakos pulled out a package of cigarettes, extracted one, put the cigarette package back in his pocket. "I think she's an employee." He looked at the cigarette, as if seeing it for the first time, slowly laid it down on the table in front of him.

"Chinese?" asked Carruthers.

Dikeakos shrugged. "Native, I'd guess," he answered. "Maybe a mixture."

The slide clicked; the next one showed the same four, obviously taken only a few seconds later. And still, thank God, Salal's back was to the camera.

I'd recovered from my shock, but I'd decided to get angry. "Who took these?"

Dikeakos looked at me. "I did."

"When?"

He started flicking through his notebook.

I turned on Menzies. "The night I phoned you, right? The night they knew he was there." Now they were all staring at me, except Dikeakos, who was still flipping through his notebook.

"Friday," he finally answered me. "I was there Friday night." He looked from my face to Menzies'. "Camera's pretty small," he assured me.

"You were seen!" I retorted. "Believe me, I heard all about it." I turned back to Menzies. "You've been trying to make out that if this raid doesn't come off it'll be my fault. But I'm telling you now, just for the record, that if this operation's a flop it'll be because you went to some trouble to let them know we were coming."

Menzies didn't answer, but eyed me, balefully, like a bull about to charge. Everyone watched us, silent. Out of the corner of my eye I saw Dikeakos pick up his cigarette, tap the end of it against the table, stick it in his mouth. But he made no move to light it. "Let's move on," he said finally, the cigarette dangling from his lips.

As if automated by a switch, Menzies resumed operations, turned away from me and changed the slide. "Last one," he announced, as a full-face portrait of Caesar lit the screen. He stared at it—exactly as he'd stared at me only the moment before. "What the hell's this in here for?" He turned to Harry.

Now it was Harry's turn to get difficult. "Just in case. We're not expecting to find this guy," he explained to the others. "But there's a chance. If you do see him, sit on him. Hard."

"That's Grice, isn't it?" asked Dikeakos.

"Yeah," said Harry. "Caesar Grice—also known as Charles. Well over six feet, blonde hair— "

"Mr. Universe," I put in.

But Harry didn't want help. "Broad shoulders," he continued doggedly, "good physique— "

"You know," said Dikeakos, cutting him off, "that reminds me. I heard a story about Grice—about Grice and Haswell in fact—glad you reminded me. From Pinko."

The name meant nothing to me, but looking around the table I deduced that Pinko was well-known—probably an informant.

"He told me that those two had fallen out," Dikeakos continued. "Apparently Caesar held out on him once too often and Haswell bought off another dealer. So— " His gaze returned to Harry, remained there, inquiringly.

Clearly, Harry was taken aback, but not about to admit defeat. "Fallen out, eh?" He tugged uneasily at his earlobe.

"So he's not going to be there." Menzies spoke with finality.

"Actually," I said, "my informant told me that same story."

"He did?" Harry turned on me. "Then why didn't you tell us?"

"Because it didn't seem relevant. Not the way I heard it. And my information seems to be a little more up-to-date. My informant told me that the fight had been made up, and that Caesar was delivering again—more punctually, in fact."

"So!" Harry nodded, meaningfully, at the others. "Keep your eyes open!"

"But I was given no reason to believe that Caesar would be there on Tuesday night," I warned him. "That's not part of the plan."

"Exactly," Menzies said dryly. He switched off the projector; for a moment we sat in darkness. "Anything else?" he asked. In the ensuing silence he began dismantling the projector. "All right, that's it. Mrs. Lacey, you'd better go off and sign a release form; Carruthers, you go with her. Everyone else—tomorrow night, nine p.m. downstairs." Chairs scraped, papers shuffled, Dikeakos lit his cigarette. Maschak opened the venetian blinds; bars of sunlight striped the table; coils of cigarette smoke unravelled towards the ceiling. "Oh and Mrs. Lacey— " said Menzies.

I turned, but couldn't see him for the dazzle from the window behind him. I stepped sideways to get out of its glare.

"Don't forget to tell him that we're coming."

At first I didn't get it. "Who?" I asked. Then, when Menzies didn't answer, but continued watching me, looking as cute as he knew how, I got the so-called joke.

"Oh yeah," I said, picking up my bag, "I'll give him a call. Thanks for reminding me." And much to my surprise he grinned from ear to ear, his tongue protruding salaciously.

I stalked towards the door where Carruthers was waiting for me, and walked out, feeling his grin, like slime smeared down the backs of my legs.

CHAPTER TWELVE

THERE were nine of us in the back. I was sitting by the doors, from where I could get a view—of sorts—out the back windows. The van turned right off Pender, then waited across from the alleyway to make a left turn; I could hear the ticking of the blinker from up front. Just before we turned I caught sight of a vintage white Plymouth, circa 1958, a convertible with the top pulled up. It was parked across the street, not ten yards from the entrance to the alley. The van turned; the white convertible was cut from my sight. A moment later we were reversing into our appointed parking spot. The driver shut off the engine. Silence.

Ten fifty-four; five minutes to wait. We crouched like fetuses in the womb of our van, listening to the clamor of downtown all around us, its alarms and disturbances muted, but reassuringly familiar. Carruthers was right beside me; Maschak was up front next to the driver; I'd forgotten the others' names as soon as I heard them. There were the five guards, the officer appointed to go with Maschak, the other appointed to accompany Carruthers, myself and the driver. Eleven in total. And no one to whom I could very well say: "Why that looks like Johanna's car! What a coincidence that it should be here on the very night that...." Coincidence? I felt a familiar unease in my belly. How many other people in town owned a 1958 Plymouth, white with a black top? I wished, belatedly, that I'd thought to look at the license number.

Ten-fifty-seven. Carruthers announced the time, and around me police officers adjusted their parts: straightened cuffs, loosened collars, dug holsters out of their ribs. In a low voice Carruthers went over the main points of the plan, reminding the guards where to go and how to get there. The radio up at the front emitted static and garbled voices; Carruthers looked at Maschak inquiringly, but he was shaking his head. She turned to me. "You stick close by me," she instructed. "Anders will be behind you." Again the radio crackled; Maschak signaled with his hand. "Let's go," Carruthers commanded. I leaned into the back door handle; the doors opened with a squeak. We piled out two at a time.

We lined up quickly, Carruthers at the front, the guards at the back, and started moving at a jog along the north side of the alley, keeping in the shadow of the New Brighton Hotel. As we passed the Smithrite, I peered around Carruthers' back and saw the other team approaching from the opposite end of the alley, a sinister black centipede passing in and out of the shadows.

We reached the door. A few seconds later, Harry, leading the other team, arrived at the westside alley door. He and Carruthers looked at each other; they turned their doorknobs at the same time.

Immediately we were moving again—heading up the stairs. Without looking back, I felt the sudden absence of the guards behind us; at my heels Anders was breathing heavily. At the second floor landing Carruthers stopped and watched as Maschak stepped up to the door—again the knob turned. Now there were only three of us, and I was in the middle. We climbed the last flight of stairs to the third floor landing; Carruthers opened the door at the top. There before us was that ugly, fluorescent-lit hallway. My stomach churned like colored wash.

We proceeded down the corridor, looking—just as I'd done the last time—into each room as we passed it. Today the rooms seemed smaller and even more depressing than I'd remembered them: panty-hose and falling plaster, mold-filled cups abandoned among the paint chips. I thought of the cops on the floor below, also proceeding from east to west through the building, and I glanced at the ceiling, hoping to hear some clue to the activities taking place on the fourth floor. Then I did hear something: voices, and music—a television was on in one of the rooms up ahead. I saw Carruthers and Anders glance at each other; Anders' hand moved to his hip.

The smaller rooms were all empty, but when we entered the big room where the television was blaring, we found a girl lying on the sofa in front of it. She was eating potato chips. She had two black eyes and a graze along her jawbone. When we walked in, her eyes widened—with fear, but also excitement. "Cops!" she whispered, and seemed to know in that instant that a chapter of her life had just ended.

"Get up," ordered Carruthers.

The girl climbed quickly off the sofa, stood before us in a lime-green nightie, a shapeless sweater hooked over her shoulders. Her bare arms were prickled with goose-flesh, her wrists mottled with bruises; her hair hung in lank dark strands down her neck.

Carruthers stepped forward and gave her a perfunctory frisk. "Put on the sweater," she said. "Have you got anything for your feet?" While the girl fished beneath the sofa for a pair of shoes, I glanced at the television, saw that the bad guys had just flipped their car off the cliff and the hero was peering over the edge, saying the things that heroes say when their enemies bite the dust. There was a loud thump on the ceiling.

We all glanced up. The thump was succeeded by a crash, then all hell broke loose above: screeches, thumps, yells, pounding feet. Followed by a gun shot and screams.

"Take her downstairs then follow me up," Carruthers shouted, already sprinting across the room towards the far corridor. Ignoring Anders' protests, I followed right after her. We entered the stairwell; behind us the sound of the television ceased.

Again up the stairs. We covered the first flight, rounded the corner just in time to see a table come sailing through the open doorway at the top of the stairs, right into the cops that were gathered on the landing outside it. The table was followed by what looked like half a houseful of furniture, one piece after another, the cops ducking and scattering before the onslaught, deflecting what they could down the stairway at us. There was wood screeching, splintering, glass breaking, someone shouting, a chair that narrowly missed my ear, a table that smashed high against the wall then bounced straight towards us and right after it, bodies, literally flying down the stairs. I had no time to determine who they belonged to, but there was no mistaking the fist coming at my face.

Automatically I grabbed it, crouched, pivoted, flipped the body attached to it over my shoulder. Normally, in such circumstances, I would have let go of the arm as the body passed over me, but for all I knew this was Haswell getting away—so I held onto it. When he landed, he screamed with such fervor that I almost let go of him, before I recovered my professionalism and pinned him, gently but exactly, into an inextricable position. Carruthers materialized beside me. She was breathing hard; her lip was bleeding and a purplish lump was coming up over her cheekbone. "Give him to me," she said, giving my assailant a frisk and sticking a gun in his back. "Are you all right?"

"I'm fine," I gasped.

She put a hand on my assailant's shoulder and pushed his face into the wall. He cried out, and cursed profusely. "I think he's injured," I explained.

"Lady broke your elbow, did she?" Carruthers commented unsympathetically. She gave me a glance that was almost resentful. "What were you doing—jui-jitsu?"

"Aikido."

I looked around then and saw that on the stairs, just above us, there was another man with his face in the wall and a uniformed cop poking a gun into his back. But everyone else had disappeared. There were no cops on the landing; the door to the fourth floor stood wide open. Carruthers' gaze followed mine.

"Here, Billy," she said to the cop on the stairs above us. She gave my assailant's arm a yank. "Move," she said, pushing him up the stairs in front of her. She handed him over to Billy. "Take both of them down to the boys at the bottom."

She met Billy's eyes; he nodded. Then she looked at me. "Let's go."

I followed her up the stairs, scrambling over the pieces of furniture that littered it. When we reached the top landing, we flattened ourselves against the wall, peered around the door frame. We were staring into a huge room, which looked like it had been bombed. In the front half of the room were the remains of the movie set, props flung helter-skelter, screens lurching at desperate angles, cables dangling like cobwebs, and movie equipment everywhere—tripods and spotlights sprawled upon the floor waving legs and helpless tentacles, like insects struck with pesticide. Among this debris, the cops had concealed themselves, taking cover behind whatever came to hand. Their backs were towards us, guns cocked. In the back half of the room, beyond the movie set, was what appeared to be storage area: costume racks, furniture, stage-sets, props—in the midst of which, undoubtedly, our quarry had concealed themselves.

"Get out here!" a voice roared. I glanced towards its source and recognized Menzies' bulk squatted behind a sofa about ten yards to my right. "Come out with your hands up!"

There was a silence—dense with racing heartbeats and suppressed panting. Some cops were now moving deeper into the room, fanning out like hunters, scuttling from one object to the next. I imagined the movie crew hidden in the back, panic-stricken, fingers clenched, breathing in smells of must and old clothes.

"You've got thirty seconds!" Menzies bellowed. "Get out or we'll shoot you out."

A figure rose up in the far back of the room and started walking towards us. It was one of the girls. When she reached the edge of the movie set, she stopped, looked back over her shoulder. "Come on!" she called impatiently. "They're not going to go away!" Then she faced forward and smiled—like an actress receiving ovations from an audience beyond the footlights. I recognized her from one of my earlier surveillances. She had a pretty, heart-shaped face, black hair that gleamed beneath the lights, the ungainly grace of puberty, bony knees and big feet. She was wearing a man's vest and a pair of yellow bobby-socks. Nothing else.

There were furtive scuffling sounds, whispers, a sudden outburst of sobs and terrified giggles; someone—probably one of the girls—had succumbed to hysterics. More figures were coming forward. There was a silhouette in the back that kept appearing, then disappearing, as if engaged in an argument with somebody else. By now there were four girls on the set, clutching their meager garments, trying not to cut their feet on the shards of broken glass. In the back the sounds of terrified weeping continued, and the bobbing silhouette had disappeared altogether.

"Last chance!" Menzies shouted. "Come on—get out here!"

As if by unanimous consent, the men came out from hiding. Technicians, actors—most of them dressed casually in T-shirts and jeans, one of them—probably an actor—in a three-piece suit. Their average age was around thirty; their primary emotion seemed to be one of embarrassment. Their hands dangled in the air; they shuffled into an untidy line along one wall of the set, casting sideways glances at each other's feet as if they were members of a chorus line and had forgotten their steps. Now in the far back the silhouette reappeared, this time dragging someone with her who was kicking and resisting—clearly the hysteric—whose steady shrieks of terror slipped like ice cubes down the back of my neck.

"Carruthers!" Menzies commanded, looking around the room.

But she was already on her way towards them. Another cop stepped out to cover her; others sought new places to conceal themselves. Then I saw Haswell. He was leaning against the wall on the right-hand side of the room, arms folded across his chest as if he'd been there throughout, as if he were—like me—an observer, not a participant.

I opened my mouth to warn Menzies—but he must have seen him the same moment I did.

"Hey you on the wall! Get your hands above your head and get over with the others!"

Haswell straightened, but didn't uncross his arms, began

sauntering across the room towards the set. A shot—blank, I hope—exploded throughout the room; Haswell jerked like a puppet, stared wildly about for its source. "Hands up!" Menzies screamed. And Haswell's hands finally lifted, trembling, into the air.

By now Carruthers was coming forward with a girl on either hand, like a mother escorting toddlers across a busy intersection. The one on her left had stopped screaming, but was still weeping unrestrainedly; the other was talking earnestly, as if she'd known Carruthers all her life. Carruthers looked grim. She led her charges into a corner of the set, called the other girls over to join them. The girls approached warily, picking their way through the glass like cats negotiating snow. Carruthers looked around. "Anyone finds a broom, we need it over here," she called out to the room at large.

There were now a dozen or more people standing on the set, and the cops were on the move again, getting increasingly bolder, coming out from cover, kicking aside stray bits of furniture, peering behind partitions, making sure they'd flushed everyone. Menzies unstrapped the hand-set from his belt, spoke into it for some time. A cop emerged from behind a clothes rack, carrying a broom; Menzies lowered the hand-set from his mouth. "Bonini!" he called. "Go down and show the photo and fingerprint crew the way up."

"Yes, sir," said Bonini, then stood looking at the broom as if wondering whether to take it with him.

"Give the broom to Carruthers," Menzies said acidly. Carruthers, on the set, heard her name and looked over at them.

"There's another girl and two men at the bottom of the stairs," she told Menzies.

"A girl?"

"Yeah. And the two guys who made a break for it. I sent them all down to the bottom to get them out of the way."

Menzies looked at Bonini. "Tell the lads at the bottom of the stairs to bring whoever they've got up here."

"Yes, sir," snapped Bonini, and marched off towards Carruthers, holding the broom over his shoulder like a rifle.

Menzies looked at Harry, who had appeared beside him. "I might as well get started on the movie crew, eh?" Harry asked.

"Yeah. But leave Haswell."

Harry nodded, turned.

"Oh and Jarnell—"

Harry looked back at him.

"Send someone down to help Dikeakos. He says he'll be there all night if he doesn't get reinforcements."

Harry nodded. He pulled out his hand-set, issued a few orders, then strolled over to the set.

I wandered into the room and, uncertain of my welcome, tried to find myself an inconspicuous place to sit. I finally perched on the ledge against which Haswell had been standing, from where I had a good view of the room. The movie crew—the male half of it—were being searched by a couple of constables; the girls were still gathered around Carruthers, who was asking them questions, writing down the answers in her notebook. The floor was being swept. Only Haswell stood alone, still exempting himself from the proceedings, lounging against the wall, his hands manacled behind him. He was being ostensibly ignored—but I noticed that none of the cops nearby ever really took their eyes off him.

Throughout the rest of the room policemen were still prowling, poking their sticks into cupboards, curtains, and costume racks. I saw some disappear through the doors at the far end of the room and wondered what was beyond them. Darkrooms? Dressing rooms?

The interrogations were getting underway. Harry had been joined by a plainclothes detective and together they'd set up a table and some chairs in the corner. They were now seated, side by side, conferring with their heads together. Carruthers was rounding up and distributing clothes; the girls were getting dressed. The photo and fingerprint crew arrived, hurrying into the room like rush-hour commuters, carrying what looked like tool chests and attache cases, with other assorted equipment strapped across their chests. They took off their suit jackets, opened their boxes, rolled up their shirt-sleeves. Watching them, I happened to glance over their

171

heads and saw a uniformed policeman emerge through one of the doors at the other end of the room. The policeman closed the door behind him, looked around the room, then headed towards Menzies.

Something about him—perhaps his air of self-importance—kept me watching that cop all the way across the room. As he approached the fingerprint crew, the men standing around Menzies parted to let him through. Menzies and the policeman talked for a moment, then started back towards the door through which the policeman had emerged, Menzies' shambling, bear-like figure advancing with unwonted vigor through the maze of assorted props. They shut the door behind them. Two minutes later the cop reappeared. He toured the room, his eyes searching the faces of each group he passed. He finally walked up to Carruthers, asked her a question. She pointed straight at me.

I watched him approach. "Mrs. Lacey? Would you come with me, please."

I slid off my ledge, followed him around the movie cameras, past the costume racks, over some cables, all the way to that far door. What had they discovered? Why did they want me? I braced myself for the worst.

We went through the door, which opened into a small hallway; there were more doors on our right. The first stood open, and through it I could see what must have been an editing room, two plainclothes detectives inside it. The second was shut; the third, likewise—but on this one the constable knocked.

"Yeah?" Menzies called out, and we entered without further invitation.

"Good," said Menzies, looking up as we came in. "Now go get Stusiak. And tell the others I want prints of everyone in the place."

As the cop turned and left, Menzies put a hand beneath my elbow, directed me to the desk, the middle drawer of which stood wide open. But before I got to the drawer, I noticed the girl. She was sitting on the floor, huddled in the corner, knees drawn up to her chest. I recognized her face from the stills: Laurie, the "current star." She was just what Salal had described, an Alice-in-Wonderland type; with her hair tied up in pigtails she looked about nine years old. She was watching us, tense and still, as if hoping she might yet remain undiscovered. And on the carpet, about two feet away from her, lay a hypodermic needle. Emptied of its contents.

I turned to Menzies in mute protest.

"Yeah, I know. I've seen her. But I want you to look at this desk."

I looked down at the desk, at the drawer hanging askew, and saw that it contained pens, paper clips, thumbtacks, a comb, assorted keys, a teaspoon, a wrist watch, and a small paper bag, the contents of which had spilled throughout the largest compartment of the drawer. Capsules. Enough to keep several dozen junkies happy for a week.

"Must have been payday," Menzies commented laconically.

I stared at the capsules—Haswell's private supply? I glanced at the girl, at the needle beside her on the floor, looked up to find Menzies watching me.

"You said Caesar supplies this."

"That's what I was told."

"You know how it was done? Did he make the deliveries himself?"

"Yes," I answered. "At least, I certainly got that impression. But I don't think—"

There was a knock on the door; the face of one of the fingerprint crew appeared around it. "Hi, Stusiak," Menzies greeted him. "Get in here and do this desk. And the young lady while you're at it." He indicated the girl with a tilt of his head and I saw her fingers curl, like claws trying to retract.

Stusiak glanced at the girl, decided to start with the desk.

After watching him for a moment, Menzies turned to the girl. "All right, Laurie. You told me this is Haswell's office. So what are you doing here?"

Her eyes slid guiltily towards the needle still lying beside her, returned to Menzies' face. She said nothing.

Menzies heaved a sigh. "Yes, I've seen the needle. You've

173

been helping yourself to a little smack, is that it?"

She didn't answer, but her eyes admitted it.

"You've been using smack; you know it's not good for you; you know the stuff is illegal. I know all that already. But why did you come back here? To get the smack?"

Her answer was inaudible.

"Laurie," said Menzies, assuming a melancholy face, "I'm an old man, and I'm going deaf. So you're going to have to speak louder. Did you come in here to get the smack? Yes or no?"

"Yes," she said clearly, then looked frightened by her own audacity.

"You knew that it was here?"

She hesitated, then nodded.

"Was that drawer open like that when you came in here?" He jerked his thumb at the drawer over which Stusiak was working, his paraphernalia on the floor beside him.

Laurie shook her head.

"Then who opened it? You?"

She nodded.

Stusiak turned and looked at her, at the needle, at her hands. "You got gloves?" he asked her.

Again her fingertips hid themselves—but the question seemed to bewilder her.

Menzies looked at him. "Why do you ask that?"

Stusiak straightened. "There's two sets of prints on this desk. Hers—which are perfectly clear, and only on the drawer itself. Then a mess of someone else's, all over the place, some of which, however, have been subsequently smudged. By what looks like someone else, wearing gloves."

Gloves, I thought, and something surfaced in the back of my mind, but before I could catch it, it had disappeared again.

Menzies stared at Stusiak for a moment longer, then strode towards the door. He stuck his head out into the corridor. "Get me Haswell," he ordered, to someone outside. "And Jarnell." He closed the door again, leaned with his back against it. He was watching Laurie.

"So who told you that stuff would be in there?" He had ceased being fatherly, jerked his head in the direction of the drawer.

"Nobody." She looked scared, pressed back deeper into the corner. "But—" She stopped.

"But what?" Menzies asked, sharply.

"But I saw *him*," she whispered, and I noticed that she was trembling.

"Saw who?" Menzies demanded. "Haswell?"

Laurie looked confused, but nodded again.

"You saw Haswell? In here?"

"No, I—I was in the studio, and I saw Danny going through the door to the corridor. I followed him—but he disappeared."

"Wait a minute." Menzies rubbed both hands over his face as if surfacing from under water. "Go back. *When* did you see Haswell going through that door?"

"When you and—when you guys bust in."

"You mean, right when we arrived?"

She nodded.

"You followed him into that corridor out there," Menzies pointed towards the door, "and then what?"

"He was gone. I couldn't find him."

"Why were you following him?"

"I thought—maybe—maybe he'd give me some smack."

Menzies stared at her. "In the middle of a police raid, you wanted some smack?"

Laurie dropped her eyes.

"So when you couldn't find him—then what did you do?"

Laurie didn't answer.

"That's when you decided to help yourself," Menzies concluded. "But how did you know that the junk would be here?"

"Because I saw *him*." Her eyes lifted. "Caesar."

"*Who?*" Menzies' face contorted. There was a knock on the door behind him, but he ignored it. "You saw who?"

Laurie's eyes darted nervously from the door to Stusiak,

175

back to Menzies. "Caesar," she insisted.

Again there was a knock. "One moment!" Menzies yelled, not taking his eyes off the girl. "When did you see Caesar? Tonight?"

She nodded.

"You sure about that?"

She was sure.

Menzies puffed out his cheeks, put a hand on the doorknob, turned it. He ushered in Haswell, still manacled, and Harry, right behind him.

Immediately Haswell saw the girl. His eyes passed over her, narrowed when they came to me, as if trying to remember where he'd seen me before. Then he noticed the needle. His eyes jerked back to Laurie, returned to the needle, and stopped.

Harry was at the desk, surveying the contents of the middle drawer. "Now, isn't this nice," he observed.

Haswell glanced at him, saw the drawer, took a step towards it, and froze. He managed to maintain control of his facial expressions, but not of his blood, which rose, as if dammed, right to the roots of his scalp.

"So, Danny," Menzies greeted him, "I hear Caesar's paid you a visit."

A muscle twitched at the corner of Haswell's mouth.

"Seems he left you a present."

Haswell's eyes flickered, took in Stusiak and his paraphernalia, returned to the desk drawer.

"And where is he now?" Menzies scanned the ceiling as if Caesar were a fly. "He wouldn't walk out on you, would he?"

"I told you I'm not answering questions." Haswell seemed to have difficulty speaking.

"As I'm sure you've every right," Menzies agreed unctuously. He seemed to consider, looking at the desk drawer with an air of bewilderment. "But I didn't know you were trafficking," he added, sadly, as if Haswell had disappointed him.

Haswell said nothing.

Menzies began walking around Haswell, as if inspecting

the fit of his suit. "If you can clear yourself, Danny," Menzies continued, in a conversational tone of voice, "why don't you do it? Let's face it, you're small fry compared to some that I could name."

But Haswell only swallowed, his face a swarthy shade of pink.

Menzies turned back to Laurie. "Where did you see him, Laurie? Exactly where, and when?"

Laurie looked at Haswell, whose eyes were glued to her face. She glanced at Menzies. "You mean—" Again she looked at Haswell.

"No, not him," answered Menzies. "Caesar."

But she continued to stare at Haswell, as if expecting him to provide the answer.

Menzies returned to the office door, summoned the cop standing outside. "Take him back," he said to the cop, indicating Haswell. The cop escorted Haswell out; Menzies closed the door behind them. Turning back, he glanced at Harry—and suddenly, they both grinned.

It was an exchange that took me completely by surprise, like catching a glimpse backstage in the middle of a play. I'd forgotten that police officers are often only fulfilling their parts, their real feelings very much at variance with their behavior. Seeing that grin, I remembered that, from their point of view, the evening was going well.

Menzies returned to the desk, where Stusiak was now on his knees, working on the bottom drawers. "You done the top?" Menzies asked. Stusiak nodded. Menzies settled himself on the corner of the desk, rested his palms upon a well-fleshed thigh. "Now," he said to Laurie. "When did you see him, and where?"

She cleared her throat, nervously. "Out in the—it was when we were rehearsing. Or they were. I wasn't in that scene so I was kind of off the set and I just looked over across the other side of the room, and I saw him, walking this way. Along the wall."

"Were you under the camera lights?"

"No. Just outside of them."

"And were the room lights on?"

"Ah—no."

"So it was dark out there. Right? You sure it was him?"

"I—I thought it was. He's so big."

"Along the wall," repeated Harry. "You mean coming down to this corridor."

"Well, I didn't—I couldn't see that far—not all the way to the door. But he was coming this way so I thought—" Her eyes flitted anxiously from one face to the other.

"When?" snapped Menzies. "Three hours ago? Half an hour ago?"

"I told you, it was when we were—"

"Yes, but when was *that*? Just before we got here?"

She frowned, thinking. "Maybe fifteen minutes. At the most."

"Fifteen minutes before we got here?"

She nodded. Menzies and Harry exchanged glances. Menzies spread his fingers and rubbed them up and down his thigh. "Is that his usual procedure? He walks in, takes the dope to this back office and leaves it here?"

"Well—" She looked confused. "No. I mean, I don't know. He just gets it to Danny and Danny gives it to us."

"But when you saw him, you assumed he was bringing the smack."

Laurie looked puzzled. "Why else would he be here?"

Menzies gave a snort. "To see Haswell? To watch your shoot?"

"But we were *expecting* it!" she said indignantly.

"You were?" Menzies' eyes widened. "Why? Who told you to expect it?"

Suddenly she looked uneasy, as if afraid she'd said too much. "Word just gets around."

"You were expecting to get the smack tonight?"

"Not necessarily tonight, but—"

"But when?"

She shrugged. "Soon. Today, maybe tomorrow."

Menzies sat back, regarded her thoughtfully. I was doing the same. Harry took over the questioning.

"Did anyone else see Caesar tonight?"

Laurie looked at him. "I don't know. Maybe. But really

178

everybody was busy except me, so they might not have noticed him."

"Did you tell anyone else you'd seen him?"

"No."

"Did you see him again? Did you see him leaving, per-haps?"

She shook her head.

"Laurie." A forefinger tapped irritably upon Menzies' knee. "You saw Caesar heading towards this office, and later you saw Danny Haswell coming through that door into the corridor out there. And then you followed Haswell, right?"

"Yes."

"And you never saw Caesar or Haswell again after that?"

"No."

"What did you do? You came into this corridor—"

"And I looked in the editing room and the darkroom and then I came in here."

"And you never saw Danny or Caesar again."

She shook her head.

"Never heard them? No footsteps outside? Nothing?"

She frowned, cocked her head. "I don't know," she said at last. "It was so noisy—everywhere. Maybe there were footsteps."

"Think," commanded Menzies. "You were going through that drawer, you found the bag and the needle; you were working as fast as you could trying to get that stuff into you before you got caught. Remember?"

She watched him intently, as if hearing this story for the first time.

"Now think. Think about what you were doing—go through it in your mind. And this time, listen. Try to remember if you heard anything."

Her eyelids lowered. She looked at her hands, began twisting the ring on her finger—a small, cheap signet ring, the letter L engraved into the metal.

Menzies watched her for a moment, then turned to Stusiak, who had finished the desk and was awaiting further instructions. "You want me to take her prints now?"

"In a minute," Menzies answered. "How did you know those prints were hers?"

Stusiak looked puzzled.

"On the drawer. You said they were hers—but you haven't taken her prints yet."

"Just a guess. Small hands—and the prints were fresh."

"You're still sure about those gloves?"

At that point I remembered. "Why Caesar always—"

There was a loud knock on the door; it opened without invitation. One of the detectives confronted us in the doorway.

"Yes?" said Menzies.

"Boys have found a trap door. In the washroom down this corridor."

We stared at him as if he were speaking in tongues.

"Above the toilet," he persisted. "Hidden behind a removable panel. And it's been used."

There was a long—very long—silence. "You've sent men up?" Menzies asked finally.

"No. We can't get it open. We're still trying."

"But you say it's been used. Recently?"

"Must be bolted—from the top."

"Then break it!" Menzies exploded.

The detective eyed him steadily. "I told you. We're trying."

"Get a ladder!"

"A four-story ladder," the detective agreed, dryly.

Menzies unsnapped the hand-set from his belt, flicked the switch. It crackled. "I want a fire truck," he ordered, "with a long ladder. Immediately." He recited the address, then switched it off.

"Thank you," said the detective and vanished from the doorway.

Nobody moved. The girl inspected each of us with wary curiosity; the rest of us avoided each other's eyes. Finally, I felt Menzies' gaze move to my face and station itself there—like a cat outside a mouse hole.

"No trap doors, eh?"

I finally looked up; his eyes were distinctly unfriendly. I said nothing.

"Mrs. Lacey, I think we've had enough of your assistance."

I watched him, waited.

"You may go," he said.

For once I decided not to argue with him.

CHAPTER THIRTEEN

I DELAYED my departure as long as I could. I kept out of Menzies' sight, hoping to see what they found once they got onto the roof. But as it turned out there was a huge fire that night at a sugar refinery on the docks and there were no fire trucks to spare. At two a.m., when I left, the cops were still waiting for their ladder. There was plenty going on; the building was swarming like an ant-heap: police and their affiliates poking about in the basement, crawling out of closets, plundering files, emptying vaults, dissecting equipment, interrogating the staff. The customers at Kinky's downstairs had been carted away in an endless succession of paddy-wagons, but the movie crew on the fourth floor was still being detained, questioned and re-questioned as new evidence of Haswell's operations came to light.

The cops found a gun, chucked into the back of a costume wardrobe; undoubtedly one of Haswell's employees (or Haswell himself?) had had the good sense to get rid of it before surrendering to the police. I don't know how much information they got out of it; when I wandered by the table where it was being examined, the conversation stopped, and as I wandered away again, I felt eyes on my back. Finally Harry came up to me and said, "Meg, you're pushing your luck. You'd better go home."

"You've found a gun," I said. "I heard gun shots earlier, when we were still downstairs. Who was doing the shooting?"

Harry just looked at me.

But walking away was a very strange feeling. Once I was out of the building, through the police cordons and press photographers and past the flashing lights, the whole scene seemed to drop off the edge of the world behind me. I guess I wished it would. After all, my job was over—now supposedly in the hands of those most competent to deal with it. And Salal was gone. Safe? As I crossed the first traffic light, I remembered to look south for the white Plymouth convertible—but of course it wasn't there. I tried to add it all up. What happened to Caesar? Why had Salal lied about the trap door? But my mind balked at the sum and went perfectly blank.

My walk, that night, was a surreal experience—as if for an hour, I had stepped into someone else's life, and out of my own. No one knew where I was, no one was expecting me; I was alone in a world of fluorescent-lit streets, with only the sound of my footsteps and my shadow, like a moon, orbiting around me. I felt free, weightless. I passed between rows of mute, curtained houses; breathed in the smells of late summer in the city: carbon monoxide, warm asphalt, garbage, dog shit, and the occasional whiff of fresh cut grass. It was such a relief to have it all over with, such a relief to be alone.

But the relief was short-lived. I'd started out intending to go home. But when I reached the corner of Clark and Venables, I realized that I was within half a mile of Johanna's house—and with that realization, the questions started up again, swarming over me like red ants. That trap door, goddammit! Had Caesar escaped through it? Again I thought about Johanna's car. I stopped walking and stood in the middle of the sidewalk, staring up the empty street. The streetlights hummed over my head; the panels on a nearby billboard flipped to present me with another advertisement. It was as if everyone had died, and only the machinery were left functioning.

I headed south, toward the railway cut. The sidewalks were deserted, but lined with parked cars that seemed to watch me like guard dogs, protecting the interests of their absent owners. I was getting nervous, mentally marshaling my arguments for the confrontation ahead of me—and meanwhile checking and re-checking the streets and alleyways around me. A dog locked in someone's basement barked as I went by; every so often I spotted a light in a window. But I'm always surprised, when I'm out at this hour of the night, to discover how many people spend their nights asleep. It seems uncharacteristically human.

However Johanna was not one of them. As I approached her house, I noticed that there was a lamp on in the living room and that the kitchen window was shaded, but lit. Her car was parked out front. I peered into its interior, placed my hand on the front hood. The metal was slightly warm. I turned and studied the house. Should I try the back door, or the front? I chose the back, because it was invisible from the street, and was further concealed by a large cypress tree that threatened to consume it. Standing on the porch, I could hear a low murmur of voices coming from the kitchen on the other side of the door. When I knocked, the voices stopped.

The back door contained a small, four-paned window. A hand pushed the curtain aside, Johanna stared at me through the glass. I could see she was surprised (and not pleased) to find me there; she turned her head and said something to someone in the room behind her. Then she turned back, and her lips enunciated the words so that I could read them: "Go away."

I'd anticipated this. "No," I said.

"You want to get us into trouble?" I could barely hear her—but her lip movements were explicit. "Go away."

I held her eyes and shook my head. The chain rattled; she was unlocking the door.

She opened it six inches; her body filled the crack so that I couldn't see who or what was in the room behind her. "What are you doing here?" she hissed at me. "You mustn't come here—you know that!"

"I'm alone," I said. "I wasn't followed here. And I think you owe me some answers."

"Fine." she agreed, but raised a hand to keep me at bay. "We'll meet in a couple of weeks; I'll tell you everything you want to know. But not now—it's not safe."

"No?" I said. "Well let me tell you something. It's not too safe for me out here. I've got the whole Vice Squad knowing who I am and where to find me, and wanting to know why I gave them misinformation."

She looked wary. "Misinformation about what?"

"There was a trap door, Johanna! There was a trap door that shouldn't have been there and someone got through it!"

"Who?"

"They don't know who! They can't get it open! The point is that Salal *told* me that - "

"Shh!" she admonished me. "You don't have to shout. You'll wake the whole neighborhood."

"Then you'd better let me in. Hadn't you?" I threatened.

Margot's head appeared behind Johanna's shoulder. "Hi, Meg." She actually succeeded in sounding friendly. She put a hand on Johanna's arm, tried to draw her back from the door. "Let her in," she said to Johanna.

"She wants to ask questions," Johanna objected, resisting Margot's grip and maintaining her position in the doorway.

I realized then that she was scared. We both were. But I'd never seen Johanna frightened before. Something inside me crumpled. "I thought we were friends," I heard myself pleading with her.

"We are friends," she insisted, but she looked distraught. I'd penetrated her guard. "But please don't ask questions. There'll be time for that later."

We gazed at each other, searching for trust, for reassurance. Finally, I nodded. She opened the door and let me in.

Someone was standing by the kitchen table, her back turned to us, her head bent. Salal. She was wearing a blue dressing gown—Johanna's, by the size of it—and her hair, her most distinctive feature, was in the process of being cut. There was already more of it on the floor than on her head, and what was left on her head stood up in ragged tufts, as if she were molting. As we entered she glanced up—but immediately returned her attention to whatever it was that she was doing. As I moved to the other side of the table to see what this was, Johanna strode towards her—and together, we watched Salal slowly extract the hypodermic needle from her arm. She placed the needle on the table, closed her eyes and took a deep breath.

"I thought you were going to wait." Johanna's voice was sharp.

"I did wait," Salal answered, her eyes still closed. I saw Johanna and Margot exchange glances. Salal opened her eyes, fixed them steadily on Johanna's face. Johanna didn't say any more.

Salal looked pale—paler than I'd ever seen her. But she had a strange air of calm about her—as if all her nervous, restless energy had been ironed out of her like wrinkles.

"Back to work," commanded Margot, going to the counter and picking up a pair of hair-cutting scissors.

Salal turned, proceeded obediently back to the stool that had been placed in the middle of the kitchen floor, the hem of her dressing gown cutting a wide swath through the hair clippings. As she settled herself onto the stool, she looked at me for the first time. "Hello, Mrs. Lacey," she drawled. "Where've you been?"

Her question, and the tone of it, took me aback. "I've just come from Kinky's," I answered, finally. "Congratulations. The raid was very successful."

Her smile faded. She watched me, as if puzzled—and then her eyes unfocused and slowly slid away from me. They came to rest upon the cupboards behind Margot's head. "Oh—" she said softly, with an intonation that could have meant anything.

I looked at Johanna, who was leaning against the fridge. "They're drinking tea," she said, indicating the teapot on the table. "It's probably gone, but I can make more. I'm drinking scotch." She raised the glass in her hand to prove it.

"I'd love a drink," I admitted.

Johanna turned to get the bottle out of the cupboard, poured me a scotch. I sat down at the kitchen table. "They got everybody," I said, addressing Salal again. "Including Haswell. It went pretty well. But once they got in they discovered that—"

Johanna stood right in front of me, her stomach parallel

with my nose, her body blocking my view. She handed me my drink. "Thanks," I said. Looking up at her face, I read the warning in her eyes and understood that the topic of the raid was off limits. Having shut me up, she walked back to the fridge, took up her former post against it.

I looked at Salal, but she was still staring at the cupboards, apparently unaware that I'd been talking to her, oblivious to the fact that I'd been interrupted. I took a gulp of scotch.

Margot cut hair as efficiently as a professional. Black locks showered steadily onto Salal's shoulders; the hair on one side of her head was now an even length all over, cut high above the ears, and Margot was making the other side match it. A silence descended. There was only the snipping of the scissors, the hum of the refrigerator, the sound of a train shunting and screeching in the railyards half a mile away.

I watched Salal's profile and thought of the questions I'd wanted to ask her: "Did you know about the trap door? Did you know Caesar was there?" Funny how, here, in this cabal of women, my questions lost their urgency. But if I couldn't ask questions, why be here at all? Why had I insisted upon coming in? I realized, then, how important it was to have some alleviation, however meager, of the loneliness of the past month. By letting me in, they'd acknowledged that I was one of them.

"Very trendy," I said suddenly, as Margot's intentions revealed themselves. Now both sides were short, and Margot was working on the top.

"She's even getting a tail," Margot said, tugging at the lock that she'd left long at the back of Salal's neck.

"And longer on the top?" I suggested. "With lots of gel in it to make it stand up on end?"

"I want pink tips," Salal said, dreamily. "Pink and turquoise tips."

"What would your granny say?" Margot rebuked her.

"Will my granny recognize me?" Salal sounded worried. "She's never seen me with short hair."

"I don't think I'd recognize you," I admitted, staring at her. "It's such a different image."

"Wait till you see the clothes," Margot said, looking at me over the top of Salal's head. "They are *the* latest. I had a lot of fun picking them out."

"In my next life I'm going to be a mannequin," Salal said to the cupboards. "I'll be the first-ever, half-breed mannequin. I'll be beautifully dressed and very empty inside. I think that'll be an improvement." She said this as if she meant it.

"Don't be silly." Margot rapped her lightly on the head with the comb. "It's a costume, that's all. And when you've finished with it you'll take it off, and be yourself again."

Johanna pushed herself off the fridge and started pacing around the kitchen, which immediately seemed too small for her. She finally came to a stop in front of Salal, leaned back against the counter, crossed her arms. "What's your name?" she asked.

Salal's gaze drifted from the cupboards, settled on Johanna's face. "Louise," she answered. She spoke the name slowly, as if tasting it.

"Louise who?"

"Louise Mandawan," Salal replied. Then, as Johanna continued to gaze at her, she became nervous. "I got papers," she said, as if Johanna needed convincing. "I can prove it!" Her hands were clenched into the folds of Johanna's dressing-gown, and she was kneading the cloth, like dough.

"But you don't *say* that," Margot said. "You only use the papers if you need them. Johanna wasn't asking for proof."

Salal didn't respond, continued to stare at Johanna, as if still waiting to find out whether she'd given the right answer.

"And where are you going?" Johanna asked mildly.

"Fort St. John," Salal answered, quickly, triumphantly, like someone scoring points in a quiz. "At least that's where the bus goes," she amended, after a moment. "I think I been there once before. But I don't really remember it."

"*You* were there? Or Louise?"

Johanna's tone was gentle—but Salal took offense. She dropped her eyes, stared at her hands. There was another long silence, during which she submitted to Johanna's scrutiny and mine—while Margot continued clipping busily.

188

"Take my radio walkman thing—with the earphones," Margot suggested, measuring the length of one lock against another. "It's pretty hard to strike up a conversation with someone hooked up to a walkman."

"I'm not going to be talking to people anyway," Salal said, sullenly. "I never do."

Johanna watched her for a moment longer, glanced at the clock above the fridge. "We've got twenty-five minutes," she said to Margot. The clock said four-fifteen.

"And I'm done," said Margot, reaching for the comb again. Johanna and I watched her as she combed and clipped, pulled up swatches of hair with her fingers, snipped the ends even. Then she went at it with the comb again, flipping the locks one way, then another. "There," Margot pronounced. "That'll have to do." She glanced inquiringly at Johanna, then made Salal turn her head so that I could get a front view of her.

The change was really remarkable. I'd met people that claimed that whenever they got their hair cut, acquaintances didn't recognize them—but this was the first time I'd witnessed such a transformation for myself. Now, instead of seeing hair, I noticed the shape of Salal's head, the structure of her neck and shoulders. The hairstyle itself was a competent duplicate of one that was being worn all over town: very short at the sides and back, much longer on top, with locks of uneven lengths falling over her forehead. It suited her. But more importantly, it made her look completely different. "It's perfect," I said to Margot.

"My neck is cold," Salal complained, twisting her head experimentally. "Feels like my head is coming off." She gave an abrupt, wild giggle.

Margot placed her hands firmly around Salal's head. "You'll get used to it," she said, "and it will help you to remember that you're Louise. And when you've finished being Louise, you can grow it long again. O.K?" She peered around into Salal's face.

Again Salal was quiet—too quiet, as if snuffed. She watched Margot, her face expressionless.

"Stand up—and I'll brush you off," Margot instructed

189

her. Salal stood up, allowed herself to be brushed.

Margot blew the hairs off Salal's neck. She put a hand on her arm to turn her around—but Salal resisted being turned, was in the grip of yet another mood, staring intently at Johanna.

"You said you'd get me two caps—one for now and one for later. You said you'd get me another one." She sounded both accusing and frightened.

"I did," said Johanna. "I'll put the other one in your purse. You won't be needing it for a while."

"Don't forget," Salal threatened—but her voice was unsteady.

"I'll do it now, while you're changing."

"It's the last one," Salal murmured. She looked down at herself, frowned, started picking hairs off the dressing gown, at first with an air of fastidiousness, abstraction, and then with increasing urgency, as if she were being harassed by a plague of fleas. "No junk up there," she said quickly, breathlessly, twisting, peering over her shoulders, her fingers plucking frantically. "I couldn't get any even if I wanted to." Abruptly her hands dropped to her sides; she bit her lips, began shaking her head vehemently. She looked up at me and I was shocked to see that her eyes were swimming with tears. "I been through it before! I know what it's like! You feel like you're going out of your mind!" Her voice was raw with fear.

It was like getting an unexpected glimpse of the blood and guts concealed beneath her skin. "Your granny will be there!" I reminded her, my need for reassurance almost equal to her own. "She got you through it the last time. Remember?" Salal's facade, I was discovering, protected others as well as herself.

Salal's eyes clung to mine—and their expression reminded me of the time I'd forced my daughter to put her head under water, an act I subsequently regretted. "She'd better be there," Salal threatened. "She'd better be—"

Margot's arm was around her shoulders. "She'll be there," she said quietly. "And if she isn't, you can turn around and come back here." She glanced at the clock. "Now let's get going." She led Salal out of the kitchen.

I looked at Johanna—who was carefully not looking at me. She stood slumped against the counter, her empty scotch glass still in her hand.

"How can she come back here?" I asked. "Wouldn't that be dangerous?"

Johanna placed her scotch glass on the counter. "We'll cross that bridge when we come to it. And let's hope we don't." She fingered the glass for a moment, then let go of it.

I looked at the vase of flowers in the center of the table; I stroked the petal of a blood-red dahlia that drooped over its rim. I thought of the raid—presumably still going on—light years away from here.

"What is she so afraid of?" I asked.

Johanna was still watching me. "Heroin withdrawal."

"Besides that."

"Getting caught."

"By whom?"

"Anyone. The cops, Caesar's henchmen, Haswell's henchmen... She's just pulled the plug on quite a few people. They're not going to appreciate it."

All of a sudden I was very tired. I looked at the window and saw that dawn was already seeping in around the edges of the blind. It was time for me to go. But my questions were still unanswered—the trap door, the heroin, Caesar... Johanna's car. Yes—that was what had brought me here in the first place. I looked back at Johanna; she was staring at the floor, her eyes glazed with thought.

"I saw your car," I said, tentatively.

Her eyelids lifted.

"Half a block from Kinky's."

She studied me, wearily—and I saw that I wasn't going to get anywhere.

I gave up. I glanced around the kitchen. Someone was going to have to clean up this mess, get rid of all this hair. And someone else was going to have to get Salal out of the house and onto the bus. But not me. I had to get myself home before the cops came looking for me.

"I'd better go," I said.

"Yes," Johanna agreed. Her gaze traveled down my

body, stopped at my feet. "Make sure you're not taking any hair with you."

I inspected my pant legs, my shoes. "I'll brush myself off when I get outside." Johanna didn't move; I wasn't sure how to make my exit. I took a step towards the door, hesitated. Johanna watched me.

"Do you think she'll be O.K?"

Johanna's expression became sardonic. "Do you?"

We stared at each other.

"Well," I said, putting my hand on the doorknob, "wish her good-bye and good luck." It sounded so inadequate.

"Good-bye and good luck, Maggie," Johanna repeated, not unkindly.

I accepted defeat, and left.

By the time I reached my house, the day was well underway. The paper boys (and girls) were out, dragging their carts along the sidewalks; the morning shift workers were accumulating at the bus stops. I unlocked my front door, stepped across the threshold—and wanted to turn right around and walk back out again. Now that I was home, they knew where to find me. I'd felt safer out on the streets.

I made myself some hot milk (good old mother Meg), sat in the kitchen with my feet up and watched a summer breeze ruffle the bush outside my window. Presumably Salal was on the bus by now, climbing out of the Fraser Valley, entering the mountains. I pictured her dwarfed by her high-backed bus seat, sealed within her headphones—a small, lonely figure, her dark eyes fixed on the windows. But perhaps she felt better now that she'd left the city behind her, now that she could feast her eyes upon limitless miles of forest. Hmm, I thought. I could have used a change of scenery myself.

I took stock of my position. Were the cops finished with me? After all, I'd delivered what I'd promised: a porno movie business and a night club full of minors. So what was I worrying about? It wasn't my fault that Caesar had been there, and it wasn't my fault that he'd escaped. Salal hadn't known about the trap door and hadn't expected Caesar to be there. But if Laurie knew that Caesar was coming, surely Salal would have known it too?

If Salal knew about the trap door, she'd known the whole operation was in jeopardy. Danny Haswell could have escaped. In fact, why hadn't he? Someone had used that trap door—presumably Caesar—and if Caesar knew about the trap door, wouldn't Haswell have known about it too? After all, he owned the building. And Caesar was not—at least not to my knowledge—more than a business acquaintance. Even so, given their line of work, it was conceivable that Haswell might have taken Caesar aside one morning to show him the alternate exit. In which case, why hadn't he used it himself?

Perhaps Caesar had reached the trap door first and had bolted it after him so that by the time Danny got to it.... Yes, that seemed plausible. Caesar would have bolted it to give himself more time to get away, to stall the cops behind him—but knowing, also, that in doing so he was hammering the final nail into Danny's coffin, leaving him with the dope, and no way to get out. Not exactly the action of a friend in need but the two men weren't friends—not any more.

At the back of my mind a thought was niggling, a thought I didn't want to look at—but now it was staring me in the face. What if Salal and Caesar had been in cahoots against Haswell? Had planned the whole thing together? But...I closed my eyes. No, I said to myself. I couldn't have been that wrong, couldn't have misjudged her to that extent. Salal had hated Caesar, I'd seen that for myself. And Johanna had said he was a monster. Yet a few weeks later I'd caught sight of her on Hastings Street, leaning on Caesar's arm.

I stood up and walked to the window. Had Caesar helped them? Conspired with them to get the heroin in the desk, to bolt the trap door so that Haswell couldn't get out? I couldn't—I didn't want to believe it. It wasn't Caesar's style to team up with the law; he had other, more secure ways of settling scores with his enemies. By putting him in jail, he'd deprived himself of a customer, a customer who might very well bear witness against him. Yet what a coincidence that he'd timed his visit so well, that he'd escaped with such finesse. No, it couldn't have been a coincidence. But if it wasn't—what was it?

By now the sun was well up over the housetops, and my eyes felt full of grit. I went upstairs and undressed, climbed into bed, stared at the ceiling. I tried to close my eyes. I rolled onto one side, then the other; I lay flat on my back and counted inhalations. The events of the evening kept replaying themselves like a scratched and jerky newsreel: cops scuttling like crabs, tables bouncing from the ceiling joists, half-naked girls huddled like refugees. My brain was stuck in a groove and wouldn't move on to the next cut.

By mid-morning I was no closer to being asleep and the heat of the summer's day had infiltrated my bedroom, making me feel stupid and muggy-headed. I heard Ben get up, and decided to get up myself. I went downstairs and found him standing by the kitchen sink, downing a liter of milk for breakfast. He was on his way to work. Seeing the shirt he was wearing, I searched through his drawers until I found a clean one, ironed it while he waited. Then he was gone. I made myself some toast, nearly fell asleep with my chin in the butter dish. I went back to bed. But when I closed my eyes I saw Haswell's building again, cops swarming over it like maggots. Again I got up, ran myself a hot bath, climbed into it and stayed there.

"Look, Meg," I said. "You had reservations about this business right from the very beginning, but you believed Salal's story and you wanted to do something about it. You reacted like a liberal and Salal and Johanna treated you like one. They knew you were the type to give a pan-handler sufficient change for bus fare—but not enough for a beer. They acted accordingly. They told you some of the truth—but not all of it. What else did you expect?"

I sat up and reached for my washcloth, sloshed up some water, pressed the cloth over my face. I felt the heat soak into my pores. Maybe you've learned a lesson, I thought, blinking up at the wall where the shadows of the leaves outside fluttered in a square of sunlight. Maybe after this you'll be more willing to make friends with people with whom you have something in common. Maybe you'll stop being so determined to find out how the other half of the world thinks. Maybe you'll accept your limitations. Maybe you'll condescend to get married and knit booties for your grandchildren.

I lay back down and rested my skull against the bottom of the bathtub; the prospect of knitting booties sounded downright idyllic. The water lapped around the perimeter of my face; my eyelids began to droop. Now I'll be able to sleep, I promised myself. I lay there a few minutes longer, watching the reflected sunlight ripple across the wallpaper, finally sat up, reached for the soap. The phone was ringing.

Whoever it was must have really wanted to talk to me. The phone rang a good ten times before I finally plowed out of the bathtub, grabbing a towel on my way into the hall. It was still ringing when I got to it.

"Mrs. Lacey?"

"Speaking."

"This is Detective Sergeant Menzies' office. Will you hold the line, please?"

I held—and heard Menzies come on the phone. His secretary told him who I was.

"Mrs. Lacey? Detective Sergeant Menzies here. We'd like you to come down and talk to us. Something new has come up."

"S-s-something new?" I stammered, feeling the adrenalin prickle through my veins.

"Not something we can discuss on the phone, Mrs. Lacey."

"Oh—yes, I see. When did you want me to come?"

"Now."

I hung up, cursing, my hands already cold and shaking uncontrollably.

CHAPTER FOURTEEN

I DROVE down to the station suffering acute stage-fright. I felt as if I were in free-fall, my foot on the accelerator skittering like a hockey-puck. "Now just keep calm," I kept saying to myself, my teeth chattering in my head. "Just remember not to make any spontaneous remarks. Think before you speak." But the words were meaningless and made no more impression upon me than the recitation of multiplication tables—which was what I tried next. "Seven times six is forty-two; seven times seven is forty-nine; seven times eight is..." I couldn't remember.

I found a place to park in a downtown parkade, walked the three blocks to the station. I stood outside the door of Menzies' office, my legs vibrating like cello strings. I knocked—loudly—and the door opened so suddenly that I almost fell into the room. "Here she is," announced Harry, stepping aside to let me past him. I entered, warily; the three men in the office appeared to have filled it to capacity. But Harry found me a chair and a place to put it, closed the door again and wedged his own chair in front of it. Menzies was behind his desk, Dikeakos sitting to one side of him. They were both watching me closely.

"Did you get some shut-eye?" Harry asked, hitching up the knees of his pant legs before he sat down.

I eyed him with disfavor. I hate people who, before telling me something that they know I'm not going to like, inquire after my health. "No," I answered.

"Neither did we," said Menzies, thus dispensing with the pleasantries. He picked up his pen, twirled it moodily between his fingers. "One thing kept leading to another all bloody night. And we've got some bad news for you." His eyes lifted, held mine—like leeches clamped to my face. "Your informant is dead."

The world ground to a stop. I felt my heart slowing with it: bump—bump—and then it ceased altogether and I hung, suspended—could hear a fly buzzing behind the venetian blind on the other side of the room. Then, as if dragged into a current, everything started moving again: my heartbeats rushed and subsided, my cheeks felt hot. Informant. *My* informant. *Did they know who that was?*

I became acutely aware of their collective scrutiny, was afraid to breathe for fear of giving something away. I tried hard to think— but the eyes on my face effectively paralyzed my thoughts. I saw Dikeakos glance at my hands; I tried to pry my fingers apart from each other.

"I don't understand," I said finally. "Who *was* my informant? And how do you know he—" I stopped, made myself look at each of them in turn. I swallowed.

There was a pause—which lasted forever. Finally Menzies cleared his throat. "He was murdered."

He! I almost cried out with relief, tried—too late I'm sure—to suppress the glee that must have broken out all over my face. "*Murdered!*" I cried. "*Who* was murdered?"

"Caesar Grice," intoned Harry, dropping the words like lumps of lead. I gave him a look of utter incredulity; I no longer needed to act.

"Caesar?" I whispered. Unable to believe it, I looked at the others for confirmation. "He's dead? He didn't get away?" I was understanding less with every moment. "But why are you saying that Caesar was my informant?" Encountering their flat, unyielding stares, I slipped into a moment of intense paranoia, wondered if I'd fallen into the hands of lunatics. I took a deep breath. "You'd better begin at the beginning," I suggested.

"No," said Menzies. "*You'd* better begin at the beginning, Mrs. Lacey."

This remark was followed by another long silence. Again I looked at their faces, was aware that my knees were shaking uncontrollably. I crossed one knee over the other, twisted my calves tightly together. I stared Menzies in the eye. "You've got it wrong," I informed him. "I don't know what you're talking about. I don't know who my informant was—or is," I corrected myself, "but I never had any reason for thinking it was Caesar. Which, if I understand you, is what you are now suggesting."

"Think about it," said Menzies.

I was scared, all right, but I was also getting angry. "Look," I said to him and heard my voice rising, "you're the one with all the answers! He's dead, you say. You say he's my informant because he's dead! Well then you know a hell of a lot more than I do!"

"On the contrary," sneered Menzies. "We know very little. But we can put two and two together. He got out, didn't he? Through a trap door that he told you didn't exist. After informing on an ex-buddy of his that had been two-timing him, after arriving at just the right time to unlock all the doors for us, after filling Haswell's desk full of smack, after bolting the trap door so that no one else could get out. But it seems that someone *else* was onto him." He leaned forward across his desk, glared at me fiercely. "*Who?*"

I was shaking my head. "Wait a min-minute," I stammered. "This is all news to me. All of it." I lowered my eyes, tried to understand how they'd arrived at such a startling conclusion. Caesar had been there. Therefore he could have unlocked the doors, put the office phone on hold, escaped out the trap door. But someone had been onto him, someone who knew what he was doing and didn't appreciate it. And this person had killed him? Again I shook my head, finally looked up. "Where did you find him?"

"On the trap door," Menzies spat—literally—saliva spewing out across his desk. He looked at me as if I had been personally responsible for placing Caesar there.

"On top of it? You mean that's why—"

"It was so hard to lift," Menzies finished for me.

I began to feel sick.

"And it was bolted," Harry chipped in. "He was actually in the act of bolting it when he was attacked."

I turned to look at him—but somehow none of this was penetrating. I couldn't understand it—neither the fact of Caesar's death, nor its implications. "How was he killed?" I asked, but this question seemed to have voiced by someone else, far away.

"Throat slit," pronounced Menzies, "with a very sharp knife."

There was a ringing in my ears; black spots bobbed before my eyes and began reproducing like cancer cells; the office was receding, as if viewed through the wrong end of a telescope. Next thing I knew my nose was in my skirt and there was a hand on the back of my neck, pressing my forehead onto my knees. "Breathe," a voice said, so I obediently inhaled.

"I'm sorry," I said, my voice muffled in my skirt. The black spots were slowly clearing from my vision, but I didn't try to lift my head. I felt safer where I was.

"Shock," Harry said. "I'll go get her some tea." His chair legs scraped; I heard the door open, then close again.

Now there was silence. A fly still buzzed and beat itself against the window; the fluorescent lights hummed; a siren wailed in the distance. I was suddenly much too warm, and getting warmer, like a pressure cooker—heat swelling inside me, sweat squeezing through my pores. I became intensely aware of the nape of my neck, of their gazes, resting there. I was suffocating.

Slowly, reluctantly, I lifted my head and looked straight into the pit of Dikeakos' eyes. For the first time I registered the fact of his presence, the quality of his surveillance. He was a man who studied people the way that some people study racehorses. I knew I had to get out of his sight.

"I'm going to be sick," I said firmly. I stood up and, without looking at either of them, made for the office door. Behind me, I heard Menzies heave himself out of his chair. He followed me out into the corridor.

I didn't vomit—but then I'd known that I wasn't going to. I took refuge in a cubicle, sat on the toilet, tried to figure out what they knew, and where I stood. But it took me a while. Harry was right; I was suffering from shock, and what wits I'd possessed seemed to have abandoned me. If Caesar was dead— murdered, I reminded myself— and they'd come to the conclusion that he was my informant...he would have had it all planned—the trap door, the smack. And even if the trap door were no secret, Caesar, anticipating the raid, could have made sure that he got to it before anyone else and bolted it after him. As I pondered this scenario, I began to feel more confident; here, at last, was a plot that made sense. Until I remembered that all of this was sheer fabrication because as I very well knew, Caesar was *not* my informant. I must have been very tired, because I couldn't quite manage to assimilate this piece of information. Finally I decided that I might be better off without it. Caesar was my informant. It wasn't a bad theory, and I should encourage them to hang onto it.

This was as far as I got. Already Menzies was banging on the washroom door, wanting to know what had happened to me. So I abandoned my cubicle, splashed cold water on my face, returned to my interrogators.

By now Harry was back also, and there was a styrofoam cup steaming on the corner of Menzies' desk. I sipped it gratefully, took sanctuary in its warmth, in the business of stirring it and blowing it...while Dikeakos watched. I decided to pretend that Dikeakos didn't exist.

"Better now?" asked Harry. (Now that I was in trouble, he seemed to have decided to renew our friendship.)

"Yes, thank you." I nodded at him.

"I didn't know if you took sugar or whatever—so I gambled."

"It tastes fine," I assured him. And it did. I was beginning to feel less shaky. At least I knew what they were thinking. It was a definite advantage. I turned back to Menzies.

"So Laurie was right," I said. "Caesar *was* there. Did anybody else see him?"

Menzies harrumphed for a moment, decided to answer me. "No. But that heroin had to come from somewhere."

"Why didn't anyone else see him? Why did he take such a big risk? He walked right by them—under their noses."

200

"But if you remember, it was dark. Ever stood under stage lights and tried to look out at the audience? You can't see a damn thing. Besides which, where's the risk? After all, he was expected—so no one would have been surprised to see him. And once the raid had happened, who cares how many of Haswell's employees figure out that it must have been Caesar that turned them in? What good will that do them?"

"So you figure he came up by the stairs, unlocking the doors as he went, then slipped into Haswell's office, deposited the smack, and climbed out the trap door? Then what? Where would he go from there?"

Menzies flattened his palms upon the surface of his desk. "We found a ladder on the roof of the New Brighton Hotel. As you may remember, the buildings are adjoining, but the New Brighton is about twenty feet higher. We assume that Caesar—or his murderer, but Caesar seems more likely—set up that ladder on the roof of Kinky's prior to the time of the raid. So the murderer made use of it. He went up the ladder, got onto the roof of the New Brighton, and pulled the ladder up after him. Simple. But it took us hours to find the bloody thing."

Him, I said to myself. They're assuming the murderer is a him. "And you think that's what Caesar planned to do also?"

"We're sure of it. Turns out that the entire top floor of that hotel is Caesar's private suite and it too was equipped with a hidden trap door. It's quite the establishment; our boys will probably be going over it for days."

"Right next door?"

"Handy, isn't it? Seems he owned the building."

"The New Brighton?"

"That's right."

I remembered the night Johanna and I had been there, watching the couples reel out of Kinky's, straight into the doors of the New Brighton Hotel. I told them about this.

"Yeah," contributed Harry. "We found about a dozen girls that worked for Caesar living in the hotel. One of them was eight years old. And they were all junkies, thanks to him."

"He must have had a lot of enemies," I commented.

"It's like looking for a grain of sand," Harry agreed.

There was a silence—long enough for me to realize that if I wanted to retain the initiative in this discussion, I should not allow such silences to occur. I racked my brains for another question. "But how did the murderer get onto the roof?"

"Either through the trap door, presumably before Caesar, or he came from the hotel."

"Then he must have used the ladder in order to get onto the roof of Kinky's."

Menzies shrugged. "Probably. Or he could have used a rope. Through we've found no evidence of that. The lab boys are still going over that whole area: the roof, the ladder, the trap doors."

"But then Caesar could have done that too. Could have been coming *from* the hotel, could have been killed in the act of *entering* Kinky's. Did you think of that?" As soon as I'd spoken, I realized that I was getting off track. I *wanted* them to believe that Caesar was my informant. But surely it would look suspicious if I accepted their theory too readily.

"But it makes more sense the other way, don't you think?"

The speaker was Dikeakos. I met his eyes, but could read nothing in them. "I don't know," I answered. "I'd have to think about it."

"We *have* been thinking about it," he assured me.

I could feel my hackles rising. "But you're staking everything on what Laurie said. You've cooked up a plausible theory—but it's a theory—it's not sacrosanct. No one else saw him."

"We all saw that drawer full of smack."

"But that could have been there for hours. Or someone else could have planted it. Did you find any of Caesar's fingerprints?"

"He wears gloves," Menzies answered me.

Oh, I thought, so they'd found that out for themselves. "You mean he was seen wearing gloves?"

"No. But he was wearing gloves when we found him and we were told that he always wears gloves. And the marks on Haswell's desk bear that out."

I digested this, switched to another tack. "And he was killed on the roof? Right on the trap door? Not dragged there from somewhere else?"

Menzies folded his hands on his desk, studied his thumbnails. "That's right," he said flatly. He raised his eyes. "When you cut someone's throat you make a hell of a mess. There's no disguising it."

I envisioned what they must have found: more than two hundred pounds of prime male flesh, felled in a lake of coagulating blood. "Isn't that," I asked, distastefully, "a difficult way to kill someone? Dangerous?"

"Not if you know what you're doing," Menzies answered. "And not if you're taking him by surprise. Requires skill, certainly."

"Strength?"

He pursed his lips. "Maybe. But there were no signs of struggle. It must have happened very fast."

"Did you find the weapon?"

Menzies eyed me. "Not yet."

I cast about for my next question—and then all of a sudden my mind went blank. I couldn't keep it up any more. I felt like I'd been making small talk, something I've never been very good at. Caesar was dead—case closed. I wanted to go home.

"So who wanted him dead, Mrs. Lacey?"

The question startled me. Tea splashed over my skirt and I reached for the napkin Harry had provided me, dabbed at the stain. Finally I looked at Dikeakos who, it seemed to me, hadn't taken his eyes off me for the past half hour. "Danny Haswell?" I suggested, looking as guileless as I knew how. But his question re-alerted me to my danger ("Come on, Meg, keep thinking; it's not over yet"), and I turned back to Menzies.

"Why didn't Haswell escape? Didn't he know about his own trap door?"

"Haswell knew about the trap door," Menzies answered, "and he tried to use it. We figure that's where he was going when Laurie saw him going into the corridor. There were marks from his shoes on the lid of the toilet seat underneath the trap door, and he was undoubtedly the one that didn't replace the panel properly. Which was how we found it in the first place."

"The trap door was hidden?"

"Very well hidden. By a removable ceiling panel."

"Then surely—" I leaned forward, "he must have been there, right under the trap door when the murder occurred. Or very shortly afterwards."

Menzies laced his fingers. "That's possible. But it's also quite possible that Caesar left five—ten minutes before we got there. Knowing, of course, that we were about to arrive."

"Did you question Haswell? Did he hear anything?"

Menzies exhaled—like a surfacing whale. "Mr. Haswell, being a professional, says nothing at all. And he's hired himself a very slick lawyer."

"Did you tell him Caesar was dead?"

"Yes."

"How did he take it?"

Menzies looked over at Harry.

"He didn't believe us," Harry said to me. "He thought we were trying to trick him."

"So he had nothing to do with it?"

"Hard to see how he could have."

I had to agree with him. "And what about that gun? Who did it belong to?"

"Caesar was armed," Menzies answered, "but his gun hadn't been used. The gun that was fired during the raid probably belonged to one of the film crew, though none of them will admit to it and there were no good prints."

"Caesar was armed," I breathed, thinking of the risk his murderer had taken.

Menzies raised his eyebrows. "Taken by surprise," he repeated, reading my thoughts.

I placed my cup on the corner of Menzies' desk, twisted my hands in my lap, pressed my knees together. I made the mistake of looking at Dikeakos. Immediately I was falling into the pupils of his eyes, being dragged towards him. "Keys," I said, but the word was thick in my throat and it took an enormous effort of will to verbalize the rest of the question. "Did he have keys? To Kinky's?" I meant the question for Menzies, but couldn't pull my eyes off Dikeakos.

"Yes, he had keys," replied Dikeakos. He spoke as if we were intimates, shared a special understanding. "He could have opened the doors."

I nodded, slowly, still transfixed by his dark, slightly downward-slanting eyes; again, my mind had stopped. I couldn't have thought up another question if my life had depended upon it.

"But there's another possibility," Dikeakos continued, in that same tone of voice, as if excluding the others from our conversation. He reached into a pocket of his suit jacket, pulled out a package of cigarettes.

There is? I thought, and knew, instinctively, that now the danger was right in front of me, but I felt powerless to save myself. It was as if I were sliding downstream, spinning into the middle of the river, watching the shore slip away from me, irrevocably out of reach. Dikeakos opened the cigarette package, extracted a cigarette.

"And the second possibility is that the murderer is your informant."

I watched him, heard the words, but couldn't extract their sense. "Informant," I repeated, stupidly.

He lit his cigarette, dragged on it—hard—and it was as if I took that drag with him, felt the kick of nicotine in my lungs, felt it ease through my body—though I hadn't smoked a cigarette in ten years.

"Somehow Caesar found out what your informant was up to," Dikeakos explained. "Caesar followed him out the trap door and, as they say, curiosity killed the cat."

"Are you suggesting that the informant planned to trap Caesar as well as Haswell?" Harry asked. Apparently he hadn't heard this theory before.

"Either way," Dikeakos answered, his eyes still on me. "Maybe he planned to get Caesar, or maybe Caesar just happened to walk into Kinky's at the wrong moment. Maybe Caesar caught sight of the informant and decided to follow him and find out what he was up to. And when the informant discovered that Caesar was onto him, he figured he had no

205

choice. You don't let that kind of information into Caesar's hands if you can help it."

Now, finally, his words were getting through to me; my mind was scrabbling like a panicked rodent. Could that have happened to Salal? Could Caesar have found out what she was doing? Followed her? Yet I'd thought—but why had I thought this—that Salal would have been working the other way, unlocking the doors on her way *down*, leaving through a main floor exit because...Because of the trap door. She wasn't supposed to know about the trap door. But what if she *did* know about the trap door but lied about it because she was planning to use it herself, planning to get out before the cops arrived and bolt it shut behind her so that Haswell couldn't get out. And she hadn't counted on Caesar. Hadn't reckoned on his presence there, that night, at that time, in Haswell's office, right on her heels.... Abruptly as they'd started, my thoughts stopped. I was acutely aware of my surroundings again, of Dikeakos' gaze seeping through my skull like a thin, chilling draught. Mustering every ounce of will I possessed, I closed my eyes and shut the man out.

But not his voice. "Mrs. Lacey," he said quietly, and I heard him take another drag on his cigarette, "by virtue of your special role in this investigation, we've let you ask a lot of questions, we've told you what we know about this case. But for reasons that you must be beginning to understand by now, we're going to have to ask you some questions in return. A lot of questions. Your informant may have been the murderer or the victim or neither, but one thing we're almost certain of is that he—or she—" and he paused for a second to let that pronoun sink in, "is a key figure in this case. So we want you to think back to those conversations you had with your informant; we're going to take you through them one by one; we're going to dredge your memory for anything we can find. We want to know who he is—or was; we're determined to establish that fact once and for all. We've got what we think is a comprehensive list of Haswell's employees; we think we know everyone that was in a position to give you the information you received and then passed on to us. So now, with your help, we're going to start eliminating names from the list. Then we'll see who we've got left. All right?"

I risked a glance at his face and yes, there he was; no fairy godmother had dispelled him from my sight. I licked my lips. "I'm very tired," I whispered, "and I've got a terrible memory." I sounded like a child about to cry.

"Just do the best you can. O.K?"

But it wasn't O.K. at all. Even if Caesar *had* been my informant, even if everything had happened the way I'd said it had; even then, I'm sure, I would have made a hash of that interrogation. How many times had the informant phoned me, on what dates, at what times, at my office or at my home, how had he introduced himself, how had he addressed me, where had he got my name, what other names had he mentioned, how had his voice sounded, when did I find the stills and the scraps of film, who'd suggested procuring these, who'd.... At best, they must have thought me incredibly muddle-headed; at worst, they knew I was lying. But nobody shouted at me, or became sarcastic or abusive; Dikeakos did most of it, his voice as quiet and relentless as February rain, until my story was like a sieve and retained no reliable facts at all. "I don't remember," I kept saying. "I'm very bad at things like this. At work I write everything down. I have to, or I forget."

"That's fine," he assured me. "I'm only asking you to try. Now about that last phone call...." And it would start all over again.

The whole thing lasted anywhere from an hour to ten hours; I never knew. By the time he sat back and said, "Thank you, Mrs. Lacey, you've been very cooperative," my head was splitting and I was ready to scream—which was the first thing I did when I got out of that office, out of the police station, and into the comparative privacy of my car. I howled, screamed, wept, drove my fingernails into my forearms, beat my fists against the steering wheel—anything to expel the accumulated tension, the fear, the shame. It isn't pleasant to be afraid; it's a degrading experience. People should remember that when bringing up children.

About half an hour later, I finally started the drive home. The air was still warm, smoked purple with dusk; the teenagers were out in full force on Granville Street. Boys like my son, girls like Lily Kubicek. Slowly, the thoughts that I'd suppressed, that I hadn't dared think while under the scrutiny of my interrogators, began surfacing to my consciousness. What had I done? With the best intentions in the world, I'd dug myself into a morally questionable and dangerous position—from which there was no way out. Caesar was dead—slaughtered like a side of beef. And I'd been made an accessory to the act.

CHAPTER FIFTEEN

MY PHONES were still tapped. I was followed everywhere I went; I was interrogated several times a week; my office and townhouse were repeatedly searched. Harry befriended me, phoned me nearly every day "to keep me informed," took me out for drinks and told me many things "in confidence," encouraged me to do the same. Sometimes I came very close to doing so. I have never felt more alone; I would have done anything for a safe shoulder to cry on. But there was no such thing as a safe shoulder anymore.

Now, I'd plead silently, thrashing sleepless in my bed (afraid to speak aloud even in the privacy of my own bedroom), now is when I need you, Tom, chivalry and all. But in the cold light of day I knew that even if he'd materialized, I couldn't have confided in him. In doing so, I would have compromised him, and Salal's trust, would have placed her fate in his hands. I had no right to do so. So it was just as well that he wasn't around.

Meanwhile the murder was all over the newspapers; the media were milking their one-man-Mafia for all he was worth: romanticizing his iniquities, glorifying his achievements, reveling in his demise. According to the papers, various people had been held for questioning and new evidence was being discovered daily—but none of the evidence cited was new to me, so I suspected that Menzies was merely rationing it out to them bit by bit, keeping up the supply of copy, maintaining the illusion of progress. "In confidence"

Harry had told me that a number of Haswell's former employees had disappeared: a Jamaican short-order cook who had been in the country illegally; one of the bartenders who, they'd discovered, had skipped parole in Toronto four years previously; and the secretary, known as Sally, who'd apparently had the night off and had not been seen since.

"You think one of them might be my informant?" I asked him, dubiously.

Harry blew out his cheeks. "Hard to say. The bartender, maybe. But it depends on how the murder was done, and we still haven't figured that out. The informant could have exited out one of the alley doors, entered the New Brighton, gone up to Caesar's apartment, out his trapdoor and over the roof to Kinky's. Or he could have unlocked the alley doors and then gone up to the fourth floor, walked right through the film studio, into the washroom and out the trap door."

"But then someone would have seen him," I objected.

"Not if he was careful. After all, only Laurie saw Caesar. No one else noticed him. The room was dark and there was no shortage of stuff to hide behind. Or—and this is a whole other can of worms—the informant might have had an accomplice. Let's say he was a member of the film crew. He unlocked the doors, returned to his camera and let his accomplice do the dirty work. The accomplice disposes of Caesar, then goes over the roof to Caesar's apartment, wipes the knife and sticks it back in the kitchen drawer. He washed up in Caesar's apartment—that much we do know—then changed his clothes and left."

"You've found the knife?"

Harry made a rueful face. "Problem is—we've found too many knives. Caesar owned three kitchen knives that were up to the task, lethal weapons every one of them."

"But the lab tests...?"

"Don't tell us anything conclusive. Maybe it was one of them and maybe it wasn't. Whoever this guy was, he was very tidy. Best clean-up job we've ever seen."

"No dirt, no hair?"

Harry was shaking his head. "A damp towel. A tiny bit of gravel on the kitchen floor. Lots of fingerprints—but all the fresh ones are Caesar's. For sure the murderer was wearing gloves."

"Wearing gloves when he killed him? Or afterwards?"

"That part's got us stumped. Did he kill him with his bare hands and then slip on a pair of gloves before going into Caesar's place? He must have, or he'd have left bloody fingerprints all over the place. But then what did he do with the gloves? What did he do with his clothes? He *must* have changed his clothes. You make a slice like that—I don't care how fast you are—you'll get blood all over the place."

"One cut?"

"One cut—a beauty. Straight through to the vertebrae. Caesar was practically decapitated. The murderer got him so fast that he didn't know what hit him. That takes some doing." He protruded his underlip; I stared at it, and swallowed.

As usual, I wanted to ask about Salal: Where had they searched, what had they found out about her, who had they questioned? And as usual, I didn't dare, was afraid to express too much interest in her. Harry, after all, had been assigned to my company for exactly that reason—to tempt me to ask the questions that I knew I mustn't ask. Sometimes I'd lead up to it, would encourage him to talk about the Jamaican cook or the missing bartender, camouflaging my real interest, intending to ask just one question about Salal—only to discover that when the moment came, I couldn't get the words out. It was as if she'd become taboo, a name that couldn't cross my lips.

The cops recorded the voices of ten men, called me down to the station to listen to the tape. I said it could be this one or that one, but failed to identify any one of them for sure. Later, stopping by my office, Harry informed me that two of the voices on the tape had been recorded by women.

"Women!" I protested. "But I keep telling you, my informant was a man! And you yourselves are always talking about 'him.'"

"Yeah," Harry looked reflective, "but that's just prejudice. Most of us have never met a woman with the qualifications to commit this murder. But Dikeakos insists that anyone who really knew how to use a knife could have done it. He says that she could have disguised her voice or—" He gave me a furtive look. "You could be lying about it."

I met his gaze. By now I'd become accustomed to these sly, prying barbs; they were the price I paid for having someone to talk to. "Maybe," I agreed.

Harry shrugged. "Well, he's supposed to suspect everyone. And he's a damn good detective. The best."

"But do you have any female suspects?"

Harry grimaced. "Not since we were told that the Jamaican cook had an accent you could cut with a knife. Then there's that damn secretary; we still haven't figured out what happened to her. One of the other girls could have been the informant—but it takes a certain kind of person, psychologically, I mean, to commit a murder like this one, and I doubt that any of them would have been up to it."

"What happened to the theory that Caesar was my informant? I was wondering about that when you called me in to listen to the tape. If you think Caesar was my informant, why expect me to identify any of the voices on that tape?" As I asked the question I saw something flicker across his face, and my heart skipped a beat. "Or was he—Caesar—You mean his voice was on that tape?"

Harry's eyelids lowered; he shifted his weight. Damn, I thought fervently, damn, damn, damn! Why hadn't I thought of that? But it had never occurred to me to listen for Caesar's voice among all those others; I was still living in the Middle Ages, before the advent of electronic immortality. When had they recorded him? But they'd undoubtedly been tapping his phones for years.

"So the 'Caesar as informant' theory is dead," I concluded, dryly.

"No—not exactly dead. Nothing's ever—"

"But out of favor."

"Well, to be frank with you," (again), "Dikeakos was never too keen on that theory in the first place. He says it's out of character—for Caesar, that is. Caesar wouldn't collaborate with the police. He doesn't need to. He could have done in Haswell a hundred other ways, just as effectively and without half the risk. Let's face it, compared to organizations like the Mafia, we're bloody ineffective."

After every one of these sessions with Harry—sessions that invoked as many questions as they satisfied—I'd wander about my house, seething with disquiet, trying, for the millionth time, to figure out what had happened that night, what had really happened. I tried to convince myself that Caesar's murderer could have been an outsider, one of those innumerable enemies that the newspapers made so much of. It was possible, but not likely. So then I considered the scenario that Dikeakos had suggested, the possibility that Caesar's visit had coincided with the time of the raid, that Caesar had come upon Salal just as the police were charging up the stairs, just as she was climbing through the trap door. But if this were the case, why was Salal carrying a knife? And without the advantage of surprise, how did she manage to overpower a man at least twice her size? How did she make such a perfect getaway? No, Caesar had not been killed in self-defense. Very little had been left to chance.

All right—suppose that Salal—Salal and Johanna?—had planned to kill Caesar. It was Johanna that I'd seen with him, coming out of the hotel door; it was Johanna that would have cased the New Brighton, that knew about Caesar's apartment, its trap door and its selection of knives. It was Johanna that set him up. She told him that she was planning to sick the cops on Haswell; she persuaded him to add his smack to the cause. And Caesar agreed? Maybe. Even if these methods were, by his standards, amateur, he might take malicious pleasure in adding his two bits to the crazy plan that his lady friend cooked up. Or—and this seemed more likely—Johanna didn't even tell Caesar about the raid. She thought up some other pretext for getting him up to Haswell's fourth floor at quarter to eleven on a Tuesday night. Although he did deliver the smack. But maybe he didn't. Maybe it was Salal that planted the heroin in Haswell's desk, using those same gloves that came in so handy later.

At some point—by then I'd lost all track of time, had been hanging, for millenia, from a cliff-face by my fingernails—it dawned on me that I'd lost my stooges. I was still receiving impromptu visits from officers of the law, I was still a regular visitor at the police station—but there was no longer a man waiting for a taxi in the lobby of the apartment building across the street, and when I walked to the store there was no one wandering along behind me, peering at house numbers. All of a sudden, it was possible to be alone. I began going for long walks, mostly at night, when I couldn't sleep; when I needed, more than anything else, to be somewhere—anywhere—where nobody else knew where I was. At home or in my office I was always on guard, renovating my defenses, memorizing my facts so that the next time they came I'd have my story straight. It was only when I was out walking that I felt anonymous enough to let my thoughts flow uncensored. That I was able to abandon my fortifications and really inspect my situation. I came to no comforting conclusions.

One afternoon as I was leaving the police station, having failed yet another interrogation, Dikeakos intercepted me in the corridor. He hadn't been the one questioning me that day, I'd been relegated to a minion—but perhaps he'd already received a precis of the results. "I'd like you to come in tomorrow afternoon for a lie detector test," he announced, without preamble.

I'm sure I went pale. "Is that legal?" I asked.

"If you agree to it, it is."

"I've heard that they're not very reliable," I gushed, nervously. "It might say that I'm lying even if I'm not."

"It's just a check," he said. He was neither reassuring nor accusing; he was making no apology for his suspicions of me. "We don't take it as proof. It doesn't work for everyone."

"But it works for most people?" My tongue felt thick and dry.

"Most," he agreed.

I stared at him, tried to think of something to say.

"We haven't been getting very far with you, Mrs. Lacey." He reached for one of his ubiquitous cigarettes.

"But that's not my fault!"

"Your story's a mess."

"You try!" I protested. "You tell me who phoned you on

July 31st, over a month ago. You tell me who phoned you, when they phoned, what they said. If it had been a regular business call I would have made notes. But he explicitly told me not to. And he phoned several times. It's not like remembering one event."

He watched me, exhaling a steady stream of cigarette smoke through his nostrils. "Will you agree to take the test?"

"Can I think about it? I want to get advice. I know I heard somewhere that they're not accurate."

"Either that, or you're lying," he said, indifferently. He turned on his heel. "Phone me tomorrow morning."

"Yes," I breathed, staring after his retreating, impeccably tailored back.

That night, I went out walking, and having made sure that there was no one watching nor following me, I slipped into a phone booth and dialed Johanna's number. Please be home, I prayed, plugging my free ear against the noise of the traffic outside. Her phone was ringing. She answered.

"Hello?"

"Johanna—it's Meg."

There was an infinitesimal pause. "Who did you want to speak to?"

"Johanna! It's me—Meg."

"I—I'm sorry. I don't think I know you. Are you selling something?"

"Joh—"

She'd hung up.

I stood there with my mouth open; the receiver trembled in my hand. I imagined myself hurling it through the window of the phone booth; my ears ringing with the sound of splintering glass. Then I replaced the receiver, slowly, exactly onto its hook. I stared at the dial. All right, I thought—and a clean, murderous power charged me from head to foot. I'll tell them everything I know. I'll take their damn test—and I'll tell them the truth, the whole truth, and nothing but the goddamn bloody truth.

I slammed out of the phone booth and stomped down the sidewalk. I don't think I've ever been so angry. I'd lied for them, I'd risked my own neck to save theirs. And this was how they repaid me! I couldn't believe how heartless they were—and how stupid. Because they were at *my* mercy; they were utterly dependent upon my good will. Of which I had none left.

I strode through the suburbs, down quiet, tree-lined streets, past solid, respectable houses—as out of place as a marching band. I was gesturing and arguing out loud; I kicked a tin can clear across the street into a tree trunk. If I'd had a knife, I would have started slashing tires. After about a mile of this, I considered the possibility that Johanna hung up on me because she considered me stupid enough to be calling her from a tapped phone. It didn't make me like her any better. After about another mile, it occurred to me that Johanna might have reason to think that her own phone was tapped. She hadn't told me that I'd got the wrong number (which would have been the obvious response), she'd denied knowing me. If she thought her own phone was tapped, then she couldn't deny being herself (because they knew who she was), she could only deny knowing me, however implausible that seemed.

But how had they got onto her? Had someone seen her with Salal? Or, more likely, had someone seen her with Caesar? As I had. Serves her right, I thought bitterly, satisfied to think that I might not be the only one suffering the attentions of the police. Not that they'd get anything out of her. Johanna was good at keeping her mouth shut. I could vouch for that.

Reluctantly, I relinquished my plans for revenge. I had to give her the benefit of the doubt. I didn't forgive her—but if it were true that her phone was tapped, then she couldn't have answered in any other way. And my phone call had been a mistake.

My anger was spent, but the fear was returning—a gnawing anxiety eating through my innards like acid. What was I going to say, tomorrow, when they strapped me to that machine, when they asked me why I'd phoned Johanna last night? ("You know, Mrs. Lacey, your friend, Johanna. She's a hooker; she was involved with Caesar. Why were you phoning her?") Perhaps they'd already traced the call to that phone booth on Cambie Street; perhaps they were there now, taking fresh fingerprints from the receiver. They've got us, I thought. The game's up, we've lost. I've got to vanish, like Salal. But what about Ben? I couldn't disappear on Ben—nor could I ask him to tell lies to cover me. No wonder more mothers don't take up a life of crime.

No longer aware of what I was doing, or where I was going, or why, I started walking again. I arrived on a main street and stopped, shocked by the bustle, the glare, the traffic. In front of me there was another phone booth. I found a quarter in my pocket, heard a phone number repeating itself in my mind like a prayer: 677-1428-677-1428-677.... I stumbled into the booth, lifted the receiver, inserted my quarter. The phone rang once. Then Margot's voice materialized in my ear, her French accent, for some reason, more noticeable over the phone. "You have reached the offices of Healey, Mulligan and Proctor, barristers and solicitors. I'm sorry that no one is available to take your call right now, but if you wish to leave a message, you may do so after the tone. Our usual business hours are...." I removed the receiver from my ear; I stared at the mouthpiece. What was I going to say? "Help? They're going to give me a lie-detector test!" How could they help? What did I expect them to do? In my relationship with the police I was absolutely on my own, and had been, from the very beginning. That was the deal I'd made. But I hadn't—and couldn't have—foreseen Caesar's murder. They'd sprung that upon me afterwards. So the contract was void; I didn't have to honor it. I didn't—I couldn't!

I stood on the bright strip of sidewalk between the streaming cars and the storefronts. The city swirled around me like a whirlpool, the neon lights, the rushing cars, the couples reeling out of restaurants, the line-ups inching into the movie-theaters. I thought of Salal, pleading with me to save her—but how could I save her when I couldn't save myself? I started to cry. The neon lights swam and shimmered through my tears; three teenage girls passed and glanced at me, curiously, an older couple was approaching...Oh my God, I thought, I'm making a scene. I plunged back into the sidestreets. I saw a taxi stopped in the middle of the road, its interior lit, its engine idling. I gave the driver my address, then huddled into the corner of the back seat. As soon as I got home, I headed straight for my bedroom, burrowed myself under the bedclothes and bawled.

I've had many a good cry, but none quite like that one—as if I'd been hauled inside out and wrung like a dishrag, as if I were decomposing, returning to the liquids that engendered me. Afterwards, I slept.

When I woke up the next morning, I felt detached, light-headed. I drove to my office, searched my files and came up with the name of a criminal lawyer. I phoned her. I asked her about lie detector tests, the legal ramifications involved in taking them, and refusing to take them. She told me that as far as she knew, they weren't used anymore because the results weren't admissable as evidence in court.

"Then why did he suggest it?"

"Not for court purposes. He's probably doing the obvious—trying to verify your information. Either that or he's trying to intimidate you."

When I finished talking to her, I phoned Dikeakos and told him I wasn't going to take the test. I offered no explanation; he accepted my decision without comment.

After that, the cops seemed to lose interest in me. Harry's visits became more infrequent, Menzies' secretary stopped making appointments for me, and the detectives stationed on the doormat turned out to be proselytizing Mormons. The newspaper articles retreated deeper and deeper into the back pages of the paper: "Caesar's Killer Still at Large," "Detectives Stumped." A day passed in which I forgot to think about the murder at all. Then a new serial killer began roaming the suburbs: a child in Surrey disappeared, two bodies were found in Delta. Presumably these new murders occupied the minds of the police as well as the front pages of the newspapers. Life goes on; even murderers get usurped. It was over.

Almost over. One evening I got a phone call.

"Meg? It's Johanna."

As soon as I heard her voice I was right back there in that phone booth, rage blasting through me like an explosion of breaking glass.

"You've got the wrong number!" I blurted, and hung up, fast.

Unfair? Well, let me tell you something. If Johanna's phone was tapped that night, I never heard about it from the police. Which is odd—don't you think? If you were a police detective, wouldn't you have followed that up? A connection between me and a hooker that serviced Caesar?

As far as I was concerned, she didn't deserve another chance.

CHAPTER SIXTEEN

HASWELL was tried and convicted. I heard that he made a good impression in the witness box, looking as boyish and penitent as he knew how. But there was no shortage of evidence against him and the judge, a woman, gave him a stiff sentence. Three years later he was out on parole. The jails are overcrowded; well-behaved prisoners, regardless of their crimes, are let loose upon the public as soon as possible.

I didn't go to the trial. I didn't want to see Menzies or Dikeakos ever again. I felt like someone who has survived a war or an earthquake; I craved boredom and security, I appreciated things that I'd formerly taken for granted: the relative safety of my home, the health of my children. And when Tom finally returned from the Northwest Territories, he found me much easier to get along with, less defensive, less proud. After some soul-searching and many frank conversations, we got back together again. He's learned not to offer help unless I ask for it, and I've stopped getting angry at him for caring what happens to me.

Summer rolled round again. The economy was recovering, and business was picking up. Ben enrolled in a computer drafting course, Katie found a new boyfriend. I got a letter from Portugal, where Joau and Victor Goncalves were visiting relatives. Enclosed in the letter was a photograph of the two of them, both scowling into the sun, standing before the whitewashed cottage in which they were born, with their diminutive and aged mother smiling proudly between them. Would that more of my cases ended in family photographs.

But I now specialized in divorce cases. I never went looking for missing children anymore. When distraught parents phoned me, begging me to help them find their progeny, I referred them to someone else. I wouldn't—I couldn't talk to them. If I did I'd start screaming: "Go find your own kids! I'll tell you where they are! They're out selling ass and stealing to pay for their drug habit—you need me to tell you that? Don't you read newspapers? Don't you know anything about the society you live in?" It was a subject that rubbed me raw, a topic I couldn't discuss without getting bitter and righteous. And I refused to investigate the reasons for these emotions.

But the past doesn't go away. (At least mine never does.) If not properly exorcised, it slides into the future and crouches in the wings, waiting to stage a relapse. So I was dismayed—but not surprised—when I got ambushed.

I was attending the opera. I don't like opera—but Tom likes opera and sometimes persuades me to come along, assuring me that *this* particular opera will surely win me over. It never does—but I enjoy watching Tom watching the opera, a glazed look in his eyes, a little smile on his lips, contentedly tapping the beat on my forearm and humming, not quite inaudibly and definitely out of tune. The second act was over and we'd been herded out into the lobby again where, along with everyone else, we were sipping drinks and inhaling second-hand cigarette smoke. Tom was accosted by an acquaintance and they began comparing this production to productions they'd seen before, discussing the merits of the singers. I was pretending to listen, and meanwhile following the progress of a truly stunning blue gown—when I felt a touch on my shoulder.

"Meg?"

It was Margot. Her plain but pleasant face was beaming up into mine; she was wearing a charming, round hat with a little feather in the front of it, a hat that, by the style of it, she had inherited from her mother.

Taken aback, and not knowing how to greet her, I

pointed to the blue gown. "Look at that," I said.

"Mmm." She nodded. "But you'd have to be tall to wear it." She indicated Tom and his acquaintance, standing a few feet away from us. "Are you with them?"

"One of them. The one with the beard." I watched Margot appraise him.

Was she here alone? I wasn't going to ask. If Johanna were here, I didn't want to know about it.

"I came with a friend," she explained, helpfully. "She's in the washroom. But Meg—" She touched my sleeve. "I want to see you. I've been thinking about you. When can we get together?"

I felt the heat spreading up my neck. "Why do you want to see me?" The theater beeper started beeping, signaling that the intermission was ending.

"To talk."

I stared out across the lobby, avoiding her bright, watchful gaze. People were downing their drinks, stubbing their cigarettes, searching out ashtrays and garbage cans. "I don't want to talk."

"But I do." She was emphatic. "I'll come see you at your office. When?"

Tom was parting with his acquaintance; the crowd was milling slowly towards the doors that led into the theater.

"I don't know, Margot. I really don't think that anything productive can—"

"In the evening? Tomorrow evening?"

Tom was standing in front of us. "Time to go?" he suggested, looking at both of us, inquiringly.

"Yes." Margot nodded at him. "Seven-thirty," she said to me. "I will be at your office at seven-thirty. O.K?"

I gave her a look of exasperation. I was still unwilling to see her and determined to say so—

"Oh!" Margot cried. "There she is!" And like a bird she took flight, pursuing an older, grey-suited woman towards the far theater doors. "Genevieve!" Margot called out, waving her program. Genevieve stopped at the doors, waited for Margot to catch up. As they disappeared into the theater, Margot gave me a wave.

The beeper continued insistently; the lobby was emptying fast. I looked at Tom, who was looking at me. "And now for the gory climax," he announced, happily, taking me by the arm.

I didn't want to see her. Phone her and tell her so, I said to myself. Phone Mr. Healey. I bet you still know his number by heart. But I didn't phone Mr. Healey. And later that day, I thought: Well, maybe I should find out what she's got to say. After all, I'd never blamed Margot as I'd blamed Johanna and Salal; there'd been no contract between us, no friendship to betray. But even so, I didn't want the memories stirred up. "Don't go," I encouraged myself. "You never said you'd meet her. She has no right to expect you." But when seven-thirty rolled around, I was there in my office, pretending to be catching up on my paperwork.

"So," I greeted her, in no mood to mince words, "have you come to confess all?"

She gave me a dubious glance, took off her coat and deposited it over the back of my sofa. "I came to talk to you about that phone call. The time that Johanna hung up on you." She sat down.

I propped myself on the edge of my desk; I felt my eyelids droop, a sardonic expression congeal upon my face. It was Johanna's expression—it was her look, not mine—and I tried to get rid of it.

"We thought the phone was tapped," Margot explained earnestly.

"I thought you thought that."

"Not your phone—her phone."

"I understand," I assured her, not at all understandingly. "But it wasn't," I pointed out. "Tapped," I added.

"No, I guess it wasn't. But we couldn't know that until afterwards. At the time... You see, the cops had just left."

"Left where? Johanna's house?"

"Yes! They showed up out of the blue! They wanted to talk to Johanna. And they hadn't been gone five minutes when you called. So as soon as the phone rang, Johanna said:

223

'It's tapped.' Because we thought that you must have—" She stopped.

"That I must have what?"

She clasped her hands in her lap. "It was a terrible evening. It was very confusing. The cops showed up at the door—but they weren't asking about Salal, they were asking about Caesar! And they wouldn't tell us why they were there or who'd told them about Johanna—"

"Someone had seen her with Caesar," I said, filling in the blanks.

"Yes!" She looked surprised.

"Well they weren't exactly discreet. I saw them myself."

"Yes, I know. So that's why we thought that you—"

"Ah!" I interrupted her. Now I got it. "You thought *I'd* sicked them onto her."

Margot's forehead buckled. "No—at least—we didn't know. Johanna couldn't think who else would have— We thought the pressure, you know? We knew you were under a lot of pressure and that the cops might have—"

"Did you?" I interrupted her, sliding off the desk onto my feet. There was an intense, high ringing in my head. "You knew, did you?" I walked over to the windows, digging my fingernails into my palms. "You knew I was being interrogated every goddamn day, making up lies left, right and center; you knew I was being followed everywhere I went, that my house and office were searched, that my phone never stopped ringing, that I was afraid to talk out loud, that I couldn't eat, couldn't sleep, that they were threatening to give me a lie detector test—" I turned on her. "That's why I phoned you!"

Margot's expression hadn't changed—but her face was turning pink.

I leaned against the wall. "I'm sorry. But I told you I didn't want to talk about it."

"*I* am sorry," Margot apologized, much more sincerely than I had. "I see that it was much worse than we knew. We thought that, being on their side—"

"*They* didn't think that I was on their side. They thought that I was withholding information. They weren't after me—

224

they wanted my informant. And they didn't believe that I didn't know who he was."

"But he phoned you anonymously. I thought you told them that."

I looked at her pityingly. "Margot, that story was pretty thin. It was good enough to get the police to organize a raid, but it was no protection in a murder case."

"A murder case?" Margot looked startled, sat back. "Oh. Yes. I see."

"But let me assure you," I added. "They never found out about Johanna through me. She can't blame me for that."

Margot was nodding. "We never blamed you. Not for anything. But we couldn't accept that phone call. Because we thought—"

"I understand that," I said, holding up both hands, surrendering. "I do. I didn't at the time, but—" I shrugged. "You thought the phone was tapped. An understandable fear, in the circumstances. But for me—" I stopped. Did I really want to get into this? Margot was watching me attentively. "For me that phone call was the last straw."

"What do you mean?"

I looked at her for a moment, struck, yet again, by how nice she was, how sincere—at least that's how she appeared. "Nobody trusted me," I answered, finally. "Salal told me lies—lies that I passed onto the cops, lies that they blamed me for, afterwards. And Johanna wouldn't tell me what the hell she was doing! The three of you stuck me out there on the front line like cannon-fodder—but no one had the courtesy to tell me what was going on."

"But you knew what was going on! You were in on it right from the beginning. We were going to shut down Danny Haswell."

"And Caesar?" I asked, sweetly.

Margot looked blank.

"You remember Caesar?" I inquired sarcastically. "The guy they found on the roof?"

Margot watched me, her forehead criss-crossed with wrinkles. "Of course," she answered, warily.

"Well?" I persisted. "That's why they visited you, right?

They wanted to know who killed Caesar. They wanted to know where Johanna was on the night of his murder. So what did you tell them?" I stared at her, aggressively.

"Johanna was with Salal at the time; she was bringing her home from Kinky's. But we couldn't tell the cops that—so I had to say that she'd been with me, at my place."

"Did they believe you?"

She bit her lower lip, glanced down at her hands. "I think so. We weren't sure. We got the feeling that they were grasping at straws, that they didn't really have anything on us—except for Johanna having been seen with—with Caesar, of course."

"And why *was* she with Caesar?"

"She said they'd just had a—a bit of fun together, nothing serious, and that she hadn't seen—"

"I didn't ask you what she told the police. What did she tell *you*?"

Margot's eyes lifted, met mine. "Nothing."

"You didn't ask?"

Again she was avoiding my gaze.

"You knew what she thought of him. Then you found out that she'd been having—what did you call it?—a bit of fun with him, and then you learned that he'd been murdered on the same damn night as the raid! What on earth did you think?"

Her eyes were downcast, fingers twisted in her lap. "I didn't know what to think." An expression of pain crossed her face. "I mean, even if they had—had killed him or whatever—I wasn't going to tell on them. So what did it matter?"

"Murder doesn't matter?"

Margot's lips compressed. "Maybe in some cases, it doesn't."

"And who's the judge of that?"

Her eyes met mine, head-on. "God."

I almost started to laugh. So there! I'd been right all along. She *was* religious. "Not the courts?" I suggested.

"The courts make mistakes." Margot's voice was low, but defiant. She knew that she was uttering heresies, but she was going to stand by her beliefs. "And these were special circumstances."

"Life is full of special circumstances," I commented dryly.

She didn't look at me, said nothing.

"So you never even asked her."

Margot shifted, sighed. "Yes, I asked. But she said the same thing. She said: 'Why do you want to know? If Salal killed him—if I killed him—are you going to turn us in?'"

"But you never asked her what she was doing with Caesar?"

Margot looked uncomfortable. "I don't ask about things like that."

"You don't? You didn't ask her why she was consorting with a monster? What a strange relationship you must have. My lover right or wrong, is that how you see it?"

"But Johanna can't tell me everything!" Margot pleaded, stung. "How could she?" Her eyes clung to mine, accusing, defenseless. "She protects me too! I protect myself!"

I stared at her—and then remembered Johanna's johns. Finally, I understood. A good part of Johanna's life was kept secret from Margot; there must have been all sorts of things that Margot didn't know. I couldn't imagine how they avoided such topics—but I now understood that they did so, that they'd found ways to get around them.

"When you live like Johanna and Salal do," Margot continued, "of course you have secrets. If you don't keep them, you don't survive. I don't expect Johanna to tell me everything she knows, everything she does. I trust that she loves me—" Her voice trembled, and she stopped, got it back under control, "I trust her to treat me fairly. Of course I may be wrong—but we all run that risk. Love is a gamble, everyone knows that."

I studied her, thoughtfully. In my line of work, one learns a lot about couples, and I know that many people insist on trusting their mates in the face of all kinds of evidence against them. Most of us judge others by the way they treat us—which was why Margot's perception of Johanna did not match my own.

"I guess I don't think that Johanna treated me fairly," I said, after a silence.

"Because she didn't tell you everything?"

"If I'd known, at the beginning, what I was letting myself in for, I wouldn't have agreed to get involved."

Margot tilted her head. "Are you so sure that, in the beginning, Johanna could have told you what you were letting yourself in for?"

I sighed. "No, I'm not sure. But she knew more than she was telling me. She said as much."

"She *was* trying to protect you—and Salal. It would have been dangerous for you if you'd known too much."

"I didn't feel exactly protected."

Margot's lips pursed. Her eyes strayed to the Aikido photographs on my walls; she sighed. "It is possible," she acknowledged, "that she misjudged the situation. I don't think she knew, any more than I did, that the police were being so hard on you."

I thought about this. I reviewed the sequence of events; I wondered if Margot had ever speculated about our chance meeting on that rush-hour bus; I wondered if Salal had kept secrets from Johanna. I wondered if any of them possessed the whole story, or if they'd each, secretly, inserted a chapter of their own—a chapter that changed the final result.

"No," I admitted, "she probably didn't."

CHAPTER SEVENTEEN

THE FOLLOWING week, Margot got in touch with me again. She suggested that we go out for out for a drink together. I was a little taken aback (Margot wanted us to become friends?), but I'd been feeling...I'm not sure—depressed, troubled? A drink sounded like a possible solution. We decided to throw in a little exercise for good measure; we'd walk from her apartment in the West End to the Sylvia Hotel. "But I want to show you something on the way," Margot said, as we set out.

"Show me what?"

"You'll see."

I gave her a suspicious glance.

"It's a surprise. You'll be interested."

So we detoured through the sidestreets until we reached Margot's "surprise." It turned out to be an older home (circa 1905, crammed between the apartment buildings), which had probably once housed a single, upper-middle class family, when families were still of Victorian proportions. Now such houses were usually converted into old age homes or divided up into apartments—but as we walked up the front sidewalk, I noticed that this one didn't appear, at least from the outside, to have suffered either fate.

Lights were on all over the house. I could hear music from inside—rock music, loud—but not unbearably loud. As we stepped onto the porch, the front door slammed open, and a group of teenagers stumbled straight into us. They were laughing, talking, smoking—I received a confused impression of dyed, gelled hair, cheap perfume, acne, black leather, skin-tight pants—youth. "Pardon us," said one, as they parted to let us through. "Welcome," smirked another, holding the door open to receive us—and then they clattered down the front steps, loud into the night.

Inside, there were more of them. Many more. At first I thought it was a party—but it wasn't hectic, like a party, and I could see no evidence of alcohol or drugs. There were at least a dozen teenagers in the living room, draped over the furniture, sprawled on the floor; the television was on in one corner, a board game was in progress on the coffee table, and a girl appeared to be asleep in the middle of the carpet. A strata cloud of cigarette smoke hung in the air, about four feet off the ground. We turned into the hall, passed a darkened room in which more bodies were visible, their faces reflecting the movie on a V.C.R. screen. But the kitchen was the real hub of this house: there were teenagers sitting at the table, leaning against the counters, squatting against the walls; they talked over and around each other while making tea, drinking coffee, buttering slabs of bread, snacking out of chip bags and cereal cartons, scraping their cigarette ashes into empty pop cans. I say "teenagers," but some of them could have been younger; there was quite a range of ages. And I could tell, looking around, that this was not a chapter of the 4-H Club, not a gathering of Junior Achievers. These were rebels and defectors. But why were they assembled here?

We were stared at, of course, but allowed to walk among them, unchallenged. I followed Margot through the rooms on the main floor, wondering what we were doing here; I stepped over the card game taking place in the middle of a hallway; I paused to read the notice posted on the bathroom door. It was a bad tricks list, a description of the johns, their cars, their license numbers...the men to watch out for. Then we turned into another dimly lit, crowded room (or was this the living room again?) and I saw a figure arise from the couch and loom towards us through the smog. The so-called surprise? Johanna.

Of course I'd considered this possibility, but I'd thought Margot more subtle. Having been brought this far, I waited, stolidly, like a horse brought to water, determined that they weren't going to make me drink. Johanna stood in front of us.

"I brought Meg," said Margot—defensively? "I thought I'd show her around."

Johanna looked at me. "Hi." She didn't sound friendly. In fact she didn't seem any more pleased to see me than I was to see her. Apparently Margot hadn't let her in on this plot.

"What is this place?" I asked her.

Johanna's eyebrows lifted; she looked at Margot—clearly surprised that I didn't know. And Margot looked wary, like a child that's been caught playing her parents off against each other. Johanna turned back to me. "It's a drop-in center for street kids."

Once again I stared around me, at two girls entwined in an armchair, at a thin, acne-scarred youth in the corner, who was working his way through a formidable stack of comic books. "But I've never heard of this place. Who funds it?"

"I do."

I stared at her, smiled, started shaking my head.

"Yes, I do," Johanna insisted. "We're also getting some money from the city, and we're hoping to get more. In fact we've applied to all sorts of people."

"But—"

Our eyes held. We'd forgotten Margot, forgotten our grievances—we were back on old ground. I was being intrigued, challenged, charmed by Johanna as I'd always been charmed—by her ability to catch me off-balance, turn my world upside-down. And she was, as usual, delighted to do so, flattered by my incredulity. "Want a tour?" she offered, casually.

I glanced at Margot. "Well, I think I've already seen—"

"Did you go upstairs?" Johanna asked, also looking at Margot.

Margot shook her head.

"O.K.—just wait a moment." Johanna glanced around, caught sight of the youth sitting on the floor, reading comic books.

"Hey, Glen," she called, softly. He glanced up at her. "Come here. I've got a job for you."

The youth got awkwardly to his feet, lounged over to where we stood. "Who's that guy over there by the window—in the blue shirt?" she asked quietly. We all followed her gaze, scanned the bodies in the living room until we located the one on the couch, wearing a light blue shirt.

"Don' know," shrugged the youth. "I've never seen him before."

"Me neither," Johanna said. "I want you to go read your comic books somewhere over there where you can keep your eye on him."

"You think he's pushing?"

"I'm sure of it. But a little proof wouldn't hurt. Will you watch him for me?"

"Sure," he said agreeably.

"Oh, and Mary Ann's in the kitchen. Jody's in there too. But if you hear Mary Ann starting up, you'd better go help Jody throw her out."

He nodded, slouched back to his supply of comic books, gathered up an armful of them, went into the living room, where he established himself in another corner, not far from the suspect in the blue shirt. I glanced at Johanna, found her watching me.

"Come on," Johanna said, and once again I was in tow, searching out a passage in between and over the bodies. I glanced back at Margot, but she'd decided not to follow us. We came to flight of stairs, the banisters heaped with jackets and coats. Johanna led me up to the relative quiet of the upper floors.

The second floor, she explained, consisted of meeting rooms, counseling rooms, an office, a girls' lounge. "But let's start from the top." She headed towards another, narrower flight of stairs; I caught up to her as she reached the bottom step.

"But this house," I protested. "It must have cost a fortune. Where did you get it?"

She stopped. "It's a gift."

"From whom?"

"One of my johns. A regular. He left it to me in his will."

"I don't believe it."

She looked smug. "He liked me. It was a revenue house. He divided it into apartments, paid off the mortgage, and then sat back and collected the rents. He had several of them. I think he figured that he was leaving me an independent income, so that I could become a landlady instead of a whore. But I had better ideas."

"What on earth did his family say?"

"What could they say? He didn't have a wife, and as for his kids—it was all legal and above board. He left me money too. But I spent that on the renovations."

"I'll bet." I looked around the landing, at the high ceilings, at the decorative mouldings and handsome banisters. It was a nice house, in pretty good shape for its age. I followed Johanna up the second flight of stairs.

The top floor consisted of several bedrooms and a bathroom. The bedrooms were carpeted, but contained no furniture other than mattresses, sleeping bags and cushions. Most of the mattresses were occupied. In the faint light from the windows I could make out clothes heaped against the walls, bodies humped under sleeping bags. Johanna and I stood in a doorway, looking in at them.

"At the moment this is my biggest problem," Johanna said softly, so as not to wake the sleepers. "I didn't intend to start a hostel—but they haven't got anywhere else. It's either here or on the streets or back into the arms of the pimp or the pusher that they're running away from. I try to shut the place up for the night and go home to my own life, but when I get here in the morning I find kids sleeping under the back porch or in the yard. I'm afraid the neighbors are going to complain. So this is my compromise. I let the kids sleep here in the daytime, or in the evenings, whenever I'm here. When I go home, I wake them up and throw them all outside. They go turn a few tricks, hang out in the all-night cafes or wherever.

It's not great, but I can't keep this place going twenty-four hours a day. I need more staff—and money to pay them with."

"You don't allow any drugs."

"I try to keep out the pushers, at the very least. But most of these kids are always high on something. I show them how to sterilize their needles, I try and get them to find out what's in a pill before they shove it into their mouth. But somebody overdoses at least once a week." She started back down the stairs.

"You're the boss," I said.

She came to a stop halfway down the staircase, looked at me over her shoulder. "It's my house," she reminded me. Then she continued down the stairs, waited for me on the landing. "They're just kids," she pointed out. "And they've lost their parents. So they use me."

"I approve," I assured her.

"Besides which," she added, opening the door nearest us, "we can't have drugs. If we have drugs, we'll get the cops. As it is they come through here several times a week." We stepped into a large, well-proportioned room—probably once the master bedroom. "This is the girls' lounge."

The girls' lounge was a mess. It consisted of a miscellaneous assortment of sofas and armchairs, side tables spilling with magazines, a bookshelf bulging paperbacks, a kitchen counter in the corner, a sink full of dirty dishes. It was inhabited. There were four girls seated around a table, there was one asleep in an armchair, another lying on her back on the floor, doing leg-lifts. "Hi." Johanna surveyed them. "I see the clean-up wasn't too effective."

"It was canceled," said one of the girls at the table. "Nobody showed up."

"There's six of you right here. Isn't that enough to clean up one room? It would take you fifteen minutes."

"Yes, Mother," the girl on the floor answered her, wearily. As she turned her head towards us, I saw that she had a fresh graze down her cheek and a whopper of a black eye.

"Where'd you get that?" Johanna asked her.

The girl watched her, shrugged. "He wanted more." I felt the hairs prickle on the back of my neck. "And he didn't pay me either."

"Did you put his name up on the list?"

"He had a goddamn stocking on his head. I don't know what he looked like."

"What about the car?"

"I didn't notice it."

"He probably always wears that stocking."

The girl returned her gaze to the ceiling.

"Do somebody else a favor," Johanna said coaxingly. "Stick him up on the list."

The girl continued to stare at the ceiling, her face set. Without warning she screamed: "I hate him! I don't want to talk about him!" Then she re-composed her features, continued doing leg-lifts. Johanna closed the door.

She gave me a glance that I couldn't interpret, then moved down the hallway, stepped into the next room. "This is one of our meeting rooms." I peered in the doorway. It contained a circle of assorted chairs, a low table in the center of them. "We've got quite a few groups going and we get people in to talk—about drugs and nutrition and sexual abuse and legal stuff. Alcoholics Anonymous is trying to get a group going. We also need one for drug addicts. But it's hard to get them off anything when they're still living on the streets. You wouldn't believe how many kids there are out there, turning tricks and stealing, sleeping on the sidewalks." She gave me a rueful glance. "A lot more than I thought."

"Judging by the crowd downstairs, this place is very successful."

"That's the problem. We're too successful."

She continued along the corridor past several open doorways, naming the rooms as she passed them. "That's another meeting room. A counseling room... And here's the office."

We'd reached the end of the corridor, and from the other side of the door in front of us, I could hear the tapping of an electric typewriter. As Johanna opened the door, the sound stopped. There was a young woman at the desk; she looked up as we entered. It was Salal.

We stared at each other, unmoving—as if we'd each seen a ghost.

"And this is our fundraiser," Johanna said proudly. "Meet Louise."

Louise, I thought, remembering that last night in Johanna's kitchen. Yes, I remembered Louise. She had papers to prove it and eyes like vortexes of fear. And here she was again, standing up slowly from her desk, approaching me—tentatively—as if I were a wild animal that might run away. She came right up close to me, peered intently into my face—while I submitted to her inspection, rigid and trembling.

Then all of a sudden she smiled—a huge, friendly smile—and I noticed that she'd lost one of her front teeth.

"It's been a long time," she said softly, fingering my sleeve.

"You came back!" I croaked.

Slowly her smile faded, her eyes grew dark. I watched them with dread, feeling myself being sucked into them. Her hand tightened around my arm. "My granny was dead."

At first I thought she was accusing me. But then, as if the news had just struck her afresh, her face crumpled, her eyes flooded with tears...and immediately mine were doing the same.

"When? Not before you—"

"I never even saw her!" She was incredulous. She still hadn't gotten over it.

"So what did you do?"

"I went into the bush. I went to her cabin. There's nobody lives there now."

"And then what? You were by yourself?"

"At first I went crazy." She was staring at a spot on the wall somewhere behind my head. "There was me, and the forest, and the animals. Then I began to starve. So I ate the animals." She frowned. "And then it was winter. I'd forgotten how cold it gets. I needed more wood and more wood. The creek froze and I had to cut out chunks of ice to get water. I killed a deer. I got so sick of that deer. But it was too far to go to town. Too cold and too far."

"So you got off the junk?"

She nodded. "I didn't think I could do that. Not by myself. But there wasn't any choice. I thought about killing myself a couple of times. But I was there, in my granny's house. And I knew she wouldn't like that. I'm the part of her that's still alive, you see?" Her gaze met mine, their expression fierce. "She wants me to live. She helped me."

Her eyes challenged mine, daring me to disagree—which I didn't. She knew that her grandmother had loved her, and it was that knowledge that had kept her alive. People are, in some ways, terrifyingly simple.

I gave her a watery smile. "I bet your granny would have been—" My voice threatened to disintegrate. "Proud of you."

She nodded, gravely, accepted the tribute. Then she dug in her jeans pocket, produced a kleenex and blew her nose.

"What made you decide to come back to the city?"

She glanced at me, sighed. "When the spring came, I went to town, and I met some people and—and I realized that I didn't belong. I didn't fit in there. I never really knew anybody except my grandparents... But I thought that maybe I'd get to know some of the people from the reservation or something...."

Her sentences kept tailing off, finally ground to a complete halt. "Anyway," she went on, getting herself going again, "it didn't work. I'm a city girl now. I never wanted to live in the city, but—I don't seem to belong anywhere else. I work here; Johanna takes care of me." She looked at Johanna who was standing, silent, leaning against the office door, then her eyes slid to me, passed me, drifted to the window, through which one could see the myriad lights of the high-rise across the street. "I've been hanging out at the Native Center. I joined a group there. I've met some people—more like me. We talk about things...." She paused, thinking, chewing her lower lip.

"How long have you been back?"

Salal's forehead creased, she looked at Johanna for an answer.

"Four months?" Johanna suggested.

"And did the cops ever—"

237

"Yeah." Salal was nodding. "They found me here. They questioned me. I just said I ran away."

"They accepted that?"

She shrugged. "They seemed to. I explained that I'd been in the bush, that I hadn't known they were looking for me. I told them that I'd gone back to Kinky's that night and found the place crawling with cops. Well, who'd stay around, eh?" She almost smiled. "They asked me a lot of questions about Haswell—" She paused. "And Caesar."

I realized that I'd stopped breathing.

"Maybe one day they'll be back...." Salal's finger strayed to her mouth; she chewed on the nail, her eyes far away, speculative.

I was hot all over. My heart was crashing against my ribs, the blood beating in my brain, and the question was rising, boiling up from my guts like vomit.

"Did you kill him?" My voice burst upon the air, raucous, crude.

Salal's gaze met mine; she considered the question, gravely. "No."

Immediately I looked at Johanna.

Johanna rolled her eyes. "Of course I'm going to say no. What do you expect? But since you didn't trust me before, don't start now."

I stared at her, turned back to Salal—and suddenly understood how much I liked them, respected them—loved them, perhaps. Which was why I'd gone to such lengths to protect them.

But love has its limits.

"I won't," I said.

About the Author

Elisabeth Bowers was born and raised in Vancouver, B.C., where she continues to live with her partner and daughter. She studied at the University of British Columbia and is presently employed at a worker-owned bakery collective. *Ladies' Night* is her first novel. She is currently writing a science fiction story for children.

SELECTED TITLES FROM SEAL PRESS

MYSTERIES

THE LAST DRAW by Elisabet Peterzen. $8.95, 0-931188-67-9

STUDY IN LILAC by Maria-Antònia Oliver. $8.95, 0-931188-52-0

FIELD WORK by Maureen Moore. $8.95, 0-931188-54-7

MURDER IN THE COLLECTIVE by Barbara Wilson. $8.95, 0-931188-23-7

SISTERS OF THE ROAD by Barbara Wilson. $8.95, 0-931188-45-8

FICTION

ANGEL by Merle Collins. $8.95, 0-931188-64-4

MISS VENEZUELA by Barbara Wilson. $9.95, 0-931188-58-X

BIRD-EYES by Madelyn Arnold. $8.95, 0-931188-62-8

LOVERS' CHOICE by Becky Birtha. $8.95, 0-931188-56-3

GIRLS, VISIONS AND EVERYTHING by Sarah Schulman. $8.95, 0-931188-38-5

AMBITIOUS WOMEN by Barbara Wilson. $8.95, 0-931188-36-9

WOMEN'S STUDIES

THE OBSIDIAN MIRROR: *An Adult Healing from Incest* by Louise M. Wisechild. $10.95, 0-931188-63-6

HARD-HATTED WOMEN: *Stories of Struggle and Success in the Trades,* edited by Molly Martin. $10.95, 0-931188-66-0

LESBIAN COUPLES by D. Merilee Clunis and G. Dorsey Green. $10.95, 0-931188-59-8

GETTING FREE: *A Handbook for Women in Abusive Relationships* by Ginny NiCarthy. $10.95, 0-931188-37-7

Available from your favorite bookseller or from Seal Press, 3131 Western, Suite 410, Seattle, WA 98121.
Include $1.50 for the first book and .50 for each additional book.